GuiltyLocks

Susan Etzkorn

Cover Art

Kaley Devon

To Rick, My biggest supporter

And to all my former students who said,
"Write the book. It would make a good story."

Preface (2004)

The first sound was sharp; a pop, then another. Sarah had just gotten in her car with Libby when she looked toward the entrance of Luxe Loom Designers, her heart slamming into her ribs. The front glass doors exploded inward, shards scattering across the floor like deadly confetti. Libby's father, John, dropped to the ground with a cry, clutching his chest, blood pooling beneath him.

Two young men rushed from a black SUV and through the doors. One carried a semi-automatic weapon, the other brandished a handgun. Their movements were practiced and precise; an orchestrated symphony of violence. The taller man shouted commands in Spanish, his voice cold and devoid of emotion. "Todas se congelan! Everyone freeze!"

Sarah pushed Libby down inside her car, her breath coming in ragged gasps. Her mind raced. Hide. Stay silent. Wait for a chance to escape. But her body trembled uncontrollably.

Mindy Bercher's voice was a desperate wail that ended abruptly with the crack of a gunshot. Blood splattered the ledger where moments ago she had been working.

Sarah stifled a scream with her hand, tears streaming down her face as Libby's mom crumpled to the ground. The world tilted. Her ears rang. She clung to the steering wheel as if it were the only solid thing in a sea of horror.

The two men grabbed the ledger and the cash from the till. As an afterthought, they broke the glass on a display case, each helping themselves to a few diamonds. When Melissa, another clerk, ran out from the back room to see what was happening, one of the men raised his gun, and just before pulling the trigger, said, "Adios, Libby Bercher."

As quickly as it happened, it was over. The black SUV sped away into the night. Sarah and Libby sat in the car for a beat, unable to move, unable to speak. Had this really happened?

Within minutes the wail of sirens pierced the night as two police cruisers skidded to a stop at the scene. Red and blue lights flashed rhythmically, bathing the jewelry store in alternating hues of urgency. Officers Andrews and Blake emerged from the first car, their hands instinctively hovering near their holstered weapons. Behind them, Officers Ramirez and

Jackson exited their vehicle, surveying the area with sharp, trained eyes.

"Dispatch, this is Unit 318, we're 10-23 at The Luxe Loom Designers on Washington Street," Andrews reported into his shoulder-mounted radio, signaling their arrival at the location. "Two vehicles on site, multiple officers present. Stand by for further information."

"Copy that, Unit 318," crackled the voice of the dispatcher.

As Andrews and Blake cautiously approached the entrance of the store, they noticed the first victim, an older man slumped on the floor. The air was heavy with the metallic scent of blood. Blake dropped to one knee, checking for signs of life.

"Victim is unresponsive," Blake muttered grimly. "Gunshot wound to the chest."

"Ramirez, secure the perimeter," Andrews ordered, his tone firm but calm. Ramirez nodded and began stringing yellow crime scene tape between streetlights, ensuring onlookers stayed clear when he noticed Sarah and Libby still hiding in their car, shaken by what they had witnessed.

"Andrews," Ramirez called out. "We have two potential witnesses." He aimed his gun at the car.

"Ladies, if you would please step carefully out of the vehicle with your hands raised."

The moment Libby saw her father's body, she collapsed. Sarah was crying uncontrollably. "I-I-I saw everything. I saw who did this."

Ramirez holstered his weapon and placed a gentle hand on Sarah's arm and helped her to the back of the cruiser. Jackson rushed over to assist Libby.

Officers Andrews and Blake continued through the store and located two more victims, both women.

"Unit 318 to Dispatch," Andrews continued, keeping his voice steady and professional. "We have one male victim, approximate age mid-fifties, and two female victims, one approximate age mid-fifties and one, mid-twenties. Gunshot wounds, no pulse. Requesting paramedics at the scene. Secure additional units for crowd control." He paused for a moment, assessing the surroundings. He and Jackson searched through the remainer of the store. "Scene appears stable, no active threat. Apparent robbery. Securing the witnesses."

"Copy, Unit 318. EMS and backup enroute," came the prompt reply.

"Blake, get a visual on any shell casings or evidence markers. Watch your step," Andrews instructed.

Blake nodded, drawing out a flashlight and scanning the ground. He spotted small, glinting brass objects near the door. "Found a couple of casings," he said, carefully marking the location with a yellow evidence card.

Ramirez leaned into the cruiser keeping his voice calm but authoritative. "I'm Officer Ramirez. Could you tell me your name? Why are you here?"

Sarah nodded. "I'm Sarah Martin. I work for John and Mindy Bercher. They own this jewelry store. This is Libby, their daughter." Libby was in complete shock and sat motionless staring into the black night.

"Can you tell me what happened here?" Ramirez asked.

"Um, we had just left the store. We work here and we were going home when a black SUV pulled in and a couple of guys jumped out and starting shooting."

"Two men, that's helpful," Ramirez assured her. "Did you get a good look at the men? Can you tell me anything about their appearance?"

Sarah thought for a moment, still not believing what she had witnessed. "They were Hispanic. I heard them shouting in Spanish. One was taller than the other. It all happened so fast. The last thing I heard them say, before they shot Melissa, was 'Adios, Libby

5

Bercher'. They thought they shot her!" Sarah said pointing to her friend.

Back in the store, paramedics arrived and confirmed the victims were deceased. The coroner was notified. Andrews spoke into his radio again. "Unit 318 to Dispatch. Coroner required. Victims confirmed deceased at 9:30. Evidence secured; officers conducting witness interviews. We'll continue holding the scene for forensic investigators."

"Copy, Unit 318," came the dispatcher's reply.

As the officers wrapped up their immediate actions, Blake checked in with Andrews. "Looks like a clean shooting scene, no sign of a struggle."

"Yeah," Andrews agreed, his eyes scanning the store once more. "We'll need the detectives to piece this together."

The officers, somber and focused, continued their work as the night deepened around them. Sarah and Libby were taken to police headquarters where the night would drag into morning as the two were questioned about what they had witnessed.

The two detectives conducting the interview were kind at first, offering Sarah and Libby water, speaking in low, soothing tones. When it became apparent that Libby hadn't witnessed anything, she was moved into another room away from Sarah. Then their questions became more pointed.

"What did the shooters look like?" one of them had asked.

Sarah closed her eyes, trying to summon the image. But the adrenaline and terror had blurred everything. "There were two men. They... they were Hispanic. One was tall, the other was shorter."

"Only two? What about a driver? You're certain they were Hispanic? Could they have been Asian?"

Sarah began to doubt herself. "I heard them speaking in Spanish and they had dark hair."

The blonde detective spoke. "I can speak Spanish; does it make *me* Hispanic? Of course not. "Weren't they wearing masks? How could you know they were Hispanic if they were wearing masks?"

"They were masked?" Sarah asked.

"Other witnesses stated that they were masked. You tell me. Anything else? Hair color? Tattoos? Did you hear any names?"

Sarah's mind spun. Her memories felt slippery, as if they were coated in oil. Were there masks? She had seen something... hadn't she? A flash of red on the shorter man's sleeve? Or was it black? Had she seen their faces? Her hands trembled.

"I don't know," she whispered. "I don't know."

The detective had been insistent. "Think carefully. Someone mentioned they saw a man with a dragon tattoo leaving the scene. Does that sound familiar?"

Sarah latched onto the suggestion, her mind filling in gaps where terror had erased details. "Yes," she said slowly. "A dragon tattoo... on his arm. I think it was red."

Sarah's memory of the night began to whirl and spin into something different. She could not remember what she had actually witnessed as the detective methodically put ideas into her head. Sarah was no longer sure what happened that night.

Two men were brought in the next day on suspicion of committing the crime. Both men insisted they had alibis. They were placed in a lineup with several other men, but Sarah couldn't identify them.

As the two suspects were being held, two young college girls entered the police station to provide a sworn statement for them. One of the girls signed the following statement.

The statement read:

I, Lydia Quinn Mason, of 4544 East Markham Street, Austin, TX, declare under penalty of perjury that the following is true and correct to the best of my knowledge:

Personal Information

- Name: Lydia Quinn Mason

- Date of Birth: 3/1/1982

- Address: 4544 East Markham Street, Austin, TX

- Contact Information: (555)477-9001 LydiaQuinn@Gmail.net

Statement of Events

On 6/15/04 between the hours of 7:30 and 10:00, I was at the Alamo Drafthouse Theatre engaged in the following activity:

I was attending the 7:00 PM screening of *The Day After Tomorrow*. The movie ended at approximately 9:45 PM.

I was accompanied by Isabella Martinez, Antonio Alvarez and Victor Sanchez. I have receipts as documentation, including ticket stubs and p ctures of us in the theatre and in front of the Marquee listing the movie.
I am willing to provide any additional information, including contacts of individuals who can corroborate my presence at the mentioned location.

I declare under the laws of Austin, TX that the information provided in this statement is true and correct.

Signature: *Lydia Quinn Mason*
Date: 6/16/2004

9

With the statement, and no positive ID, the suspects were released. Sarah's statement was considered 'Not reliable.' The case was on-going as new suspects were being sought out.

Sarah would spend years in therapy trying to recover from the events of that night.

Chapter 1 (Present day)

In the dimly lit room, the air was thick with tension as Antonio Alvarez sat at the head of a polished mahogany table. He exuded an air of commanding presence, a man hardened by years of calculated decisions and ruthless ambition. His sharply tailored suit, custom-made from luxurious dark fabrics, reflected his taste for power and refinement.

His build was solid and imposing, the result of a life lived balancing indulgence and necessity, with broad shoulders and a slight paunch that spoke to his wealth and comfort. His face, weathered but striking, carried the lines of experience; deep-set eyes that seemed to read people before they spoke, framed by faint crow's feet and a subtle scar that hinted at a violent past. His dark hair, peppered with grey at his temples, was slicked back with precision.

His expression remained calm and calculating, but when he smiled, it could be dangerous; a chilling mixture of charm and menace that made it clear he was a man who had earned his place at the top, no matter the cost.

The room was adorned with decorations that spoke of wealth accumulated through the monopoly of pricing controls in his Botella de Agua International business as well as money laundering for the cartel. A large map hung on the wall indicating all his business locations throughout Mexico.

Antonio leaned back in his intricately carved chair, running his fingers over the fine leather as he surveyed the room. His sharp calculating eyes scanned the faces of his most trusted lieutenants, each of whom had earned their place through years of loyalty and brutality.

"Gentlemen," Antonio began, his deep voice cutting through the silence, "as you know, my daughter, Sofía, is to be married in October at the El Amado Hotel in San Antonio, Texas. I must attend but there are risks and I will not expose myself to unnecessary danger."

He gestured to a large map spread across the table, pinpointing his destination in Texas. "We will take our planes and land at this private airstrip. We will be stepping into unfamiliar territory, and I won't have any surprises. I need you all to ensure my safety as well as the success of the wedding. Everything must go very smoothly."

His right-hand man, the first lieutenant, Victor Sanchez, leaned forward. "Señor, you know we've got your back. What is the plan?"

Antonio's lips curled into a sinister smile. "First, we need to establish a network on the ground. I want eyes and ears everywhere. Our informants should be well-paid and loyal, gathering intelligence on potential threats and opportunities. I don't want any mistakes. Comprendé? Sofía is not to know you are even present."

The room echoed with a chorus of affirmations.

Antonio pointed to a second map that showed the El Amado Hotel and its layout in detail. "This is the main tower, the Mi Amor Tower, where the wedding party will have rooms. I will be staying down the hall from Isabella, though I am registered to her room. Luna will be with me, and I plan for that detail to be discreet as well. None of the wedding guests are to know that she is there or that she is associated with me, not my wife, not my son, and especially not my daughter. The tower has fifteen floors, and because of the expanse of unguarded space, Victor will have a room next to mine for my security."

Victor grinned to himself as he thought of Luna and their secret affair. He was glad Antonio was taking his buchona along. Maybe he and Luna could slip away for a little fun of their own. With a room next door to Antoino, it would be easier to meet Luna.

Antonio continued. "Second, we'll need a secure base of operations where I can conduct my business during the week without any unwanted attention. I have secured a room here," he pointed to the location on the map, "at the place called the El Carino. It is at the edge of the property. You will all be staying in this location as well, to fortify it. I will spend most of my time there except during the evening hours when I will be with my family or with Luna. My brother-in-law, Enrique, will also have a room in this location."

Victor raised concerns. "Has Enrique made the decision to join as business partners with you? Has he sworn his loyalty to the Guadalajara cartel? I'm worried he can't be trusted that close to our base of operations."

"Do not concern yourself with Enrique. It is just a matter of time, I assure you," Antonio spat.

"Pardon, Dom, but word on the street has indicated that Enrique has pledged loyalties to Los Zetas."

"Enrique has pledged loyalties only to himself. I will see that it changes," Antonio assured his men.

As the meeting progressed, Antonio detailed every aspect of his plan. He discussed the importance of having a reliable transportation network and emphasized the need for a skilled security detail, but one that wouldn't draw any unnecessary attention.

One of the lieutenants, Jorge Lopez, raised an additional concern. "The Texas turf is controlled by a rival gang, the Mexikanemi. We can't just walk in and expect no resistance."

Antonio chuckled, his eyes narrowing. "Jorge, that's why I've called this meeting. We have already established alliances with the Mexikanemi and smaller cartel who could be swayed. Our reputation precedes us. Our only concern is Los Zetas, but they have no alliances in Texas. We are not there to take control. We are there for Sofía's wedding. That is all."

With the meeting concluded, Antonio stood up, and his men followed suit. The room buzzed with a sense of purpose as they prepared to execute their leader's orders.

"Gentlemen? We will give Sofía the wedding of her dreams without complication, sí?"

They all shook their heads in unison. "Sí," they replied.

Chapter 2

Sarah Lawson, the teacher for Gifted and Talented students at Hudson Elementary School, stood at the edge of a table in front of a small group of her students. She was the kind of teacher every student remembered fondly long after leaving her classroom. Though small in stature, she was brimming with boundless energy. Sarah commanded attention and admiration with her infectious enthusiasm and warm spirit. Her long blonde hair, often swept back in a simple braid or ponytail, reflected her vibrant personality, always moving, always shining with life.

"Alright guys, I need to hear from each of you about your movie idea. It's time to start developing your ideas, writing scripts and casting parts for everyone. I want you to start filming in two weeks, if possible."

"Mrs. Lawson, I want to do a documentary. Would that be allowed?" asked Sydney.

"That's a great idea! I've never had anyone want to do that when making movies. What type of documentary are you thinking about?"

Sydney smiled mischievously and responded, "I want to make a documentary about this class. I plan to interview students from all the different grade levels and you, too. Don't worry about the questions I have planned, they're good questions."

"I'm sure they're excellent questions. But I'm curious about why you want to produce a documentary about *this* class," Mrs. Lawson said.

"Because I always go back to my home room excited about what goes on in here and my friends always ask about it. It makes perfect sense."

Mrs. Lawson smiled at her reasons and nodded her head.

Cooper raised his hand. "Mrs. Lawson, I was thinking I wanted to do a documentary too. If it's OK to have more than one. If not, I can use the same idea for an action movie!"

"I don't have an objection to having two documentaries, Cooper. What's your idea?"

"I think my idea slaps! I want to do something really rad dealing with the cartel. I watched an awesome series on Netflix about the cartel and drugs and stuff, and I thought maybe ..."

Sarah half-gasped as she held up her hand, color rising up her neck. "OK, let me stop you right there, Cooper. That would fall under the category of material that isn't appropriate for elementary students. The principal would certainly not approve of it, and we couldn't show something like that during a schoolwide assembly. It could be very disturbing for the younger students. Though it's definitely a very intriguing topic, and it slaps (?) as you say, it's not appropriate at this level. Maybe we could spin your idea in a different direction, perhaps along the lines of drug awareness, but let's keep the cartel out of it."

"Nah, that's OK. Forget that. I'll just do a comedy with Tyler. I know you'll approve that because we are going to have a Michael Jackson impersonator." Conner jumped up and moon walked across the room singing the famous iconic words, "Woo, oo, oo!"

Sarah, relief on her face, applauded Conner's dance moves and gave two thumbs up.

That's just how it was in her room. The students were naturally drawn to her personality and intent on pleasing her.

Sarah had spent years in therapy working to overcome an incident she experienced in college. She had witnessed the murder of her best friend's parents at their jewelry store. She would later discover that the Berchers had been working with a Mexican cartel in a money laundering scheme. Something had gone wrong, and they were gunned down by two men. Her friend, Libby Bercher, had been placed in the witness protection program after the murders.

Due to faulty questioning by the investigators of the crime, Sarah's memories had been tainted. Because of the trauma of that night, and how it was handled, she suffered from a type of amnesia her therapist diagnosed as the misinformation effect. She could no longer recall the details of what happened.

However, armed with a wealth of knowledge and a strong desire to teach, Sarah had forged ahead, trying to put her past behind her. She felt at ease in her classroom, creating an environment where she and her gifted students could thrive. It was a safe haven not only for Sarah, but also for her students.

During her planning time, Sarah sat at her desk reading through all her emails. One quickly caught her attention from NTAGC, The National Talented and Gifted Conference. It was going to be held in October in San Antonio. She had always wanted to attend a national conference to be able to network with teachers across the country.

Sarah had requested to attend the conference every year. But just as she expected, her request was denied. The funds just weren't there. The only way the district could send her to a national conference would be as a presenter, which would waive the attendance fee.

That evening around the family dinner table Sarah discussed the conference with her husband.

"This is the fourth time I've asked to attend. I should be allowed to go. Can you believe this, Michael?" Sarah complained. "They won't send me to the conference unless I'm a presenter. That's just ridiculous! I would learn valuable information and get a plethora of materials. I am not a public speaker, I have no real breakthroughs in the field of gifted education, and I wouldn't begin to know what I could possibly present. I think it's the district's way of getting out of sending me."

"Now Sarah," Michael began. "Stop being so hard on yourself. I'm sure the district would send you if it was possible."

"Mom, you're an amazing teacher and you do a ton of fun stuff with your students," chimed Jordan, Sarah's daughter. "But you don't hafta be some guru in gifted education to be able to talk to a bunch of teachers."

Zach, her son, added his thoughts. "Yeah, gurus are boring."

"The boy is right. Teachers want to hear ideas from other teachers, those in the trenches. You should definitely consider presenting one of your teaching units," Michael encouraged.

Sarah's family were her biggest encouragers and cheerleaders. Michael had a heart bigger than most people, always looking for the positive side of any situation. He bragged about his wife and her gift to teach every chance he had to anyone that would listen. He believed she was truly inspiring as she put her heart and soul into teaching and raising their children.

"Well, if I really thought about presenting, maybe I could talk about my movie production unit. This year is really going to be fun. Which reminds me, one of my students wanted to do a documentary, and if not a documentary, a live action movie about the cartel. Can you believe that? He said the cartel slapped!"

"Ouch! That's a little too close for comfort. I'm guessing you shutdown that notion," Michael said.

"I shut it down right away! I don't need anyone to dig up the wrong information! Can you imagine how certain information could compromise my reputation? I have tried extremely hard to put the past behind me and move forward with my life. The cartel? I can just imagine the problems!"

Jordan was concerned. "Are you ever gonna be safe from the cartel? Mom, I know that thing happened a long time ago, way before I was even born. But I was just thinking; this conference is in San Antonio. How far from Austin is that? Is it gonna be safe in Texas?"

"Jordan, you're sweet to be so worried about me. I have tried to put the past behind me, I just hope the other people involved have as well. I was not a reliable witness. I imagine I'm as safe in Texas as I am in North Carolina. If someone was trying to get to me, I suppose I would be easy to find, and it would have happened a long time ago. I don't think the cartel is looking for me. It was the two detectives that blew my testimony and they're serving time for their crimes. My case was not the only one they tampered with, so it had nothing to do with me specifically."

"Maybe presenting your unit on movie making should be tabled. You don't need to be triggered by anything that, what did that kid say? Slaps?" Michael smiled at his wife in an attempt to lessen her worry.

Zach piped up. "Maybe you should show him how Ms. Lawson slaps!"

"Calm down, Zach. He had no idea of my connection to the cartel or the problems I faced. But you're right, Michael. No movie presentation. Besides I'd have too much equipment to carry around with me."

"That's a good point. What other units might work?"

"I could present my escape room plans. There again, how would I even begin to gather all the materials for that?" Sarah mused.

"Well, I think you should keep it simple and fun, something hands-on for the teachers. Something they could really bite in to!"

"Why don't you just show 'em how to make Dippin' Dots?" Zach asked. "Who wouldn't want to do that?"

Because Michael worked as a chemist for a fertilizer company that used liquid nitrogen in their production, he had access to it on a regular basis, and he was always coming up with fun ways to use it. He discovered a way to make the famous and delicious Dippin' Dots that kids love so much, and Sarah had incorporated it into a unit on accidental inventions.

"Dippin Dots!" they both shouted at once.

"Our son is a genius!" Sarah gleamed. "I guess I need to beef up my unit plans on accidental inventions. This will be amazing. I'll talk about all the accidental inventions that have led to greatness; Velcro, matches, Coca Cola, and Dippin' Dots! This is going to be so much fun presenting! Zach, you're the best!"

"Slow down, Sarah. You're not presenting tonight!" Michael said.

But Sarah immediately sprang into action. When the table was cleared, she grabbed her computer and began right away. If she was chosen, this would be the unit she would present at the national gifted conference, demonstrating how to make Dippin' Dots. She had used it in her classroom with great success. What teacher wouldn't want to learn how to do this? Sarah would be the hit of the conference.

She approached her application to present at the national conference with a sense of determination and grit. This was her time to shine. She wanted to share with others all she had learned inside the walls of the classroom. Attending the national conference filled her with excitement knowing she would gain knowledge from all the interactive sessions. The NTAGC conference promoted that teachers would rediscover the magic of teaching from innovative and inspirational keynote sessions. 'Take time to reconnect, play, and spark your imagination as you join your community for conversation and collaboration.' This was it. Learning to make Dippin' Dots surely sparked the imagination! Sarah completed her presenter's application and hoped for the best.

A month later, she got the news.

"Michael! I have fantastic news! I got accepted to be a presenter."

"I told you. You're an amazing teacher and you can do anything you set your mind to. It's time for the world to know just how wonderful you are," Michael said as he hugged Sarah.

"Look out people, here comes the world famous, Dippin' Dot teacher, Sarah Lawson!" Jordan cheered.

Sarah was overjoyed and possibly a bit overwhelmed. She would indeed be a presenter in San Antonio at the National Talented and Gifted Conference, but she had work to prepare; lesson plans, substitute plans, travel plans. But first things first. She forwarded the acceptance letter to her supervisor and waited to get the go-ahead. With Jordan and Zach in school, she wouldn't be able to take her family along. Michael was knee-deep in his work and couldn't afford a week away from the office anyway, so she began to devise a way to make it an adventure without them. She would ask her sister, Emily, to go with her once everything was in motion.

Chapter 3

Emily Martin had a commanding presence that naturally drew attention. With a tall, lean frame and an air of quiet confidence, she carried herself with poise and purpose. Like her sister Sarah, Emily possessed striking, golden hair that she effortlessly turned into a signature feature. As the founder and visionary behind *Savory Bytes*, an innovative culinary technology company, Emily was driven by a bold mission, to transform the way people experience food through groundbreaking technology and creative innovation.

Though both of her parents were educators, Emily had always wanted to be a chef. Right out of business college, she attended The Culinary Institute of America in Hyde Park, and it was there that she met Stephen Padilla. He was an established chef and introduced her to the best restaurants in New York. Over time, the two began a rocky relationship. Emily excelled and made a name for herself, forging ahead of Stephen. After founding her own company and selling products like the pasta maker, she created The Nitro-Chill, which utilized liquid nitrogen to freeze and transform culinary creations. She had leaned on her brother-in-law, Michael, with help in the different uses of liquid nitrogen. It was her latest and greatest triumph.

But, next to becoming a chef and owning her own restaurant, Emily had always dreamed of a romantic wedding; someplace far away, remote, and breathtaking. She thought that her dream was about to come true with Stephen. She and Stephen had been together for eight years, and things were getting serious. There were talks of marriage and going to the next level in their relationship. They had even shopped for rings together. She was thirty-five after all; it was time to forge ahead.

Emily's relationship with Stephen began right after she graduated from culinary school. After six years of working her butt off at various restaurants in the NYC area, she landed a job at one of her favorite restaurants, The Mezcal Room, in the heart of the city. She was working under the direction of Chef T.J. Steele, who mixed the tastes of New York and Oaxaca, Mexico. He lived in Oaxaca part-time and had cultivated relationships with craftsmen, cooks and farmers throughout the region. He would visit regularly and source the corn for The Mezcal Room's menu.

T.J. had invited Emily to go along with him to Mexico to see, firsthand, how he sourced his products. The state of Oaxaca was wonderful. It was home to some amazing art, savory cuisine and diverse natural resources. Sierra Norte was nearby with biking and horseback riding amid the green mountainside. And to the south of Oaxaca was a coast with sandy beaches and surfing. It was truly a magical place; one that Emily would return to visit on her own.

T.J. had a sprawling home located between the mountains and the ocean. It was a mix of warm minimalism and well-being that invited you to fall in love with your surroundings. Each of the four bedrooms had floor-to-ceiling sliding doors and an exceptional ocean view. Stepping outside from any room led you to a massive infinity pool. The outdoor kitchen created the perfect space for cooking and entertaining. This was Emily's dream.

It was just after Emily returned from a trip to Oaxaca with T.J. that things took a turn for the worse between she and Stephen.

"I just don't like the idea of my girlfriend running around in Oaxaca, Mexico with that guy. If anyone should be taking you to Mexico, it should be me. Afterall, I was born there!" Stephen's voice was escalating.

Emily was very passionate about her job. "That guy, as you put it, happens to be my boss. And for your information, I wasn't just running around. We were sourcing corn. To be able to do that was an honor and if I'm going to own my own restaurant someday, I need to learn all I can."

Stephen was a pastry chef at Balthazar, a French restaurant. His specialty was Flan Mexicano which didn't serve him well when making French pastries. Though Balthazar was a popular destination, and it was an honor to be a chef there, Stephen had wanted nothing more than to land a job at The Mezcal Room. He had taken Emily there as often as possible hoping to meet T.J. Steele. And now she was not only working there, but she was also jetting off to Mexico to source corn!

"What happened to us owning a restaurant some day?" Stephen questioned.

"You know what I mean," Emily retorted. "Don't try to put this off on me. You're the one with the jealousy problem. If I didn't know better, I would say you are jealous that I got a job at The Mezcal Room, and you didn't."

"Seriously, Emily?"

"Stephen, I didn't start this argument, you did."

Stephen was angry. "I didn't start an argument. I just said I didn't like you spending all your time with your boss. It's always 'T.J. said this, and T.J. said that.' You're fixated on the guy. You are certainly very defensive about him. And it has nothing to do with me being jealous of your job! Did you have a little too much fun drinking and partying at his little villa in Mexico? You never seemed to be able to answer my calls. What else did T.J. teach you while you were staying alone with him in his villa?" Stephen asked, insinuating that something more had gone on between the two.

"You're being ridiculous!"

"I just don't trust the guy. It just seems suspicious only having you go along to source corn," Stephen said making air quotes around 'source corn'.

"Stephen, he couldn't take his entire staff! Someone had to stay in the states and keep the restaurant open. I'm his top chef, it was only natural that he asked me to go along," Emily said defensively.

"Have you ever considered the fact that T.J. might be connected to the cartel in some way. I've heard quite a few rumors lately that his family is connected. The Aceros are notorious in Oaxaca. He certainly has lots of money and fancy homes!"

"Are you kidding me? The cartel? Now you've gone too far. T.J. happens to be a successful restaurant owner. I'm sorry I don't take personal calls when I'm working. I told you that. And what does the Acero family have to do with T.J. Steele?"

"Emily!! You have to know T.J.'s real name is Tomas Javier Acero. Right? Acero means steel in Spanish. The Aceros are a well-known crime family. Don't be so naive."

"Stephen, that's enough! Just stop it! You wanted to work for T.J. before I got a job at The Mezcal Room and now, you're making up lies about him? You may think you didn't start an argument, but you have certainly gotten us to one – again!" Emily was furious.

"I always pick a fight. Really? Who started the fight over the rights to the Nitro-Chill? It wasn't me," he said. "YOU. You started that fight, remember?"

Emily was heated now. "It wasn't a fight until you wanted me to add your name on the copyright documents. Then it became a fight. I invented it and I intend to have the rights to it."

"And where does being married and sharing everything equally fall into that?" Stephen asked quietly. "I thought we were going to be life partners."

"I want to be your life partner, and even business partners with our own restaurant, but not with my *Savory Bytes* company, and especially not the Nitro-Chill. I am not sharing something I created 100% by myself, marketed and sold all on my own. I'm not willing to give that up," she said. "That's a statement of who I am as a chef and of my own successes."

"Well, I'm not willing to stand on the sidelines and watch you take off without me. I wanted us to be a team, working together at everything, your business included," Stephen complained.

"That's right. MY business. Michael checked with his friend and attorney. He said to put the business in my name only to protect my invention. That is what I did," Emily explained.

"Emily, I guess what I'm saying is that I'm not sure I see us working out if we can't be equal partners in everything," he said.

Emily responded, "If that is really how you feel, and I'm not worth fighting for, then you are probably correct. I'm truly sorry, Stephen."

"If you aren't willing to include me in business, I am afraid you'll have difficulty including me in your life. Don't you see, I'm trying to fight for you," Stephen said.

"But you're fighting for all the wrong reasons."

"Just promise me you'll be careful. Move forward with your life and leave T.J. Steele behind. I get the feeling he's bad news. At least, I know his family is," Stephen confided.

"T.J. is my boss, and he is teaching me things beyond your grasp. He's a professional and teaching me to be. This discussion is over. Good night, Stephen!"

The night Emily walked out the door, she never looked back. There had to be something better for her out there. She wasn't sure what it was, but it had to be better. After walking out on Stephen, she was single, childless and rather preferred it that way.

Chapter 4

A week after the breakup, Emily received a call from her sister. Sarah jumped right into the conversation as soon as Emily picked up the phone.

"Emily, I want you to go to San Antonio with me in October. It will be an adventure you'll remember for a long time. Please say you'll go."

"Hello? Hello? Who's calling please? I think you have the wrong number."

"Very funny. Let me try again. Hello, Emily? This is your favorite sister, Sarah. I just found out I'll be a presenter at the National Talented and Gifted Conference in San Antonio this October. I would love for you to go along with me."

"Oh, hello, Sarah. You know, you're my only sister. I guess that *would* make you my favorite. Now, what about this adventure?"

"It could be another adventure for the Martin sisters! I'm going to present one of my teaching units on the 10th, and attend a few of the sessions, but the rest of the time will be open for some fun sister time. San

Antonio would be amazing to visit during the fall. The convention has rooms and suites at the Hotel Contessa as well as the El Amado Hotel near the Gonzalez Convention Center."

"OK..." Emily said, still not convinced.

"Who wouldn't want to go, right? The Hotel Contessa is already booked, but there are still rooms available at the El Amado Hotel. I have already reserved a room."

"What am I supposed to do while you're at your sessions?" questioned Emily. "Walking along the Riverwalk alone for an entire week really isn't my idea of a fun vacation time. This has me a bit concerned. The last time I fell for one of your fun, sister bonding times, you convinced me to do that crazy ancestry test. Your ideas are always over the top."

"Well, the DNA test was interesting, don't you think? And we always thought we were Irish Germans. I guess the test results showed otherwise. Anyway, you know I have fun ideas. We always enjoy a good laugh. And besides, I have a plan for you that week as well. The same week I'm in San Antonio for the gifted conference, the convention center is also hosting an entrepreneurial cooking week."

"An entrepreneurial cooking week? I'm not an entrepreneur. I'm a chef in one of the finest restaurants in New York. Why would I want to do this?" Emily questioned.

"Well, first of all, you can showcase your new Nitro-Chill. Just listen to their description. '*Discover a cornucopia of cultures, cuisines and innovative cooking techniques from chefs worldwide.*' You have an innovative cooking technique and, as you say, you are a chef!"

"Hmmm, maybe."

"Just think about it. You could have a booth promoting your company and showcasing your invention, you could sell a few, and network with other chefs. We both share a room; we attend our separate conferences, and the entire week becomes a tax write-off for you. But every night will be girls' night for us! We could attend some of the performances at your festival, or we could plan our own. An entire week of girls' night! No kids, no spouse, no *Stephen*, absolutely no obligations."

"A week of girls' nights has me interested. Sarah, I like how you think. That does sound like a fun week. But you don't have to worry about Stephen. We broke it off last week. He was more of a liability than a boyfriend. Now where can I find an application for the cooking week?"

"Wait, what?" You broke it off with Stephen? Why?" Sarah asked.

Emily didn't want to get into too many details, so she simply said, "He wanted different things out of life than I wanted. It would never have worked out between us."

"What things?"

"It's not important. Now, about that application you mentioned."

"Just check your email. I've already downloaded it, filled it in and sent it to you. All you need to do is submit it. And for what it's worth, I'm glad you got rid of Stephen. I think he was just after your ideas!"

Emily said, "It was a little more complicated than that, but that probably sums it up fairly well. Thanks for your help on the application, but seriously, how did you explain my Nitro-Chill?"

"I *am* married to Michael, remember. He explained it to me, and I did a nice write-up about it. I said, 'Almost every chef is familiar with the griddle – the flat metal surface that generates even controlled heat. As a chef, you likely turn to the griddle to sauté onions, churn out stacks of pancakes, and cook burgers. However, you may not be familiar with the griddle's cold cousin, the Nitro-Chill by *Savory Bytes*. This device pumps refrigerant to generate an extremely cold surface as low as -30 degrees Fahrenheit. This cold surface flash freezes sauces, foams, and purees into a solid or semi-solid state. In less than 90 seconds, the Nitro-Chill can transform liquids into morsels with crunchy outer shells and cool, creamy centers.'"

"That is exactly what I would have written. I will get it sent in and hopefully start planning a trip to San Antonio!"

The plan was set into motion. The sisters would spend the week at the El Amado Hotel and attend their separate conferences. The upcoming trip to San Antonio would allow Emily to clear her mind and hopefully, focus on her future. She was ready to move on with life, start her own restaurant, and just enjoy living.

Yes, a trip away was just the thing she needed. The evenings would be for fun and lots of laughter. But spending a week with Sarah away from friends and family would completely change their lives in ways they never imagined!

Chapter 5

Climbing into bed that evening, the memories of that dreadful night in college began to creep into Sarah's mind. Memories she had pushed away hoping never to relive. She knew she'd have a fitful sleep as her mind took control once again.

As she thought back to her junior year of college at the University of Texas at Austin, she remembered it had been an amazing three years and graduation was just on the horizon. Working for Luxe Loom Designers had helped her afford to attend college so far from home. She had become best friends with Libby Bercher, who also happened to be studying education and was the daughter of the jewelry store owners. Libby always made sure they worked the same hours.

Sarah had always thought of Luxe Loom Designers as a refuge, a place of hard work and camaraderie. But safety, she would soon learn, was an illusion.

As sleep took over, so did Sarah's dreams. Through the fog, Sarah could see that it was just after closing, and she and Libby were getting into the car when a black SUV sped into the parking lot. And that's when her dream turned into a nightmare.

She heard the first sharp sound of a pop, and then another. Sarah turned toward the entrance, her heart slamming into her ribs. The glass door exploded inward, shards of glass scattering across the floor. Libby's father dropped to the ground with a cry, clutching his chest. Blood everywhere.

Three figures in black masks rushed through the doors. Two carried semi-automatic weapons; the other man held a handgun. Their movements were like a practiced dance routine, everything moving in slow motion. The taller man shouted commands in Spanish, his voice cold and empty. "Nadie se mueve!"

This time, Sarah pushed Libby down beside her car, both of them crying and afraid. Her mind raced. Hide. Stay silent. Wait for a chance to escape. Her body trembling uncontrollably.

As she searched the parking lot for a place to escape, Mrs. Bercher took a bullet in the chest. Blood splattered across the counter as Libby's mom crumpled to the ground. Sarah strained to see. She tried to understand what was happening. She clung to the bed sheets and held on for dear life.

Sarah screamed out in her sleep and sat straight up. "NO-O-O!"

"Are you alright, Sarah?" Michael was holding her as she shook uncontrollably. "Reliving that awful time again?"

"I guess the mention of the cartel in class brought me back to this place. I can't seem to shake it."

"Was it the same dream?"

"This time there were three men who wore black masks so I couldn't see who they were, and I was outside my car, but everything else was the same," Sarah said as she began to cry uncontrollably.

Michael turned the lamp on and pulled Sarah close. He had helped her through these nightmares on many occasions and tonight would be no different. "Take a breath. Breathe in .... Now breathe out. Again .... In .... Out."

Sarah began to calm down. "It was just a dream."

"Yes, baby. It was just a dream. They aren't coming for you. They don't even know who you are, much less, where you live. It's going to be OK. Just breathe."

After the murder of John and Mindy Bercher and the police interrogations, Sarah never had a chance to say goodbye to her friend, Libby. That also haunted her.

Two men had been brought in on suspicion of the murder but there were no reliable witnesses other than Sarah, and the men provided a believable alibi. Sarah had witnessed the entire thing. She thought she could even describe the men but because of the misinformation she was exposed to by the local detectives, detectives now serving time in prison for working closely with the cartel, her memory of what she witnessed was contaminated. She suffered from a phenomenon called the misinformation effect, similar to dissociative amnesia, and therefore deemed an unreliable witness.

During the lineup, she failed to identify the two men that had killed the Berchers. The men were released and Sarah's recollection of the crime dismissed. The entire case began to crumble. The murders had never been solved, and after so many years, became a cold case. Sarah still longed for justice for the Bercher family, or perhaps it was revenge.

After the case fell apart, Sarah also fell apart. She returned to North Carolina for her senior year to finish her degree. Not being quite ready to teach, she continued her college education working on her master's degree in Gifted Education as she continued her therapy. It was during that time, at the University of North Carolina at Chapel Hill, that Sarah met Michael. He had been her protector ever since. Her therapist had told her someday she might gain her memory of that night, but so far, it had been a similar nightmare over and over, and she could never see the faces of the men.

In a therapy session, Sarah had learned that a traumatic event can affect someone emotionally, physically, and mentally. The therapist suggested that Sarah keep active as physical activity was a good way to reduce stress since stress was causing her reoccurring dreams. She encouraged Sarah to spend time with her family and to keep busy with hobbies, maybe even get away to a spot where she felt her best. Do things to help others.

Sarah had thrown herself into her work and in raising her kids. She walked dogs once a week at the animal shelter and Michael went with her once a month to help at the soup kitchen. But on occasion she needed a bigger distraction. She felt that it was her responsibility to make the world a better place to honor her friend, Libby. During those times she had crazy ideas for she and her sister. Emily had always tried to support Sarah after the incident. They had taken up jogging a few years back so they could run in a local 5K every fall to help with the Backpack program, which provided healthy snacks for kids in need. They worked together on a local telethon, giving their time for Muscular Dystrophy Make-A-Wish Foundation. Though her sister, Emily, lived in another state, it was a great way to get her to come home for a few weeks to visit and volunteer. They had been raised by wonderful parents who always made sure they did their part to help others. It became a vital form of therapy for Sarah to help someone.

Her latest venture involved a company called Strands of Hope. She had heard about it from one of her students. Hayes was growing out his hair, so he could cut it and donate it to help another kid who didn't have hair for whatever reason. Feeling ready for a change, Sarah decided that cutting and donating her hair would be an easy way to help a child in need. Sarah could always get Emily to help her cause. She would simply remind Sarah that she didn't have children so she should help those who did. It was time for another distraction from the terrifying reality of her college days after memories of the cartel had resurfaced due to the incident in class.

"Emily, this is a wonderful idea, and it only takes an hour of your time! But the best part, besides helping someone, of course, is the fact that it won't cost you anything! Girl, we were blessed with thick, beautiful hair that grows fast! I think we should start the fall season with a cute new haircut. We're getting ready to go to San Antonio so let's go with a fresh new look."

"How much of my hair do I have to whack off and give away?" questioned Emily.

"You're required to donate 12-14 inches of hair, and we can certainly do that without any problem. And just think how light and breezy you would feel if you cut that much off and helped a sweet little girl in the process. The company is called Strands of Hope. With our hair, someone could feel human and beautiful again. The company can make wigs for girls as old as 18 so this is a great cause. What do you say?"

"How do you always make it seem impossible for me to say no to you? What's a little hair, right? Okay, put me down for the donation and a haircut." Emily thought about what it would be like to have an illness that caused your hair to fall out. Devastating. Yes, this would be an easy way to give back to the community, help her sister with a little therapy, and come home with a great haircut in the process. She had just broken things off with Stephen. A new look would make her feel alive again.

Sarah was ecstatic when she made the call to the salon for two appointments. This would be the best, and easiest way to help someone.

The following week, Emily made a quick trip home to North Carolina and headed to the salon with Sarah.

"Here goes nothing," Sarah said as her hair was braided into four long braids.

"Nothing? Here goes everything," Emily commented, taking one last look at her long, blonde hair.

The sisters allowed their hair to be braided and cut off, packaged together and sent to Strands of Hope. And, in the process, they got new hairstyles. Sarah would be heading back to school for the second quarter with a new look. Emily was a chef, and the shorter cut allowed her to still have an updo, but now it was just below her shoulders which made her look more professional.

"Emily, your hair looks fabulous and hopefully we just helped someone else! You know I have fun ideas, and we always enjoy a good laugh," Sarah mused.

"I'll have to admit, cutting your hair into a short, bouncy bob, makes you look refreshed and younger. And yes, you usually have fun ideas. But girl, as far as that ancestry test? That was the best laugh yet."

"Oh, why do you have to keep bringing that up?" questioned Sarah. "Will I ever hear the end of that?"

"I always bring it up because it was the craziest thing we've done. I keep thinking it had to be bogus. How in the world could my results say that 15% of my ancestry came from El Salvador and you, 12%? Mom's grandparents came over from Germany. And Dad? He is a mix of Irish, English and a little Cherokee. Martin is one of the most common names in Ireland," Emily retorted.

"So, you're saying that the possibility of us having any El Salvadorian is a stretch?" laughed Sarah.

"It's so out of line, it isn't even a stretch! But it was fun to get the results. However, I think I'll stick with telling people we're Irish German. We certainly don't look El Salvadoran with all this blonde hair," Emily remarked.

"Well, while we're on the subject, I will say, I did some more digging after we got the results, and it seems that our great-great-grandfather may have actually come from El Salvador. I asked Dad's uncle Giles, and he said his grandparents had always been tight-lipped about the details. There was nothing else he could tell me, other than our great-great-grandfather had married in this country and shortened his name from Martinez to Martin," Sarah confided.

"Do you really believe that? Uncle Giles is senile. I don't believe anything he says. After what happened to you in college, he's just trying to make you think you're a part of a crime family. I think he was just trying to string you along, so you'd keep going back to the nursing home to visit. We're not El Salvadorian, we don't look El Salvadorian, and we're not going to discuss the possibility again. Those tests are in no way accurate. I think it's just an estimate of what your DNA might be."

"I agree, it's just that all the rest of it looked legit since it listed German, Irish, Scandinavian, English and Cherokee. But you're right, I should just let it go.

Change of subject; let's talk about meeting up in San Antonio. October is almost here."

"I'm way ahead of you on that one. My plan is to fly into Dallas, rent an SUV, stop by the *Savory Bytes* factory to gather my Nitro-Chill samples and other items, then drive to San Antonio in the SUV. It only makes sense. I have so much to haul to the convention, putting it on a plane would cost way too much," Emily said.

Sarah smiled. "Thank you, Emily. I am so glad you're going with me. I will fly out and meet you at the El Amado Hotel. Our reservations are in the main tower of the hotel, Mi Amor. We're on the sixth floor. And Emily? Please drive carefully."

"That's the only way I drive!" Emily said, giving Sarah two thumbs up.

Chapter 6

The late October sun dipped below the horizon, casting a warm, golden hue over the sprawling El Amado Hotel and the Riverwalk. The temperature was perfect at 70 degrees with the trees swaying gently in the evening breeze. The air carried the tantalizing aroma of fresh-baked bread and sizzling fajitas from nearby restaurants, where soft mariachi melodies filled the night with music that tugged at the heartstrings. You could hear the gentle lapping of the water as gondolas glided beneath arched stone bridges. The guests at the resort wandered through the vibrant courtyard, laughter of children and the chatter of adults creating a lively backdrop to the serene surroundings.

Amid the cheerful crowd, three women arrived at the hotel, each with a unique purpose for being there.

The first of the three, Sarah Lawson, had always been a woman of intellect and passion. With a determined stride, she navigated through the resort's corridors, a sense of excitement building within her. The elegant Spanish colonial architecture, terracotta tiles, wrought-iron balconies, and hand-carved wooden details filled her with excitement. She had traveled from North Carolina to attend the highly acclaimed National Talented and Gifted Conference where she would join more than 2,000 educators as they gathered to share best practices for supporting high-ability children. But it was more than that. This year Sarah would be a presenter! Her materials had been shipped the weekend before, so there was nothing left to do but show up.

Sarah's beautiful blonde hair, once flowing down her back, had been transformed into a stylish shoulder-length bob, a change she had embraced to match her determination and her maturing age. Dressed for travel, Sarah exuded practicality and quiet refinement. Wearing a plain blouse and stretchy jeans, she had a lightweight cardigan tied around her shoulders. She wore her low-heeled loafers ensuring comfort without sacrificing appearance. Her large shoulder bag was replete with all the necessities of an educator; mystery book, journal, reading glasses, lesson plans, iPad, mints, Chapstick, tissues, a small first aid kit complete with bandages and aspirin, a various assortment of colored pens, a scarf and, of course, a small umbrella-just in case.

In another corner of the resort, Emily Martin, Sarah's sister, was drawing the attention of passersby as she unloaded display boards and cooking utensils from her SUV. She paused for a moment to take in her surroundings; twinkling lanterns along the Riverwalk and the scents of savory foods drifting through the air. In this place where old-world charm met the vibrancy of a festive town, she felt both connected to history and swept up in an ambiance that transcended time.

Emily's hair, a golden-streaked blond, was in a French twist with a few whisps escaping. She wore a midi-length tailored dress paired with matching low heels that blended comfort and versatility while maintaining a professional, polished appearance. She looked both approachable and authoritative. Emily was an innovator, an entrepreneur who had made waves in the culinary world with her groundbreaking invention, the Nitro-Chill. She was a featured guest at the International Food & Wine Festival, a magical taste tour that promised to whisk you across six continents and beyond, as you sampled mouthwatering delicacies.

As the founder of her own culinary technology company, *Savory Bytes*, Emily was determined to revolutionize the way people experienced food. The Nitro-Chill, which utilized liquid nitrogen to freeze and transform culinary creations, was her latest triumph. Emily was there not only to showcase her revolutionary invention, but to also spend quality time with her sister, Sarah. They had forged a plan to meet up at the El Amado Hotel for a week of learning sprinkled with evenings full of sisterly bonding.

And finally, Isabella Martinez-Alvarez, who stood in a quiet corner of the resort's garden, gazing at the moonlit waters of the Riverwalk. Her Black hair fell in waves to her waist, a stark contrast to her fair skin and elegant attire. She wore a custom ensemble by Adam Lippes, a dark grey textured silk suit accented with pearls and a swooped neckline. Isabella exuded an air of elegance and grace, fitting for a middle-aged woman who was about to embark on a journey of great significance.

Isabella was at the El Amado Hotel for a different reason entirely. Her daughter, Sofía, was set to be married in a lavish ceremony that would take place in just a few days. As the mother of the bride, Isabella had thrown herself into the preparations, ensuring that every detail was perfect. She would not let the fact that her husband smuggled in his newest bochona ruin things.

"Antonio thinks I don't know she's here. He's loco!" she thought.

Isabella would make her daughter's wedding day special even if it killed her. And she would do her best to keep Antonio's girlfriend a secret from her daughter and her daughter's future in-laws.

As the sun dipped lower and the shadows grew longer, the three women continued to navigate their individual worlds within the resort. Unbeknownst to them, their paths were about to intersect in the most unexpected manner. Though it was a coincidence, Sarah and Emily together, along with Isabella, had rooms on the sixth floor in the main tower of the hotel, next to each other. And down that same hall, Antonio Alvarez, Isabella's husband, was sharing a room with his newest love interest, Luna Aguliar. But beneath the laughter, beneath the celebration and excitement, a dark undercurrent was beginning to churn, and the fate of these women would soon be inexplicably woven together by threads of intrigue and suspicion.

In the heart of this idyllic setting, where dreams were meant to come true and happiness was meant to flourish, a dark storm was gathering, ready to disrupt the lives of Emily, Sarah, Isabella, and Antonio. Without their knowledge, the next few days would unravel a web of secrets, lies and unforeseen connections that would challenge their understanding of truth, loyalty and the depths of human nature.

Chapter 7

Isabella Martinez-Alvarez stood on the cusp of a bittersweet milestone; her baby girl was about to marry and step into a life of her own. The days ahead promised a whirlwind of celebrations: a lively rehearsal dinner, a spirited dance, and the grand wedding that many were already calling the event of the century. Sofía, her daughter, was marrying Samuel Anderson, a young man from one of Texas's most influential and affluent families. Isabella couldn't help but feel a swell of pride in the choice Sofía had made, her heart brimming with a mother's love and hope for the future.

Isabella had met her own husband, Antonio Alvarez, at a young age and their love story was a central part of her life. Though she was from El Salvador, their fathers were business partners and made sure they found each other. After attending the University in Austin, she returned to Oaxaca, Mexico, where she and Antonio took the final step and married. They started their own business and relocated to Culiacán where they established their business headquarters.

Isabella's marriage to Antonio, though by choice, found her in the world of the Mexican cartel. To the outside world, Antonio was a businessman owning one of the top grossing companies in Mexico specializing in the production, distribution and wholesale of beverages and purified waters. Through Botella de Agua International, he had the only company of this type in all of Mexico, but he was also one of the biggest money launderers for the Mexican cartel.

Isabella's home in Culiacán reflected both immense wealth and constant vigilance. The property was enclosed by towering, reinforced walls topped with barbed wire, and heavy wrought-iron gates that were guarded around the clock. Within the walls, a sprawling Mediterranean-style home spread across an expanse of property adorned with terracotta roof tiles, arched windows, and manicured gardens filled with tropical plants and fountains. Inside, the grand entrance boasted polished marble floors, a sweeping staircase with wrought-iron railings, and an opulent crystal chandelier.

The living spaces were richly furnished with oversized leather sofas, silk and velvet textiles, custom-carved wooden tables, and walls adorned with fine art and family portraits.

Security was paramount, with a sophisticated surveillance system, a panic room, and quarters for armed guards. A discreet helipad was at the edge of the property to provide swift escape. Her home was a grand testament to both the opulence and peril inherent in Isabella's world.

Their daughter, Sofía, believed that her father was an important businessman. She had been kept sheltered from the real business dealings of her family. Marrying Samuel would ensure that she was safely out of Mexico and away from the danger. With her son, Antonio Jr., out of Mexico and enrolled in college in Cambridge, Massachusetts, Isabella needed only to worry about herself and of course, her brother, Enrique.

Getting married at the El Amado Hotel and resort was not a choice that Isabella would have made. She had always imagined a wedding in their home with Sofía walking down the grand staircase, her wedding dress flowing behind. However, she relented to the wishes of Sofía. She had wanted a 'magical wedding', and what better place to get married, than along the Riverwalk in San Antonio. Isabella was certain that Samuel's mother had put that idea in her daughter's head. But, getting married in Culiacán, Mexico would be dangerous. With the worry of Los Zetas, and their threats to her family, having the wedding celebration in the States seemed like a safe decision. Antoino wasn't on the FBI wanted list yet, he was merely on a watch list. Hopefully, it would stay that way.

Sofía, like her mother, Isabella, was striking with her long, jet-black hair, and dark, expressive eyes. Her demeanor was graceful, and her style was a blend of traditional Mexican fashion and modern elegance. They both preferred tailored dresses and extravagant statement jewelry. From the back, it would be difficult to know if you were seeing Sofía or Isabella. A confusion in which Isabella took great delight.

Isabella, herself, was a mix of strength and vulnerability. She was deeply committed to her children, but her loyalty to her husband was wavering. She continually found herself in the role of mediator and peacekeeper within her family. Her brother, Enrique Martinez, was slowly getting mixed up with Antonio and his dealings with the cartel. He was a vital part of the cartel's plan to move deep into El Salvador.

Isabella spent most of her time trying to prevent unnecessary violence. She had a strong moral compass and was conflicted by the violence and harm caused by Antonio's enterprise. She never wanted to be a Narcos wife. She didn't love that life, or the danger and she certainly didn't want to call the shots! But worst of all, she was appalled that Antonio would bring his bochona to San Antonio for their daughter's wedding. He believed she knew none of this, but she was informed of everything. She had allies in the company.

Facing Antonio this week would be difficult at best. He and his lieutenants would be at the wedding watching her every move. Her Catholic faith kept her committed and faithful to her marriage, but his commitment was definitely lacking. Being Dom Alvarez, she knew he had inappropriate relations with his buchonas. His newest girlfriend was flamboyant and loud. The fact that he brought her to San Antonio and made the decision to share a room with her had Isabella in a state of rage. Isabella was his wife, which guaranteed a home and security. But Luna was the recipient of his love and affection. She would just have to make it through the week and then see where things stood between them. A divorce would be the death of her – or him if she had a preference! Besides, the cartel would never allow a split without a death. She held too many secrets. She put the depressing thoughts out of her mind as she headed down to the pre-wedding party. As she entered the courtyard, she thought she spotted the buchona flirting with Victor, one of the cartel members. Great, she thought. Antonio will ruin this celebration with his anger as usual if he sees them together.

The wedding was just a few days away. Surely, she could make it until after the ceremony. At this point, she would focus all her attention on her daughter, Sofía. If things got too out of hand, she would call on her brother, Enrique. He was a man of great importance in El Salvador and would be attending the wedding. Hopefully, Antonio would listen to reason.

As Isabella was deep in thought, she ran right into her dearest friend and former college roommate, Lydia.

"Oh, Lydia! It's so good to see you here. I'm honored that you came to Sofía's wedding. Where's Evie?" Isabella said as she slipped her arm around her dear friend.

Though their personal lives were now worlds apart, Lydia was Isabella's confidante. They spent considerable time together sharing life's ups and downs since graduating. Lydia had been the maid of honor at Isabella's wedding and was the god mother to her son, Antonio, Jr. as well as Sofía. Isabella was Evie's godmother and spoiled her every chance she had.

"Isabella, honey, you know I wouldn't miss this event for anything. Your children are very special to me; almost as special as you. Evie is over there with that group of young people."

Isabella searched the courtyard looking for her god daughter. "I don't recognize her. Tell me which one she is."

"Oh, darlin', I haven't told you the good news. You've been so busy with wedding plans. Evie is there in the blue dress. She finally got her new wig, and she feels human again! You see her?"

"Ay dios mío! She is absolute asombrosa. I am so happy to see her enjoying life. Alopecia is such a terrible disease to happen to such a beautiful soul. How long has she had this new wig?"

Lydia responded, "She just received it days before we left. She was so thankful to have it in time for the wedding. And I tell you, I have never seen her happier. And how is my little Antonio Junior doing these days?"

"I don't see him by the pool now, but earlier, he was having deep conversations with Enrique. Little Antonio is still living in Massachusetts, working on that law degree. But he doesn't use the name Antonio Jr. He simply goes by A.J. I don't think he cares too much for his heritage. He has said he will never return to Mexico, but we shall see," Isabella said.

Lydia responded, "I am so proud of him getting his law degree. But honey, I thought he would surely return to Mexico, as that would be helpful for the family business, yes?"

"Antonio is banking on it! He thinks a lawyer under his wing will ensure that no legal trouble comes his way. However, A.J. is adamant that he will not be a part of the business. Only time will tell." Isabella confided.

Lydia just frowned and shook her head.

"Thank God Sofía and Samuel will be living in Austin alongside his family. I worry most about her safety. Culiacán is no place for her. But in just a few days, she will be married and starting a life of her own as Sofía Anderson. I want her to have the life I dreamed of having." Isabella looked around to make sure Antonio's men weren't listening to her conversation. She noticed Jose lurking nearby and knew she needed to move away from him. "If you will excuse me, I need to ensure everything is running smoothly. I will have more time to talk after the ceremony. I have much to tell you."

"Until we speak, dear friend, I'm here for you," comforted Lydia. As Isabella disappeared into the crowd, Lydia navigated through the courtyard enjoying the party and all the ambiance it had to offer. "Yes," she thought. "She and Isabella needed some privacy to speak openly." She felt in her heart that something was not quite right with her dear friend, and she was determined to help her through this rough patch.

Chapter 8

Late that afternoon, Lydia walked along the Riverwalk trailing her daughter as she popped in and out of boutiques. Evie was headed to college in the upcoming semester and having the perfect wardrobe was all she could think about. Lydia's mind began to wander as she recalled attending college herself for the first time.

The sun blazed mercilessly over the sprawling sidewalk, and it took Lydia's memory back to the campus of the University of Texas at Austin. She was a petite blonde with sharp blue eyes and a smile that seemed too big for her small frame. She had been determined to make a name for herself on campus in her suede cowboy boots and miniskirts. She saw a lot of herself in Evie, as Evie shopped for the perfect look.

Lydia remembered she was midway through her freshman year, and though far from her parents' Hill Country ranch, she felt at home in Austin. She thrived in the bustling city, where street musicians played soulful blues, and the scent of barbecue lingered in the air. Her curiosity about the world extended far beyond the borders of her upbringing, and it was that curiosity that led her to cross paths with Isabella Martinez.

Isabella, with her jet-black hair cascading down her back and eyes as dark as midnight, possessed an effortless elegance that turned heads wherever she went. Her family had sent her to Texas for an American education. Beneath her polished exterior, however, Isabella carried the weight of secrets that would shape her destiny.

The two women met in an economics class. Lydia, eager and slightly nervous, had offered to share her notes with Isabella after noticing her struggle to keep up with the rapid-fire lectures. "Honey, you look like you could use a little help." Lydia had said with a grin.

Isabella had hesitated, her pride tugging her in one direction, but something about Lydia's openness disarmed her. "Thank you. I could use a friend more than anything."

From that moment, an unlikely bond formed between them. Lydia's warmth and relentless optimism complemented Isabella's quiet, measured grace. They became inseparable, studying late into the night, sharing secrets over tacos from a food truck near campus, and wandering the city under the neon glow of Sixth Street.

As the months passed, Lydia noticed shadows creeping into her friend's life –whispers of late-night phone calls and urgent meetings with mysterious men. Isabella's answers to Lydia's questions grew vague. "It's just family business," she would say, her tone cutting off further inquiry.

One evening, as they sat on the worn leather couch of their shared apartment, Lydia confronted her. "Isabella, honey, are you in trouble? If something's wrong, I want to help. You know I'm here for you."

Isabella's eyes softened, and for a moment, the mask slipped. "It's complicated. My fiancé... is involved in things that are dangerous. Things I can't walk away from."

Lydia reached for her hand. "We're in this together, Isabella. You're my best friend. We'll figure it out. You know there isn't much I wouldn't do for you."

"Would you be an alibi for someone if I needed you to be? I hesitate to ask, but my family may be getting into unspeakable trouble." Isabella whispered, as she was ashamed to speak any louder.

"For you, my dear friend, I'll do it. No questions asked. Just tell me how I can help."

Relief washed over Isabella's face. "I'll be forever grateful. Here is the plan ..."

It was at that moment that their friendship was sealed, and Isabella knew she could count on Lydia for absolutely anything. Lydia knew she was wading into dangerous waters, but she had sworn her loyalty to her friend.

Despite the dark currents running beneath their friendship, the two women stood as each other's pillars. Isabella introduced Lydia to her sprawling, tightly knit family during a visit to Mexico, and Lydia invited Isabella to her family's ranch, where they rode horses under the vast Texas sky.

Graduation came too quickly, and with it, the choices that would separate them. Isabella married young, her wedding a lavish affair to a man whose eyes were as sharp as the blade of a knife. Lydia watched her best friend walk down the aisle, the weight of knowledge pressing heavily on her heart. But she stood at her side, ever a support to her dearest friend.

The bond between them never broke. When Lydia married her college sweetheart in a simple ceremony beneath an ancient oak tree, Isabella stood by her side as maid of honor, her laughter bright and pure. And when their children were born, a fiery-eyed boy for Isabella, followed by a dark-eyed girl, an exact image of her mother, and then a cherubic girl for Lydia, they became godparents to each other's most precious gifts.

Through the years, their lives spiraled in opposite directions; one rooted in quiet Texas ranch life, the other entwined in the ruthless world of cartels and power. But their friendship endured. Late-night phone calls crackled with laughter and tears, and the rare visits were filled with stories of simpler times.

When Lydia's husband was killed in a ranching accident, Isabella was there to comfort her friend. She helped her pack up her life on the ranch and relocate to Austin with her daughter. 'Anything to help my friend' had always been their vow to each other.

One summer night, while the cicadas sang and the stars blinked above her home, Lydia sat on the porch, her daughter asleep on her lap. She dialed a familiar number and waited.

"Lydia," Isabella's voice came, soft but steady.

"I miss you," Lydia whispered. "Come visit soon. Let's remember what life felt like before everything got so... complicated."

Isabella sighed. "There have been complications in our lives. Many that we don't want to relive. Si? Things have gotten very difficult for me and my family as you may have realized but I will try to visit. One day. I promise."

But they both knew that some promises were harder to keep than others.

The two maintained close contact through phone calls and letters, but it wasn't until this wedding that they were finally able to reconnect face to face after the passage of many years.

Chapter 9

At 23 years old, Antonio Jr. possessed striking features with his dark, expressive eyes, thick eyelashes, and jet-black hair, often a disheveled mess. He had a well-defined, chiseled jawline that gave him an air of confidence and strength. His olive skin radiated a healthy, sun-kissed glow, reflecting his Hispanic heritage and adding to his undeniable allure. He was a captivating blend of rugged masculinity and sensual elegance.

As a third-year law student, being at Sofía's wedding was costing him valuable time away from school, but his mother had insisted he come for the week. During the pre-wedding party, he decided to pass the time by the pool area checking out the girls.

With champagne in hand, he headed to a chaise lounge near the pool. The area boasted a large pool and, in the center, a 50-foot replica of a Mayan pyramid. Even in San Antonio, at one of the nicest resorts, he couldn't get away from his Hispanic heritage. He sat and watched the water stream down the steps of the massive stone structure into the Lost

City of Cibola and listened to the screams and laughs of children as they plunged headlong into the water on the spitting Jaguar Slide.

"Anglos think Mexico is so full of charm," he thought. "But they never think about the cartel."

As a student of the law, he was becoming more and more aware of just how powerful the Mexican cartel could be. His law professor had recently led a discussion on the Mexican cartel and cartel detection. The government uses what is referred to as cartel screening to identify collusive patterns in firm conduct such as prices and bids. His own father owned the largest wholesale distribution of beverages in Mexico, Botella de Agua International. There were no other companies like it. He had always had suspicions that his father was involved in the cartel because he controlled all the wholesale prices. He had companies all over Mexico, maybe even in his mother's homeland of El Salvador. As he pondered these things, his uncle, Enrique, joined him.

"Enjoying the view, I see," Enrique said as he sat down in a lounge chair near the pool next to A.J. "Is everything OK, you seem to be deep in thought."

Enrique Martinez was Isabella's older brother. He was a man of striking charisma and smoldering intensity. His dark, wavy hair framed a face defined by sharp cheekbones and a strong, square jaw. Deep-set, expressive eyes, almost black in color, conveyed both charm and a simmering edge of danger. His confident smile, with just a hint of mischief, had a way of disarming even the most skeptical. Standing with an effortless grace, Enrique carried the air of someone used to being in control—whether in business or in matters far more perilous. His tailored suits and polished demeanor masked a fierce loyalty to his family and a quiet, dangerous resolve when the stakes were high.

A.J. snapped out of his trance, "Oh, Enrique, I didn't see you walk up. Yes, everything is fine. I was just thinking about school and the coming semester."

"Are you learning much about the law?"

"Yes. As a matter of fact, I have a paper due soon. I was just thinking about it," A.J. confessed.

"So, tell me, what have you learned, that you will write about?" Enrique asked.

A.J. sat in silence for a moment thinking about what to say before answering. "My paper is about criminal violations of antitrust laws. Did you know that under the Sherman Act, Section 2, it is illegal to monopolize or attempt to monopolize in a business."

"Antitrust laws can be a tricky thing," Enrique commented.

"You know about antitrust laws?" A.J. asked incredulously.

Enrique responded, "Of course, I'm in business. I know of these laws. You must be very careful in business, controlling market prices and colluding with the wrong people. Very careful."

"I have suspicions that my father is colluding with the wrong people. What do you think?" A.J. confided.

"I cannot speak on behalf of your father. But I can tell you this; Stay in Cambridge where you are safe and do not speak of your suspicions again. Sometimes the walls have ears." With that, Enrique rose and headed back to the party.

As he reached the main lobby, he thought he spotted one of Antonio's men lurking around. He was about to approach him when he passed a beautiful woman speaking with the concierge about a bar called *The Moon's Daughters*. She was planning a night out with her sister in a couple of days and wanted to go to someplace fun.

"*The Moon's Daughters*, huh? I might need to have a fun evening out as well," he thought as he walked back towards the wedding venue.

A.J. remained poolside deep in thought. Not soon after Enrique left, Samuel joined him.

"Hey, little brother!" he teased.

"Hello, Samuel. It won't be long before I *am* your brother. I'm sure Sofía is a mess right now with all that is going on. She's definitely high maintenance."

Samuel chuckled at the comment. "High maintenance doesn't even come close when it comes to this wedding and your sister. Everything has to be perfect, a real fairytale affair. That's why I'm staying out of the way. My job is simply to show up and say yes."

A.J. considered his comment. "You are saying yes to a lot of things. You have no idea."

"Considering the amount of time I've spent with Sofía and your family, I have a pretty good grasp on what I am saying yes to. But love is the most important thing."

The two sat silently in thought and contemplated their situations until Samuel's phone pinged.

"Duty calls! I guess slipping out of the party for a quiet moment isn't allowed. See you later, Bro." he said as he sprang from the lounge chair and headed inside.

"Duty," thought A.J. "Duty to whom? Sofía, the Alvarez family, the cartel?" That was a tough question, with an answer A.J. didn't have.

Antonio saw his son by the pool and decided it was a good opportunity to talk about family business with him. He needed Antonio Jr. home as soon as he graduated to begin duties at his company.

"Hola, hijo," Antonio said as he sat down next to A.J.

"Hello, Papá," he replied.

Antonio jumped right in, telling A.J. what was on his mind. "You are to graduate soon, sí?"

"Yes, Papá, I have one more semester and then I can take the bar exam."

"Excelente!" Antonio exclaimed, clasping his hands together. "When that is done, I have a position for you in my company."

A.J. was torn. "I plan to make my own way in the world, just as you have done. I will not be joining you in Mexico."

Antonio began to get angry. Color rose from his neck to his face. "This is not up for discussion. You will return to Mexico and represent my company as our attorney. There is no other plan."

"But Papá, I want to follow my own dreams. I have already discussed this with Mamá, and she agrees," A.J. said.

"Your Mamá? Your Mamá?! You are not a bebé. You do not discuss matters of business with your Mamá,"

Antonio spat. "You discuss them with me, man to man. But there is no discussing this. You will return to Mexico and take your position within *OUR* company. The plans are already set for you to be the legal representative of the company. And in time, the company will become yours." With that, Antonio rose and walked away leaving A.J. alone with his concerns.

Enrique and his mother advised him not to return to Mexico, yet his father had insisted he return. A.J. had been having doubts about the legality of his father's company and this was just another strike against returning home. It was certainly not the life he wanted for himself.

A.J. headed back to his room before anyone else showed up to give him advice. As he was leaving, he noticed that he was being watched by one of his father's people. The walls definitely had eyes and ears!

Chapter 10

The day of the presentation was upon Sarah. Her nerves were running through her body like lightning! She was beginning to second guess herself, and she could feel her blood pressure going up. Was this presentation good enough? She had heard so many wonderful speakers this week.

"Emily, I can't calm my nerves!" Sarah exclaimed.

Emily smiled. "A quick call to Michael might calm you down."

"I don't know what I'd do without you ... or Michael for that matter. I'm calling him now."

As soon as Michael picked up, she started, "Oh, Michael, I'm so worried I won't do a good job today. I'm nervous as a cat..."

"... in a room full of rocking chairs?" Michael chuckled, trying to lighten the moment. "Sarah don't fret. You've got this. Just look at it as a conversation, not a performance. Just have a conversation like you do with me when you're telling me about a unit or lesson you are going to teach. You're just speaking with people, teachers like yourself. You're not speaking TO them. Watch their reactions as you talk about your unit. See the interested looks on their faces, just like you do with your own students. Share a joke or a laugh. Enjoy yourself and enjoy your audience. Sarah, I'm telling you, you've got this!"

"I wish you were here to give me a reassuring hug. You're the best," said Sarah.

Michael replied, "I love you too, now go knock it outta the park! Call me when you're finished so you can tell me how well you did."

Sarah was reenergized and she knew she would get through this. She had presented different units at the state conference, and this would be no different. She gave herself a peptalk as she walked along the Riverwalk all the way to the Stars at Night Ballroom at the convention center. Along the way, she passed two Hispanic men in a heated discussion.

"I'm telling you!" yelled the first man. "Break it off with Luna. If Antonio finds out, he will have you killed!"

"He's not going to find out! He's focused on the wedding, not on me. I'm his top lieutenant. Nothing wrong with having a little fun."

They immediately stopped talking when Sarah neared them. They crossed their arms and watched her walk past, with an air of suspicion. She felt nervous and uncomfortable, so she sped up her pace and kept walking.

"Stupid Gringo!" the first man muttered under his breath in her direction.

"Did he just say killed? I never imagined having to worry about the cartel at a teacher's conference. My mind has gone into overdrive," Sarah thought. It gave her a very uneasy feeling as she looked back over her shoulder. Although it had been years since her best friend had gone into protective custody, she was still worried about her own safety. But she quickly put the notion out of her head as she remembered why she was there and started from the beginning and presented her unit to herself once again.

When Sarah was out of sight, Victor grabbed Jorge by the arm. "Did you notice that gringo? Did you see her face?"

"No, I do not notice gringos. They do not interest me."

"Perhaps you should take notice. That was the one. She has to be! She was the girl that witnessed the hit in Austin at the Luxe Loom all those years ago. Do you think she has remembered? She looked right at us. We need to let Antonio know that she is in San

Antonio. If she should suddenly be able to identify us, we are dead."

"Si! He will want to know. I will follow her and see where she's going. I will get word to you when she is located. In the meantime, stay away from Luna. Ciao!"

As Jorge headed in Sarah's direction, Victor quickly headed back to the hotel, to the secure location in the El Carino wing. He had many things to discuss with Antonio.

By the time Sarah arrived at the conference, she had presented the unit to herself three or four times. It was a welcome to the convention that Sarah would never forget. The sign outside the lecture room read, NTAGC Annual Convention, Accidental Inventions with Sarah Lawson, North Carolina. She quickly had someone snap a picture of her next to the signage so that she could text it to Michael. She would later notice the mysterious man standing in the background of the picture watching her.

The conference room began to fill up with lots of excited teachers chatting about speakers they had already heard or ones they were looking forward to hearing. Hopefully, they would be excited when they left this one. Dressed in her accidental invention themed 'OOPS t-shirt' and slacks, she put on a smile and stood before her audience.

"Good morning, friends. What a happy accident that I have been given this opportunity to speak with you. It wasn't my original plan to be a presenter, but sometimes the unexpected events in our lives seem to work out for our benefit. So, let's get started with this serendipitous adventure."

Sarah took a deep breath before continuing. "I'm Sarah Lawson, GT teacher from North Carolina. Let me ask you: Have you ever wondered how Coca-Cola or potato chips were created? It is probably not how you might imagine it. Did you realize that cheese puffs, bubble wrap and Post-it notes were accidents? What about Play-Doh? Now that's a fun accident."

Sarah continued with her unit, presenting all the different accidental inventions. She showed pictures of her students at their invention convention, elaborating on all the wonderful ideas that her students developed. She then introduced the idea of Dippin' Dots and had them all up creating their own tasty treat. It couldn't have gone any better. The group was lively and excited about her presentation, full of questions and even some ideas of their own. She was a hit at the conference.

So many teachers were talking about the amazing unit that the conference committee asked her to do a repeat performance for teachers that missed it and were asking when it would be presented again. Sarah left that day with a long list of new teacher connections; teachers that wanted to stay in touch and share ideas. Laurie from Washington, Karen from Arkansas, Amy from California, Laura from New Mexico; the list was endless. She couldn't wait to call Michael. Afterall, he was expecting to hear how well she did.

"Hello?"

"Michael, I did it! Thanks for all your encouragement. I presented my unit, and they have asked me to do a repeat because so many others heard about it and want to attend." Sarah was overjoyed.

"What have I always told you? You're the best teacher around. I'm not surprised that you've been asked to give an encore performance. Record it this time. I want to see you in action!"

Sarah laughed. "I'll do my best."

"Who knows, maybe you could add some of it to the documentary that your little kiddo is doing at school. It would truly show the real you!"

"Speaking of me, you'll never believe who I met today. None other than Joseph Renzulli, founder of the Renzulli Center. I also met Ann Robison. I know you've heard me talk about both of them."

"That's exciting for you," Michael commented.

"Actually, it *is* exciting. I follow all of their work."

Michael was truly encouraging. "Nice. Glad you are meeting people who inspire you to be a better educator. I can't wait for you to get home to tell me all about your experiences."

"I love you, Michael," Sarah said.

"I love you, too, Sarah! And keep those selfies coming! When I see how much you are enjoying the convention, it makes me happy that you're there, and I'm not as lonely. Make the most of your time and soak up as much knowledge as possible. I can't wait for you to come home!"

Later that evening, when Sarah returned to the hotel, she was reminiscing over the day she had experienced. Looking though the photos she had taken, she was suddenly shaking, and her skin was crawling. In one of her pictures, lurking behind the signage in the foyer of the convention center, was a man that seemed to be familiar to her. He was looking directly at her, but she couldn't quite place him. She just knew it left her feeling strange and uneasy.

Chapter 11

Smoke curled lazily through the dimly lit hotel suite, weaving its way between the figures of men gathered like shadows around their boss, cigars smoldering in their hands. Antonio stood apart, tension carved into the lines of his face, his unease palpable. Every fiber of his being strained against the calm he was forcing himself to maintain, his fury bubbling just beneath the surface. His voice, sharp and edged with desperation, cut through the haze. "Again, Victor. Tell me again."

"Señor, of this I am certain. It was the same person that police say witnessed the hit in Austin, and she looked directly into my eyes with a sense of recognition then she began to walk with urgency."

Antonio banged his fist on the table. "How could that be? She could not identify either of us! We have an alibi, remember?! The investigators assured us that we were safe."

Victor was unsure. "I know she could not identify us then, but what about now. We weren't guaranteed forever, and the investigators are serving time for their crimes. Jorge is trailing her and will keep us abreast of any updates. We will discover where she is and what her motives are. I assure you I will not rest until this is dealt with. She will not live to remember anything of the past."

"No mistakes! Do you hear me? No mistakes on Sofía's big day. Now get out of here and find that woman. Pronto!" Antonio screamed as he threw back a shot of tequila.

Chapter 12

That night, sleep did not come easily. When Sarah finally drifted off, her mind dragged her back into the nightmare.

The night was dark and suffocating as black smoke swirled around her. She felt the heat of her own breath against her hands as she crouched inside her car trying to stifle a scream. The sounds returned: the snap of gunfire, the shattering glass, the thud of bodies hitting the ground. She peered through the car window, her heart thundering. The men moved like shadows, swift and merciless.

She tried to focus on their faces. They shifted in her vision, warping and swirling with the smoke. She reached out to pull a mask away, but when her fingers grasped the edge, there was nothing underneath. Empty voids stared back at her. Dragon tattoos on the arms of the men.

She screamed; her voice lost in the dark.

Sarah's eyes flew open. Her body was drenched in sweat, her breath coming in panicked gasps. She pressed her hands against her eyelids, but the images clung to her mind like a film she couldn't rewind. She still couldn't see them. The men remained faceless phantoms in her memory.

Emily sat up with a start. "What happened? I thought I heard you scream?"

Sarah took a big, cleansing breath. "I think I'm ok. I just had a dream."

"Oh, sweetie, are you sure you're OK?" Emily questioned. "You look terrified."

"Yeah, I'm OK, it was just a dream. I'll be fine."

Emily pressed, "Are you positive? Do you want to talk about it? I can turn the light on if you want."

Sarah lay back down and rolled over, turning her back to her sister, tears filling her eyes. "It's OK, go back to sleep." She stayed that way the remainder of the night.

Chapter 13

"Sofía, hold still so I can braid this small section of your hair," Isabella said. "This may be the last time I get to do this for you. Estar quieto."

"Mamá, you will braid my hair many more times. I am only moving to Texas. I'll see you all the time," Sofía said.

"Dear Sofía, mi amor, I know this is what you say, but you will be busy attending to your new husband and your new life. I pray you do not forget your familia. But remember that sweet Lydia also lives in Austin. She can be there for you when I cannot."

"I'm so thankful for Lydia, but I am not losing my familia, Mamá. I am just gaining more! Now, how do I look?" Sofía asked.

"Hermosa, beautiful! Just as you imagined in your dreams. Samuel is a lucky man. Now come. It is time for you to get married," Isabella said as she put her arm around her daughter's waist and placed a kiss on her temple.

Just then, there was a knock at the door. Samuel's mother, Mary Lou Anderson, was standing there with her big Texas charm and her dazzling smile.

"Hello ladies! Oh Sofie, don't you look beautiful in your dress," Mrs. Anderson said in her southern drawl. "I just had to come sneak a peek at you before the start of the wedding."

Mary Lou Anderson was a true picture of a southern woman. She was strong and passionate about her family as well as her community. Her faith in God was obvious to anyone who took time to notice. She was admired by her friends for her hospitality and manners, sumptuous meals and lovely garden. Mary Lou liked to joke that she never left home without her face made up and her lipstick on. Standing at just under six feet, she was lean and attractive. She wore a long evening dress made of linen in a beautiful shade of light blue which accentuated her dark blue eyes and silver hair.

Sofía smiled in her most charming way, "Thank you. It was my Mamá's dress. I hope I look as stunning as she did when she was married."

"Oh honey, I can't imagine a more beautiful bride than the one I'm looking at right now. My Sam is one lucky man. Isn't she pretty, Belle? Your people do call you Belle, don't they?" she asked Isabella.

"My people?" Isabella said with a hint of annoyance in her voice. "No, my people, as you put it, call me Isabella. That is my name," replied Isabella.

"In Texas we shorten everyone's name, Belle. Isn't that right, Sofie? Unless, of course, you have a double name like me." she smiled.

Isabella was getting uncomfortable, and a bit upset every time Mrs. Anderson said Sofie instead of the beautiful name, Sofía, that she had given her daughter. Lydia was from Texas and she never did that, but Lydia was special.

"But as I was saying, Sofie, you are such a beautiful bride. We're so blessed to have you in our family."

"Thank you, Mrs. Anderson," Sofía said.

"Darling, you're soon to be family now. Please, call me Mary Lou, or just Lou if you prefer," she insisted as she gave her a big squeeze.

Sofía was hesitant. "Alright,... Mary Lou."

The string quartet began playing softly, signaling to the ladies that the wedding was about to begin. "Girls, I think it's time for the wedding," Mrs. Anderson hugged Sofía once more and said, "See you in there, Belle, Sofie," then she left and headed toward the wedding venue just as Antonio came around the corner.

"Hey, Tony, prepare to see a beautiful bride in there," Mrs. Anderson said with a huge grin on her face. Antonio looked at her in confusion and shook his head. "Who is Tony?" he said under his breath.

Entering the bridal room, Antonio paused a moment taking in the beauty of his daughter. What a momentous day. Even his wife was breathtaking. But shaking his head he said, "Isabella, you must go. Antonio Jr. is waiting to seat you, so the wedding can begin." He stepped aside and allowed his wife to leave the room.

Isabella took one more moment to gaze at her daughter, and pressing a kiss to her forehead she said, "Mi amore." She patted her hair into place, wiped a tear from her eye, and headed out the door.

Antonio took Sofía in his arms and held her for a moment. Then, placing a kiss on each side of her face, he extended his arm and the two of them left the bridal room.

"You are the most beautiful bride I have ever seen," Antonio said.

"What about Mamá? Was she not the most beautiful?"

"Sí, two beautiful brides. You favor her so much, it makes my heart proud," Antonio confided.

"I love you, Papá," Sofía whispered.

"Yo Tambien te quiero, I love you too, mi amor."

Together, they headed out of the bridal suite and into the beautifully lit courtyard where their guests were waiting. The quartet began playing Canon in D as Antonio escorted his beautiful daughter down the aisle. Everything was perfect.

But lurking in the corner, were two of Antonio's men being the eyes and ears for him. Nothing and no one would get past them. There would be no surprises per Antonio's orders.

Chapter 14

The wedding of Sofía Alvarez to Samuel Anderson was a spectacular affair that captured the essence of their love and the stark contrast between their two worlds: one of wealth and privilege and the other of danger and intrigue. Sofía had been sheltered from the darkness of her family's business and raised with the belief that there was more to life than the power and wealth that surrounded her. Samuel was a wealthy businessman with an empire of his own, working side-by-side with his father in Austin. He was known for his kindness and philanthropic efforts, the opposite of Sofía's family. He couldn't have imagined that the woman he was marrying was the daughter of a Narcos kingpin. But together they found solace, love and the promise of a brighter future.

The venue chosen for the wedding was the lush courtyard of the El Amado Hotel along the Riverwalk in the heart of San Antonio. Its towering trees and blooming gardens created a picturesque backdrop. The courtyard had been transformed into a wonderland of flowers, fairy lights, and cascading greenery, creating a whimsical atmosphere that brought a touch of magic to the occasion. Sofía had always wanted a magical wedding and today her wish was coming true.

The beautifully adorned courtyard featured a golden altar that was covered in white roses and calla lilies. Gold Chiavari chairs also boasted roses and lilies along the aisle. White rose pedals covered the red-carpet runner leading to the altar.

Sofía, radiant in her exquisite lace wedding gown, made her way down the aisle on her father's arm. Her beauty was breathtaking, as her veil cascaded over her dark hair like a waterfall, with one small braid running around her head.

"This is your day my sweet mijita."

"Papá, I am so happy. Thank you for this day and for honoring my wishes," Sofía replied.

Her eyes misted with tears as she paused and presented her mother with a red rose, a symbol of her love and devotion to her family. "Mamá, for you. Te Amare por siempre, I will love you forever."

Isabella replied, "Mi dulce hija, te tengo en mi Corazón." (My sweet daughter, I hold you in my heart.)

Samuel looked regal in his tailored black tux. It was a stark contrast to his fair skin and light hair. His deep blue eyes shone with love and admiration as he watched his bride approach. He had never seen a more beautiful princess. She was the essence of beauty and love. This day would be long remembered and cherished. He took her hand and placed a kiss on top. "I love you, Sofía."

The priest stood before the gathering, his presence, one of reverence and holy devotion to God. "And who gives this beautiful bride away?"

Antonio, eyes filled to the brim with tears, responded, "Her Mamá and I."

The priest made the sign of the cross and said, "Let us pray."

During the prayer, as Antonio moved next to Isabella on the front row, one of Antonio's men slipped in behind him and in a hushed voice, whispered into his ear. "We have eyes on her." Antonio simply nodded.

Samuel spoke his vows first. "Sofía, from the moment I saw you, I knew my heart had found its home. Your kindness, your courage, your fierce love for life have taught me what it means to be whole. I vow to stand beside you in joy and sorrow, to share every triumph and every trial, and to love you as fiercely in the storms as I do in the calm. I give you my heart, my faith, and my forever."

Sofía's eyes glistened as her lips trembled into a smile. Her voice, soft as the breeze, carried the weight of her heart. "Samuel, you have been my strength and my peace, my laughter in times of joy and my shelter in times of fear. I promise to honor you, to trust you, and to walk with you wherever this life leads us. I will love you with my whole soul, through every season and every storm, until my last breath and beyond."

The river murmured in the background as they slipped rings onto each other's fingers. A sudden breeze stirred the wisteria, and petals rained down like blessings from heaven. The world held its breath as Samuel leaned forward, brushing a kiss on her lips, gentle and sure, binding their promises with love. The gathered family and friends erupted into applause and cheers, but to Samuel and Sofía, there was only the thrum of their hearts, beating as one.

The love shared between the bride and groom was evident to all in attendance. It seemed to transcend the differences in their backgrounds. Sofía's family, clad in elegant attire, watched proudly as she found happiness with a man who embodied everything they could have hoped for. Isabella was especially thankful that Sofía was marrying an honorable man. Samuel's family celebrated their son's union with a woman whose charm and grace had captured their hearts.

Following the final blessing from the priest, Samuel and Sofía turned to their guests, smiles on their faces.

Sofía presented Mrs. Anderson a rose as they made their way back up the aisle. They were now Mr. and Mrs. Samuel Anderson.

After the ceremony, the guests were led to a sprawling candlelit courtyard along the Riverwalk for the reception.

Sofía and Samuel shared their first dance. It was a memory they both cherished deeply. As the couple embraced and shared a kiss, fireworks lit up the night sky. It was truly a magical evening.

Well before the party ended, the couple boarded a private gondola on the river for a short cruise before taking a limousine to the airport. A private jet awaited them that whisked them off to Paris where they would spend the next two weeks on their honeymoon. It couldn't have been a more perfect wedding.

But looming in the background of it all were Dom Alvarez's men guarding the courtyard and running interference. A threat from the Los Zetas was ever present in Antonio's life, and nothing was beneath them. His men's orders were to ensure that the wedding was beyond perfect in every way. When the event was winding down, and everyone began returning to their respective rooms, Antonio's men could relax and enjoy their surroundings while maintaining a low profile. All but one. Jorge was on guard on the sixth floor keeping an eye on the girl from the past.

Victor took the opportunity to find Luna, who was waiting at the bar. He loved her and wanted her for his own. Sneaking around Antonio was dangerous and could end in disaster. He must be careful until Antonio tired of her and moved on to someone else to fulfill his needs. It seemed to him that life was full of waiting. With Antonio still at the reception, this would be the perfect time to meet up with Luna.

Luna Aguliar was a vision to behold, and her appearance demanded attention. Her dress clung like liquid gold, a designer piece that cost more than most people's annual rent, the kind of fabric that shimmered with every movement, as though it shared in her confidence. She had diamonds in her ears, heavy but carefully chosen –*never too much.* Even excess required discipline.

Her hair cascaded in bleached, luxurious waves, perfectly styled to fall just past her shoulders. Not a strand dared stray. The rich blonde gleamed under the overhead lights, touched with golden undertones that hinted at long afternoons spent in sunlit gardens; gardens she didn't have to tend herself. Luna's makeup was applied like a masterpiece. Her brows arched and precise, framed eyes that smoldered with dark liner and shadow. Her lips were painted a fierce red, the kind of red that didn't kiss and tell but left a mark, nonetheless.

But it wasn't just her aesthetics. Luna was a force. Confidence radiated from her, unshakable, like the heat rising from desert sands. She moved as if the world bent to her whims—and often, it did. There was power in that. Buchona; It wasn't a label. It was a crown, dazzling and deadly. And it fit her perfectly.

"Victor, my darling," Luna purred, extending her hand. Victor took it, momentarily feeling the cold weight of rings adorned with emeralds and rubies, stones that could have been plucked from the depths of a pirate's treasure chest. "I've been waiting for you."

Chapter 15

"**I**' m sorry I had nightmares last night. They come on without warning most times, but I tell you, that man in the picture means something to me. My therapist said when the misinformation effect ended, if it ever did, I would begin to gain my memory of what really happened the night of that horrific murder. Could that be what is happening? It's been so many years. At this point, I didn't think it was possible. Could he be tied to the murders?"

"Sarah, I don't know. This whole misinformation effect is baffling to me. But I do know this. I will protect you, no matter what the cost. That guy doesn't know what he's in for with the Martin sisters. If he shows his face, I can assure you, he'll wish he hadn't! But I think this is something you will have to discuss with your therapist when you're back home. Now let's forget that creep and have an exciting night to finish off this wonderful week."

It *has* been a wonderful week," Sarah mused as she dressed in her nicest dress. "I have met some wonderful teachers; made some new friends and I have some amazing lessons I plan to use when the week is over. This has been the best place to network with like-minded people. What about you, Emily?"

"It has certainly been a profitable week for me! I've written orders for several Nitro-Chills so far and I have met some fabulous chefs! It *has* been amazing. The Nitro-Chill has been such a hit. But I can tell you what *isn't a hit.* It's that dress you're wearing. Seriously, Sarah?"

Sarah asked, "What is wrong with it? It's fun, it's flirty and it's not something I could wear in the classroom." She swished around allowing the skirt of her dress to move and flair out just below her knees.

"Girl, you shouldn't wear it in the classroom or ANY WHERE ELSE! You look like Mom. Please! Flirty? If you call a Peter Pan collar and sensible shoes flirty, then we're in trouble. We aren't going to Parents' Night. Here, put this dress on," Emily said, pulling another cocktail dress from the closet. "It will do wonders for your appearance and will draw some attention. You have a great figure, why not show it off."

"Emily, I am not seeking attention, and I don't think I could pull that off for a second! In case you've forgotten, I'm a mature woman in my forties." Sarah complained.

"You may think you're mature, but you still have a great body. You're wearing this cocktail dress and you're wearing these shoes! We are going out to have fun not to conference with the parents of a troubling child."

"Why would you have two cocktail dresses on this trip?" questioned Sarah.

"I've got more than two. Besides, I like choices, and I know you. I knew you wouldn't have a fun dress to wear that was appropriate for going out. And while I'm at it, let me do your hair and makeup. Let me show you how it's done." Emily pulled Sarah back to the mirror and began her magic.

An hour later Sarah looked stunning. Her makeup was on point and not one hair was out of place.

"Emily, I wouldn't believe that this was me had I not witnessed your amazing skill! Take my picture. I want to send it to Michael," Sarah said as she twirled in front of the mirror. "No one would ever recognize me this way. I look beautiful."

"Sarah, you've always been beautiful inside and out, you just haven't let your beauty shine through," Emily assured her. Before they left for their evening, Sarah made a quick call to Michael. Emily seized the moment to slip her Glock into her handbag. She wasn't taking any chances. If there was someone lurking around her sister, she intended to take care of it. Then, arm in arm, the two sisters headed out the door together.

"First stop, *Rita's on the River*, then *The Moon's Daughters*, and then who knows where the wind will take us. I am going to show you what fun really is," Emily said as she made her way past her sister heading to the elevator.

Sarah was trying to keep up with Emily not only in fashion, wearing a pair of high heels and a short little cocktail dress, but also at speed. Emily could powerwalk in four-inch heels! Midway down the hotel hallway, Sarah stopped to adjust her shoes. She used the door handle of another room to keep her balance.

"Emily, wait! My shoe strap needs adjusting! If you don't stop and help me, I'm going to fall on my face. I just hope no one is in this room! I'm creating quite a disruption! Emily!"

As Sarah adjusted her shoe, the hotel guest across the hall peered through the door peephole to see who was causing the ruckus. Mrs. Underwood couldn't see much, just a blonde woman in high heels and cocktail dress, holding onto the door across the hall and cursing. She was hoping it was her grandkids returning from the Riverwalk.

"Oh, commercial is over, back to the tv show," she thought as she headed back into the heart of the hotel room.

"Sarah, I told you to take it easy in these shoes. You've spent half your life wearing sensible footwear!

Playground shoes as you so aptly call them." Emily returned to her sister to offer help. As she waited, she pulled lipstick from her clutch purse for a refresher. After reapplying her lips, the tube slipped from her fingers and rolled under the door.

"Damn! I dropped my favorite lipstick, and it rolled under the door. Knock and see if anyone answers."

Sarah knocked quietly on the door, but no one answered. "I owe you a lipstick, now let's go have some fun before I change my mind!"

Jorge was lurking around the corner near the stairway keeping an eye on the girls. When Sarah knocked on the door, he realized it was Antonio's room, and he was on high alert. She was definitely the one, and she must know that Antonio is here.

Sarah saw Jorge in her peripheral vision, but when she turned back to get a better look, he was gone. Had it been her imagination? Something was definitely at play here.

As they stepped off the elevator and walked through the lobby, they noticed that a wedding had taken place in the courtyard. There were still a few people dancing at the reception and lingering in the courtyard. It was a beautiful sight to behold.

"Oh, Emily. Isn't it the most romantic setting! If Michael and I had to do it all over again, I believe an outdoor wedding might make the top of my list. I just love all the twinkling lights and beautiful flowers," Sarah mused.

Emily retorted, "If I ever get married, and that's a BIG IF, it won't be in a hotel courtyard, I can promise you that."

She got a faraway, dreamy look in her eyes as she continued, "I would want my fairytale wedding to be at Castell de Tamarit. It's a castle just outside of Barcelona, located on the Mediterranean. It has a tiny, incredibly atmospheric church which was built in the eleventh century, with an amazing watchtower and village built just to protect it. The views over the Mediterranean Sea would be memorable and romantic."

"Sounds like someone has done some research. Are you..."

"NO, end of discussion. Our Uber is here."

"You called an Uber?"

"Seriously, Sarah, you could barely walk down the hallway in the hotel. I can't imagine you walking the ten blocks down the sidewalk."

As the two climbed into the Uber, Emily instructed the driver to take them to *Rita's on the River*. Sarah caught a glimpse of the same Hispanic man lurking in the foyer of the hotel watching their every move. He was talking on a cellphone and looked quite agitated.

Emily's thoughts were of Stephen as their wedding plans played out in her mind. Had she made the right decision to break it off with him? Sarah hadn't even known that she and Stephen had discussed marriage. No, it wasn't a mistake. It was better this way. Emily wiped a tear from her eye and put on her happy face when she suddenly noticed the man in the hotel drive, point at them and get into a taxi. She needed to forget about Stephen once and for all. Tonight, all of her attention was focused on Sarah.

Both sisters were quiet on the short ride to Rita's. Sarah couldn't shake the uneasy feeling that she was being watched. Was her past catching up to her?

Chapter 16

Enrigue Martinez sat alone at the bar watching Luna Aguliar flirting with one of Antonio's top men, Victor, while the wedding reception was winding down and the guests were drifting back to their hotel rooms or out of the hotel for more entertainment. Victor had his arms around Luna's thin waist as he was whispering into her ear and nibbling on her neck. "Antonio is going to be so angry," he thought. "Someone should stop them, but not me, not tonight."

He looked up as he heard laughter, and he noticed two beautiful women arm-in-arm heading to the front of the hotel. He overheard the younger woman mention dinner and drinks. "Hmmm," he thought. "I believe she was the same woman I saw earlier today asking about the bar, *The Moon's Daughters*. I should stop in for a drink. With any luck, I could come back to the hotel with a beautiful woman on my arm- or perhaps even two."

As he began to formulate a plan for the remainder of the evening, he took a swig of his DeLeón Tequila.

Out of the corner of his eye he caught a glimpse of one of Antonio's men in the foyer watching the two ladies get into a car. "What was that estúpido hombre up to?" he wondered. It was at that moment he noticed Luna and Victor slip out just as Antonio was walking in. Disaster avoided.

Antonio sat next to him at the bar. "Enrique," he nodded.

"Antonio, beautiful wedding tonight for Sofía, huh?" Enrique was making small talk.

Antonio nodded, "Sí." He motioned to the bartender and held up two fingers indicating that he wanted a drink for Enrique and one for him.

As the drinks were set before them, Antonio said, "We need to talk. We have an important matter that needs to be settled."

"I'm going to say this one more time, Antonio. I don't want to be a part of your 'other business'," Enrique said making quotes in the air.

"You are familia. You have no choice. We need a presence in El Salvador, and you have been chosen," Antonio said as he took a swig of his drink.

"I want no part of this," Enrique said as he looked Antonio in the eyes.

Antonio simply said, "It's done."

"Then undo it! I never agreed to launder your dirty money. Does Isabella know of this?" Enrique asked.

"Isabella is of no concern to you," Antonio warned.

"Isabella is my sister. That makes her my concern. And what of this Luna person that you bring to your own daughter's wedding? You're losing control, Antonio. It needs to stop!" Enrique yelled as he jabbed his finger into Antonio's chest.

"Enrique do not threaten me! You do not realize who may be listening. The cartel? They are everywhere," Antonio said as he lowered his voice. "No one is safe. They have resources and they will track you down if you don't do as I have instructed. Our only choice is live and comply unless you'd rather die."

"You should have thought of that sooner. I'm done with you, familia or not," he spat, as he slung back his drink and left the bar.

Antonio sat a moment longer in thought. "You will do as I say, Enrique, and Antonio Junior will also do my bidding."

After his second shot of tequila, he knew he needed to spend some time with Luna. "That will settle me down," he thought.

He had one more shot of tequila and headed to the elevator. One of his men was waiting in the wings.

"The dama has left the hotel, but I must warn you. She is staying on the sixth-floor next door to Isabella. A sign outside of the meeting room said her name was Sarah, same as the Luxe Loom witness, but the last name was different. But I believe it is the same dama. Jorge saw her knock at your door tonight. Something doesn't feel right. He is following her now."

"Gracias, Juan. We cannot let her out of our sight until the threat is eliminated. Comprende?"

"Si, Señor. Eliminación."

Then, before taking the elevator, Antonio turned back and asked the bartender for a bottle of wine and two glasses. Luna saw him get into the elevator as she turned her attention back to Victor.

"Just a few more minutes, mi amor. Antonio will be expecting me. After I take care of his needs, and he has fallen asleep, I will slip into your room. Then, I'll be all yours."

Enrique walked to the front of the hotel and got into an Uber. "Take me to the place called *The Moon's Daughters.*"

Chapter 17

After a week of workshops and training sessions, Sarah was ready to unwind. Emily had promised her a night to remember. The night was a whirlwind of activity. First stop: *Rita's on the River.*

"I guess margaritas would be a great way to start the evening!" Sarah cheered.

"I hear it's one of the most iconic locations on the Riverwalk. The colorful tiles and hand-painted murals are exquisite. It is so warm and welcoming," Emily pointed out.

She showed her international experience and culture by ordering a Mojito with Mezcal, while Sarah stuck with what she knew. "I'll have a Princess Peach Margarita. Sounds yummy!"

As they sipped their drinks, they enjoyed the lively mariachi music playing in the background. The aroma of sizzling fajitas and street tacos wafted in from the kitchen. The girls ordered a plate filled with al pastor, carne asada and pollo tacos. Each bite was a burst of flavor.

Partway through their meal, the mariachi band moved throughout the lounge, wearing their iconic charro outfits, they began to serenade the patrons. The sound of their trumpets, violins, and guitarron filled the room, creating an atmosphere of joy and celebration.

"Oh, Sarah, listen. They are playing Cielito Lindo! This song is like an emblem of Mexican culture. I love the cheerful melody. From my understanding, the lyrics encapsulate a sense of joy."

"Since when have you been able to speak fluent Spanish and sing Hispanic songs?" Sarah questioned.

Emily laughed. "I don't speak much Spanish, though I am learning on the job. However, I am a cultured person. I know the words are something about a young girl with a pair of deep brown eyes and a stolen glance. Her mouth is made of sugar and the guy singing wants to enjoy the sweetness. He wants to hug her before her mother comes. And here's my favorite part: Ay, ay, ay, ay sing and don't cry, heavenly one, for singing gladdens hearts."

"That's truly beautiful. But seriously, tell me how you know all this."

"That's what happens when you date a guy named Stephen Padilla. Stephen used to sing this song to me. His father is Hispanic, so he taught me a lot about his culture. But that is no more. He's out of my life."

Sarah was shocked. "How could I not know that Stephen was Hispanic?"

"Dark hair, dark eyes? Padilla?? Come on, Sarah. Think about it. You know my attraction to dark haired men like that."

Sarah smiled at her sister. "I truly didn't realize Stephen was Hispanic. I thought Padilla was Italian!" she said with a laugh. "But he is definitely a looker."

They sat in silence for a moment alone in their thoughts, taking in the rest of the music. Emily scanned the restaurant making certain they weren't being watched. The restaurant had provided a lovely experience and a wonderful way to start the evening. She wasn't going to let anyone ruin that.

Rita's on the River was not just a bar, but a place where the spirit of Mexico came alive through the music, food, and camaraderie. After having their delectable meal, a second drink and a delicious plate of cinnamon churros, the Martin sisters left the cantina and headed for their next stop: *The Moon's Daughters*, the famous rooftop bar.

"Are you sure we want to go to the roof for more drinks?!" Sarah complained feeling the effects of the margaritas.

"Oh, sweet Sarah. We are two girls out on the town. You need to live a little, sister," explained Emily.

111

"That's right, live a little. How do you know about all of these wonderful places?" Sarah asked.

"I network and do my homework. This place sounds fabulous! It is supposed to be one of the best bars in America. They have a DJ that entertains with a program called Vinyl Vibes. My friend at the tradeshow told me that they have coordinating lights that flash to the music, and your servers join in by dancing. Apparently, the specialty drinks are amazing! Uber is here!"

The sisters arrived at *The Moon's Daughters* around 10:00 P.M. but took a stroll along the Riverwalk to allow Sarah to catch her breath and sober a bit from her margaritas.

As they were strolling along, Emily realized they were indeed being followed. She thought she had seen this thug lurking in the hotel driveway and she began to have a bad feeling about the situation, remembering Sarah's earlier complaints of feeling watched and the possibility of her memory of that horrific night returning. She would not allow this uneasy situation to go unchecked.

Emily pulled Sarah into a quaint coffee shop and ordered her a cup of coffee. Sarah needed it, that was certain. After getting her sister situated, Emily excused herself to the ladies' room, but instead, went in search of the thug. She had dealt with stalkers in New York and San Antonio was no different. She would address the problem head-on, and Sarah would never know.

When Emily returned to the coffee shop, she adjusted her dress, smoothed her hair and retrieved her sister. Sarah was a bit agitated. "Where have you been? You said you were going to the ladies' room, but it seems like you've been gone for quite a while. I've already finished my coffee."

"I just ran into a little snag on the way, but problem averted. Ready to go?"

Chapter 18

That evening after the wedding celebration had come to an end, Isabella was spotted by Antonio's men leaving arm-in-arm with her friend, Lydia. She was safe, which allowed them to relax and enjoy their surroundings for the remainder of the night.

Isabella went to the room of her best friend, Lydia. She was so thankful to have her present to help celebrate the wedding of her daughter.

"We've practically raised our girls together even though they are six years apart. Tell me more about how Evie is doing. She is headed to university next semester? Si?"

"Oh, yes. And honey, she is so happy! She will be attending our old alma mater when the new semester begins. I feel so proud. I can only hope she becomes friends with someone as special as you," Lydia confided. "Now that she has finally gotten through the process of getting a real wig, from real hair, she has her self-confidence back and is ready to take on the world. Having a weak immune system has been devastating enough, but Alopecia has been the worst.

She's resting now, but you should see how remarkably the wig is made. You can't tell it's not her hair." Lydia went into the bedroom of the suite and returned with the beautiful wig.

Isabella gasped! "That is some gorgeous hair! From a distance I couldn't tell it was a wig, but even up close, holding this in my hands, it feels remarkable."

"Yes," Lydia agreed. "It is a custom-made wig from real human hair. With the right care, the company assured us that it could last for over a year before needing a replacement."

"You know, I've always admired your blonde hair, and I've even imagined what I would look like as a blonde. Do you think I could try it on?" asked Isabella.

"Oh, I don't know Isabella. Evie is very protective, and it was made specifically for her."

Isabella gave Lydia her most serious pouty face. "Oh, Por favor mi querida amiga?"

Lydia consented. "Well, maybe just for a minute just to see you as a blonde."

Isabella donned the wig. She felt like a different person. "I should wear this down to the lounge just to see if any of Antonio's people notice it's me. Just for a minute. . ."

"Isabella, I don't know. Maybe for just a quick minute. I don't want Evie to wake up and look for her wig. Just make it a quick fashion show and come right back."

Isabella seized the opportunity. She went straight to the sixth floor and to Antonio's room. If he was drunk enough, he would think she was his girlfriend. Maybe she could convince him to show his love and affection to her alone, like it used to be in the beginning of their marriage. It was worth a try. Isabella quietly knocked on the door.

"Antonio? Let me in."

As usual, Mrs. Underwood was peering through the peephole. She was still waiting for her grandkids to return, and she was getting anxious.

"Hmph," she thought. "That blonde lady is back knocking on the door. Good luck lady, he was drunk when he went into his room five minutes ago. I bet he's passed out."

As she spied through the peephole, the door suddenly opened, and the blonde was pulled inside.

"WHERE THE HELL HAVE YOU BEEN? NO ME DECEPCIONES!" the man's voice boomed. Then the door slammed shut.

Antonio thought he had a hold on his girlfriend. He had seen her flirting with his top lieutenant, Victor. But she came to this wedding with him for one purpose only and he was about to take advantage of that. He had one arm around Isabella and the other hand had a firm grip on her head. As he pulled her face around to force his mouth on her, he realized it wasn't Luna. "What the Hell? Quién eres?" he yelled as the wig pulled free of Isabella's head. "You!? What are you doing here in a blonde wig?"

"Antonio, wait! I can explain. I was ... I just ... Antonio! Mi amor! Please listen to me."

Chapter 19

The air felt thick with dread as Isabella stifled sobs, biting down on her lip until she tasted blood to keep herself silent. Even as she steeled herself to act normally, a numbness settled over her, a hollow void where her innocence once lived. Antonio rejected her love, her daughter, Sofía, was now married and gone, AJ was headed back to college, and suddenly she felt all alone in this world.

Moments later, Isabella quietly knocked at Lydia's door as she pulled the wig from her head. "Lydia? Lydia, please open the door."

"Isabella, are you alright? Honey, you look frightened," Lydia observed. "Have you been running? Is someone after you?"

Isabella quickly responded, "No, I mean sí, I'm alright. I just have a headache starting. I don't know, I don't know. I need to go to my room and lie down."

She uttered other things in Spanish, most of which Lydia could only somewhat understand.

"Can I get you anything? Are you going to be alright?" Lydia asked.

"No. No, I'll be ok," Isabella quickly responded.

"Well, at least tell me before you go, if you surprised anyone with your blonde hair."

"Did I surprise anyone? You might say that," she thought. Isabella began to feel panic rising inside of her.

"I saw no one. And please, Lydia, if anyone asks about me, I have been in your room since the wedding reception. Si?" She couldn't bear the thought of rejection by her own husband. Isabella headed to the door and looked to see if any of Antonio's men were in the hallway.

"Of course, honey. Whatever you need, I'm here for you. Always," Lydia responded as she hugged her dear friend one last time. She closed the door and locked the deadbolt, worried that there might be trouble. "Antonio is destroying the heart of my friend," she thought. "He should be stopped. I can't stand by and be a witness to this any longer."

"A lo hecho, pecho. What's done is done," Isabella said to no one in particular. She took the stairs to her room, locked her door and lay on the bed and cried.

Chapter 20

The sound of the gun's explosion echoed through the hotel room. After that, only silence.

Mrs. Underwood heard the gun discharge. As she ran to the door to peek, she saw the retreating blonde hurry from the room. At least she thought it was the same woman. She had only caught sight of blonde hair and high heels. High heels, sparkling dress, stockings... As she stood pondering it all, the young bimbo returned to the room. The door was partially ajar, and as she pushed open the door, she let out a blood curdling scream.

"ANTONIO? Antonio!! Oh my god, someone call the police!"

The rest of the evening was a buzz of activity. A cadre of police arrived, and soon after, the room was cordoned off. Within half an hour the district prosecutor and a coroner arrived. An ambulance with a litter was on standby just in case it was needed. Victor saw the buzz of activity while sitting in the bar and his suspicions were on high alert. When he saw the CSI van pull up out front, he tried to call Luna.

When she didn't answer, he called Antoino. No answer. He immediately made his way to the sixth floor, but he was prevented from going down the hallway. The police were everywhere and there was police tape across the entrance to Antonio's room.

Victor promptly alerted Antonio's men and though they needed to reach Antonio, they had to maintain a low profile. He tried to reach Luna again, but she still wasn't answering her phone.

When the detectives arrived at the hotel, Luna and Mrs. Underwood were separated and questioned, as the room was searched, and fingerprints lifted. Detective Cruz agreed to question Mrs. Underwood while Detective Henderson spoke with Luna.

Detective Cruz was a middle-aged man who carried himself with confidence and authority. He had a sturdy build indicating a life of physical activity and discipline. His salt-and-pepper hair was neatly cropped, and his piercing eyes were framed by a pair of wire-rimmed glasses. He wore a dark-colored suit and a crisp white dress shirt with a conservative tie.

Detective Henderson was quite the opposite. He was a heavyset gentleman in his mid-fifties. His hair was mostly gray but balding on top. His face was weathered with deep lines and wrinkles. He had reading glasses perched low on the bridge of his nose.

121

His eyes, though tired, were kind. He wore a baggy, corduroy jacket and wrinkled pants. His shirt wasn't completely tucked in, and it sported a coffee stain. His tie was slightly askew.

"Mrs. Underwood, I'm Detective Cruz. I understand you may have witnessed what happened here tonight." he said.

"Yes, I saw things," she said. "First of all, I saw a blonde woman in heels and a sparkly dress knocking at the door. She had her hands on the door listening to see if anyone was there. I also heard her cussing."

"Did she enter the room?"

"No, I don't think so. Actually, I'm not sure. My show came back on the TV, so I went back to watch."

"Then what happened?"

"I heard that Spanish man coming back. He was drunk, dropped his keycard and started cussing in Spanish. At least it sounded like he was cussing. He had two wine glasses and a bottle of wine in his hands. He struggled opening the door because his hands were full."

"Was he alone?"

"Yes, but then the blonde came back. He pulled her in yelling at her about where she had been and something in Spanish."

"Then?"

"Then I went back to my show. At some point I heard a gunshot or something. It was hard to tell with all the fireworks going off all evening. When I went back to peek, I saw the blonde lady in heels leaving. I thought about calling the front desk, but then the young girl came back and started screaming. That's when I called the front desk. I'm telling you, that room across the hall is like a revolving door, one incident after another!"

"Are you sure it wasn't the young girl that entered the room first?" the detective asked.

"Oh, the bimbo? I know it wasn't her. She has longer hair than the woman I saw repeatedly at the door. She's just a young thing. Can't miss her with all that makeup and that tight, gold dress! The woman I saw was much more mature than her." Mrs. Underwood was certain of that.

"Thank you, Mrs. Underwood. We will stay in touch. Here is my card in case you think of anything else," the detective said.

Detective Henderson questioned Luna. "Could you tell me why this man is staying in your room when you are the only one registered here?"

"He's here for his daughter's wedding. His wife is also here, and I believe he's registered to her room, but we're, you know, in a relationship, so he was here in my room," Luna said.

"When did the wedding take place?" Detective Henderson asked.

"It was tonight. The wedding was tonight with a reception," Luna wiped her eyes with a tissue and blew her nose.

"Where were you during and after the wedding?"

"I didn't attend the wedding. Isabella would have thrown me to the wolves! I was in the bar waiting for Antonio."

"Who is Isabella?"

"Antonio's wife," she cried.

"So, you say you were waiting in the bar. Were you alone?"

"I was alone during the wedding and then I was with Victor. He works for Antonio. I waited in the bar until I thought Antonio would be back in the room. He was expecting me to be there. You can ask the bartender. He saw me. He even hit on me, so I know he'll remember I was there. When Victor showed up, he backed off."

Detective Henderson continued with the questioning. "What happened when you entered the room?"

Luna started crying. "I found Antonio on the floor with blood everywhere! Oh my God! He was already dead!"

"Who called the police?"

"I don't know! I was hysterical. I tried to revive Antonio, but it was too late. He's dead," she said with a definitive tone.

"Thank you, Ms. Aguliar. That's all I need for now, but I'll be in touch. If you think of anything else, don't hesitate to call. Oh, and Ms. Aguliar, your room is an active crime scene so you will need to find someplace else to stay but don't leave this hotel."

"Where am I supposed to go if I can't stay in this room?" she cried.

"That's something you'll have to figure out on your own."

As the detectives crossed the police tape and entered the hotel room, Detective Cruz noticed the lipstick behind the door. "Hey, buddy," he indicated to one of the police officers gathering evidence. "Bag that. It could be significant."

Detective Cruz lifted the cover on the victim to take a look. "Do we have a positive ID on the John Doe?"

"You are not going to believe this! It's Antonio Alvarez, known to the FBI as El Mas Loco," reported the coroner. "We're going to take the body downtown and then send it off for a full autopsy. But at this point, it looks like a single gunshot to the chest."

"El Mas Loco, The Craziest One. We are in for a long investigation. I don't think it was an accident by any means. I'm sure several cartels have a hit put out on him, especially being out of his own country without the protection of his men, Detective Cruz commented. "What is he doing in San Antonio, Texas? Enjoying the Riverwalk?"

"Naw," said Detective Henderson. "From what I can gather from Miss Aguilar, his daughter just got married here today."

"And the weapon used?" questioned Detective Cruz.

"Apparently, he was packing his own heat, an 8mm Roth-Steyr. It looks like a struggle took place. We'll have to wait on ballistics to determine if he was shot with his own weapon. But the gun chamber is missing a bullet."

Detective Cruz asked for a list of hotel guests who might have attended the wedding. "First on the list: Mrs. Isabella Martinez-Alvarez, presumed wife of the deceased, registered in a different room. "We can start there and work our way down the guest list."

Chapter 21

Sarah took a deep breath as she and Emily stepped out of the elevator onto the 20th floor of the Thompson Hotel. The polished brass doors whispered shut behind her, and she felt a hint of exhilaration, as though she were standing on the edge of a hidden world. The entry to *The Moon's Daughters* beckoned with a celestial charm; an arched doorway framed in ornate metalwork that shimmered like silver under the soft glow of hanging lanterns. Above, a crescent moon motif glimmered, its curves dotted with twinkling lights, as though stars had fallen from the sky to illuminate their path.

Sarah, still feeling the effects of the margaritas, and a bit shaky, was exhilarated with the view. The interior walls seemed to dissolve into glass, framing the San Antonio skyline like a living painting. Buildings stretched into the twilight, their lights flickering against the backdrop of a dark sky. Far below, the River Walk wound through the city like a ribbon of dark silk, reflecting pinpoints of gold from the streetlamps.

The bar stretched along the wall, a masterpiece of design. A mosaic of moon phases adorned the backdrop, each phase crafted from inlaid stone and shimmering mother-of-pearl. Bottles of every conceivable shape and hue lined the shelves, their contents glowing like captured potions in the ambient light. A bartender, dressed sharply in black with a silver tie, moved with effortless grace, shaking a cocktail shaker high above his head before pouring a stream of liquid gold into a chilled glass.

The music and atmosphere reenergized Sarah and she ordered a *Wish We Were Here* which included Mexican and Caribbean rums, passionfruit, lemongrass, and lime. Her drink also came with a souvenir glow cube which made her most happy. She was not a seasoned drinker and was still tipsy from her two margaritas earlier in the evening.

Emily went for a more adult drink and ordered a *Must Be Nice,* which featured Serrano-infused tequila, green apple, Jalisco orange, and lime. No souvenir glow cube for her. She wasn't about to play the role of tourist. She also had a shot of straight tequila to settle her nerves. What happened when she left Sarah at the coffee shop would be her secret. It was out of love and protection of Sarah that caused her to do what she did.

They were enjoying the music and the fun when Sarah noticed a patron at the bar near them. He was staring intently in their direction. Did she or Emily know this man? Was he trying to pick her up? She was a married woman. It was at that moment that she noticed the smile at the corner of his mouth and realized he had eyes for Emily.

Dressed in a black Armani suit, he looked like a young Antonio Banderas. His wavy black hair was combed back just graying at the edges. His shoulders were broad and his jaw square. His dark skin contrasted sharply with his white shirt. He had one hand in his pocket, leaning casually against the bar. His wrist was adorned with a large, diamond studded Rolex, and he had a gold and diamond ring on his little finger. He moved with a slow swagger, a man who knew what he liked and what he intended to have. His lips turned slightly up in a cocky knowing grin.

"Hey Emily, four o'clock, just your type." Sarah giggled.

"Four o'clock? What are you talking about? Four o'clock?"

"No. Not the time. I'm trying to give you code talk for the guy at the bar. The one at four o'clock. He's looking intently at you. Dark hair, dark eyes, just your type. Do you know him?"

"What guy?" Emily asked as she scanned the bar. "Ohhhh, my! FOUR O' CLOCK! Next time just say, hey, there's a handsome man at the bar looking your way."

The gentleman motioned to the bartender and instantly, two drinks appeared in front of Emily and Sarah. "Compliments of the gentleman," the bartender said as he motioned towards the man.

"O-h-h pretty!" exclaimed Sarah. "What kind of fancy drink is this?"

The bartender said, "It's a Nineteen Twenty Cocktail. It's pretty on the eyes and on the tastebuds. Enjoy, ladies."

As Emily took a drink, she glanced at the gentleman, and he lifted his shot of tequila in a toast. She batted her eyes and smiled demurely. That was all it took for the gentleman to move in her direction.

Sarah giggled again. "Don't look now but four o'clock is changing time. He's coming over!"

A suave, middle-aged Don Juan stepped up to the bar. Sarah thought he was as smooth as Tennessee Whiskey as he took Emily's hand in his and gently placed a kiss on the top of her hand. "Hello, I'm Enrique."

Sarah swooned. "I just love the way you say your name. Lord, this man is romantic!"

Emily gave her a look that said straighten up and shut up because you are liquored up! She turned and smiled sweetly at Enrique and then introduced herself. "Hello, I'm Emily and this is my sister, Sarah."

"It is such a pleasure to meet two lovely ladies. Tell me, what brings you to San Antonio?" Enrique's accent melted Sarah like butter. She *must* be intoxicated. She wanted to plant her nose into his chest and breathe him in. Somehow, she hoped Michael would forgive her.

As if on cue, *Saving All My Love for You*, began playing by the Vinyl Vibes DJ. Enrique took Emily by the hand and swung her out onto the dance floor.

As they danced, he serenaded her with his lovely Hispanic accent. He leaned in close and whispered into Emily's ear. "You're a very beautiful woman."
She giggled and whispered something back. It looked as though Sarah might be heading back to the hotel alone. Flirtation was getting heavy.

Suddenly, Enrique's phone rang. "Excuse me, I must answer," he said as his mood began to darken. His entire demeanor changed as he grew dark and allusive. "Qué? When? Tonight? ...Are you safe? Sí, I am on my way."

"I beg your forgiveness. I must go now as a family matter has come up. Ladies, it was lovely to meet you both. Enjoy the rest of your time here. If ever you are in El Salvador, look me up," he said as he slid a business card towards Emily. He kissed Emily's hand, bowed slightly, and then he was gone.

Sarah nearly fell off her barstool. "Emily, oh my goodness, that was so romantic. If he'd have kissed my hand and looked at me the way he was looking at you, I would have forgotten all about Michael and jetted off to Spain with him. He looked just like Antonio Banderas. He's my favorite actor. Michael knows my infatuation for him. He would have forgiven me. Tell me he was from Spain. Was he from Spain?"

"No. Did you not hear him say he was from El Salvador? But my god, did you see his eyes? They were so dreamy. If he'd have asked me to run off to El Salvador with him, I would have gone in a second. I guess it was a good thing he had an important call."

"What was that all about?" Sarah questioned.

"I'm not really sure. He said something about family business." Emily explained as she shoved his card into her purse. She would save it for another time.

"Oh, dear Lord! I just realized something. Remember the DNA test I made you take. It said we were related to people in El Salvador. Can you imagine having family that looked like him? I'm ready for a family reunion!"

"I think you're ready to crash because you seem to have had a bit too much of the Nineteen Twenty drinks. Let's get you back to the hotel. I don't think we need any more fun tonight." Emily hooked her arm in Sarah's, and they headed out the door.

Sarah and Emily had spent hours away from the hotel that evening. They were having the time of their lives. Sarah hadn't had an evening out like this in a long time. As a teacher, she was always careful not to overdo it in case she ran into a parent or an administrator from her school district. Here, she was free to let go and have fun. She was determined to ensure that Emily had fun after her breakup with Stephen.

When they arrived at the El Amado, police cars were leaving along with an ambulance.

"Geez, I wonder what we missed here. I hope no one got hurt. How awful to come to San Antonio for a vacation and not get to enjoy it." Sarah wondered aloud.

Emily smiled to herself. "I think the evening turned out just perfect."

Chapter 22

Late that evening the police were banging on the door of Isabella's suite. Isabella opened the door with some trepidation.

The police verified her identity and moments later, the detectives arrived to question her.

"Mrs. Alvarez?"

"Yes, that's me." Isabella replied.

"I'm Detective Cruz and this is my partner, Detective Henderson. Do you mind if we come in and ask you a few questions?"

"What is this about? Is there a problem, detectives?"

"Yes ma'am, if we could just step inside."

Isabella held the door open and at the same time held her breath.

"I regret to be the one to inform you of some terrible news. Are you alone?"

Isabella nodded yes; she was alone in the room.

"Are you the wife of Antonio Alvarez?"

Again, Isabella nodded yes.

"Your husband has been shot, and unfortunately, he didn't make it," Detective Cruz explained.

Isabella gasped and covered her face. "What?" she asked looking up. Are you sure it was Antonio?"

"We would like to take you down to the station for further questioning, and to identify the body if you don't mind. We'll step outside and give you time to gather your thoughts and change into appropriate attire."

"Who could do such a thing? Were there any witnesses?" she questioned.

"If you don't mind, we'll cover all of that down at the station. But at this point, we know a blonde woman was seen outside Antonio's door on several occasions. That's all we can tell you," Detective Henderson assured her.

A blonde woman was seen outside Anthony's door on several occasions. Several? She was not blonde, and she had somewhat of an alibi if she needed it. She would simply say she was in the room of her dear friend, Lydia, someone she was certain would lie for her if it was necessary. Lydia would be a solid alibi.

As soon as the door was shut, Isabella picked up the phone and called Lydia. "Oh Lydia, Antonio has been shot and killed! ...I have no idea what happened! ... I've been asked to go down to the police station so they can take my statement. ... Yes, I know, it's a terrible thing to happen. But listen, Lydia. They said a witness saw a blonde woman outside his room on several occasions. NO! It wasn't me. But please, if you are questioned, keep me out of this. Swear you won't tell a soul that I put that blonde wig on. You're my only alibi. ...you know how important alibis can be in a sticky situation. I must go. They're knocking on my door. Thank you, Lydia. Thank you."

"I'll be right out," she called through the door.

Her next phone call was to her brother, Enrique Martinez. "Antonio has been murdered in his room. Two detectives are here waiting to take me to the police station for questioning. Get here now! Por favor."

Chapter 23

Antonio's men gathered in the secured room of the El Carino wing of the resort, their movements tense, their voices low. The situation had erupted without warning, demanding swift and decisive action. Victor stood at the head of the group, his expression grim, the weight of the moment pressing heavily on his shoulders. A solitary light flickered overhead, its dim glow casting long, shifting shadows across the walls and the hardened faces of the men, their silence as heavy as the air.

"Our line of defense was compromised tonight. As you know, after the wedding ceremony and reception, when we thought things were quiet and secure for the evening, Dom Alvarez was murdered. Luna has informed me that his life may have been taken by his own gun."

"Any leads on who committed the murder?" Jose questioned. "Was it the Los Zetas? The Mexikanemi?"

"At this time, I am speculating that it was the Cali cartel. They are big drug smugglers in this region of the United States, but no calling card was left to indicate for sure," Victor said.

"But why Antonio? We weren't here to smuggle drugs."

Victor explained. "I say the Cali cartel because they are moving into this region, and they are known for sicaria."

"Female assassins?" Pablo whispered, his eyes full of fear. "They are cutthroat."

"Luna told me that the police believe it was a female who committed the crime. A witness saw such a woman entering and exiting Antonio's room moments before Luna discovered him dead," Victor continued.

"What about the woman from the past? Could she have done this?"

"I am uncertain. I am waiting for Jorge to return my call. He was supposed to be trailing her, but I lost contact with him. Knowing Jorge, he is probably drunk in some bar," Victor retorted.

"What happens to Isabella?"

Victor smiled viciously, "Isabella has no protection from us. Our loyalties are to Antonio. We will find out who is responsible and take our revenge." Then he thought to himself, "And I will take advantage of Isabella since Antonio is no longer her protector."

"And Enrique? What of him?"

"Enrique stands with Isabella," Victor said, as he crossed his arms. "At this time, he is not a part of our organization and considered an outsider. We have no responsibility to him until such a time when he expresses his sole loyalty to us and to the Guadalajara cartel. Our mission is very clear."

"Do we consider Antonio Jr. to be at the head of our organization, as his father's successor?" Pablo asked.

"Listen to me. As Antonio's first in command, I am directing things now. Antonio Jr. has no interest in his father's business. I heard that firsthand from Antonio today. He plans to stay in the states to practice law. I am in charge! Is that clear?" Victor questioned his men.

They nodded their understanding.

"Good. I want eyes and ears everywhere. The moment you have a name I want to know."

At that moment, Jorge staggered in with a small cut above his eye. "Where have you been? What happened to your eye?" Victor screamed.

Jorge just shook his head. "Aye yai yai! I was trailing that dama and her sister. The next thing I know, I'm waking up in an alley. I think she cold cocked me with her pistol!"

"You estúpido idiota!! Men, this may not be a hit by the Cali cartel after all. It may be a revenge hit! We will band together with the cartel in this region and declare war on the person responsible. Now go," Victor commanded. "Bring me the name of the killer!"

Chapter 24

Isabella was seated in an investigation room at the police station. She was extremely nervous. Had she left her fingerprints in Antonio's room? She was his legal wife. She did have a right to be in his room. Had she left evidence that might indicate her? Did anyone see her? Her mind was reeling with questions as the two detectives entered the room.

"Would you like something to drink, Mrs. Alvarez?" Detective Cruz offered.

"No, no thank you. I am fine," she replied.

"Very well, we will start with some simple questions and move on to the more difficult. This will all be recorded, of course," Detective Henderson said. "First of all, please state your name and relationship to the deceased."

"My name is Isabella Martinez-Alvarez. Antonio is ... um, was my husband."

"And how long have you been married to Mr. Alvarez?"

Isabella was overcome with grief at that moment. The reality was beginning to hit her. "Please, could I have a tissue?" she asked as the tears began to fall.

Detective Cruz was truly kind. He handed her his handkerchief and patted her hand. "I know this is very difficult for you. Your only daughter has just married, and your husband murdered all in the same day. Please, take your time."

"I'm so sorry. Um, we have been married for twenty-five years."

"You're doing great Mrs. Alvarez. Now, what type of work did Mr. Alvarez conduct in Mexico?" questioned Detective Cruz.

"Oh, he owns Botella de Agua International. It's one of the biggest wholesale distributions of beverages and purified waters."

"Uh-huh, and did your husband have any enemies that you were aware of? Anyone who might want to see him dead?" Detective Henderson was quick and to the point.

"No. I can think of no one that would want to hurt Antonio."

Detective Henderson continued. "Why did your husband have a need to carry a personal handgun? Did he have a permit in Texas for it?"

"I don't know if he had a permit. He was a very important businessman. He wanted his family protected. That's all I can tell you," Isabella stated.

"Did Mr. Alvarez have a relationship with the Guadalajara, Los Urbanos or Los Zetas in Mexico?" Questioned Detective Henderson. "What about the Cali cartel? Ever hear him mention them?"

"I'm not sure what you mean. Cartel?" asked Isabella. Antonio always told her to keep it simple and answer as little as you could if ever questioned by the police. Don't implicate yourself or anyone else. At least he had left her with good advice.

Detective Henderson pressed on. "Yes, the cartel. There are two groups he had been known to associate with: the Guadalajara and Los Urbanos. And he may have been on bad terms with the Los Zetas. Surely you have heard of them. Did he have a relationship with any other cartel for that matter? What about the Mexikanemi?"

Isabella became defensive. "My husband's business was legal. Why would you ask such a question?"

"Mrs. Alvarez, the FBI seems to believe Mr. Alvarez was involved with money laundering. Do you know anything about that?" Detective Henderson asked.

"I know nothing of the sort. Is there anything else you need to know? My husband was killed tonight," Isabella said defensively.

"Yes, Mrs. Alvarez, we have more questions. Could you tell us where you were this evening, after your daughter's wedding? Were you with Mr. Alvarez?"

"We were together at the reception. When the guests begin leaving, Antonio excused himself as well. I cannot tell you where he went."

"How about you, Ms. Alvarez, where were you after the reception?"

Isabella sat for a moment before answering. "I finished up with the reception and took care of matters with the hotel on incidentals. Then I visited with my dear friend, Lydia Palmer, in her suite until about 11:45. I left and went straight to my room. It wasn't long after that when you showed up at my door."

"And this Ms. Palmer, can she verify that you were in her hotel suite?"

"Yes."

"Do you happen to remember her room number?" inquired Detective Cruz.

"No, I followed her to her room after the reception, but I remember it was on the fourth floor," Isabella told them.

"OK, Mrs. Alvarez, I think that's all we need for now. We will stay in touch with you and keep you informed of our investigation. I know you have family matters to attend to, so we won't keep you. If you need anything, or have any questions, you have my card," Detective Cruz assured her.

"Officer Dutton will take you down to identify the body and then see that you get back to the hotel," Henderson said matter-of-factly.

When Isabella exited the room, the detectives sat in silence and looked at each other for a moment. "I believe there is something she's not telling. Did you get that vibe from her too?" Detective Cruz said.

Detective Henderson responded emphatically, as he nodded his head, "Oh, there's something she's hiding, and we are going to find out what. But for now, let's question Ms. Lydia Palmer. She may be our mark. She and her daughter were the only Anglos attending that wedding on the bride's side and our witness insisted it was a blonde woman she saw entering and exiting the room. I think it's safe to say the guests on the groom's side are not involved but let's not exclude anyone just yet."

Isabella was escorted back to the hotel. When she reached her room, she immediately called Enrique again. She would need his help. At this point, she would do her best to tie up any loose ends and put this disaster behind her. The beautiful memory of Sofía's wedding was tarnished all because of Antonio and his jealousy! Would he have killed her? He had a gun in his possession. She didn't even want to consider the possibility. She had warned him not to bring Luna. But that was the least of her worries now.

Isabella would also need to speak with her son. She wanted him back at Cambridge as soon as possible. The detectives were beginning to question all the wedding guests, anyone with a connection to Antonio. She feared for his life now that Dom Alvarez was dead. It was just a matter of time before the Los Zetas came calling.

Lydia Palmer was a tiny woman standing no taller than five feet. Her pixie cut hair was light brown, with frosted highlights. She had long, manicured nails painted hot pink with little palm trees on them with toenails to match. Her sundress had bright orange and yellow flowers with large green leaves. She looked the part of a woman on vacation in sunny San Antonio. She had a timid, but caring personality.

The detectives had Officer Dutton bring her in after dropping Mrs. Martinez-Alvarez back at the hotel.

"Good morning, Ms. Palmer. I'm Detective Cruz and this is Detective Henderson. I hope you're doing well today."

"Yes sir, thank you," Lydia answered quietly.

"Ms. Palmer, do you understand why you are here today?" questioned Detective Henderson.

"You wanted to ask me about Antonio? At least, I think that's why I'm here. Officer Dutton said something to that effect." she responded.

"That's correct. Now, Ms. Palmer, we will be recording this interview for our records. Is that alright with you?"

Again, she answered quietly, "I suppose so."

Detective Henderson continued with his questions. "Ms. Palmer, where were you last evening and what is your relation to the Alvarez family?"

"I attended the wedding of Sofía Alvarez. She and her brother, Antonio Jr., are my godchildren. Isabella is my daughter's godmother."

"Did anyone else attend the wedding with you?"

"Yes, my daughter is here with me. She's back at the hotel. We attended the wedding together," Lydia answered.

"How old is your daughter?"

"She just turned 18. We thought it would be fun to come to the wedding and celebrate her birthday the same week. It's the perfect place to celebrate, don't you think?" she asked.

Detective Henderson pressed. "Ms. Palmer, our suspect is believed to have blonde hair. We would like to take a hair sample from you, just to rule you out if you don't mind. And does your daughter happen to have blonde hair?"

Lydia felt embarrassed. "Well, not exactly, dear, she's bald. You see, she has a condition called Alopecia."

"I'm so sorry to hear about her condition. Oh, our forensics specialist is here for the hair sample and fingerprints as well, if that's alright with you."

Lydia gave her consent. Afterall, she had nothing to hide.

The two detectives paused for a moment and had a private conversation in the corner as a hair sample and fingerprints were being taken from Lydia.

Henderson said, "Her daughter is bald so that would rule her out, right? We won't even need fingerprints from her. Let's move on to Palmer's alibi."

"OK, that's fine by me. Wait, hold on a sec," Cruz Replied.

"Hey, Dutton," Cruz called out to the officer that had brought Ms. Palmer into the station.

"Hey. What's up?"

"When you picked up Ms. Palmer, did you happen to notice her daughter in the room? Cruz questioned.

Dutton responded, "You mean that bald girl? I guess it was her daughter, why?"

"That's fine, no reason." Cruz gave a confirming nod to Henderson.

They returned to question Lydia about the evening. "After the reception, where did you go?" Detective Henderson asked.

"I sent my daughter, Evie, up to the room. She was tired and wanted to watch tv and relax. It had been a long day after shopping and weddings. I waited in the courtyard for Isabella to finish up with the waitstaff and then we went to my room together to talk and catch up."

Henderson interjected, "What time was that?"

"I believe it was around 8:30 or 9:00 PM. We talked for several hours and then Isabella left sometime close to midnight. I went to bed after that. I was awakened early this morning and brought here."

"Did Isabella say where she was going when she left your room?"

"She said she'd had a long day, and she was going straight to her room for a shower and bed."

Henderson pressed her. "To your knowledge, did Isabella or her husband have connections with the cartel?"

Lydia flushed and brought her hand to her neck. "What? Why would you ask me such a question? They are fine people and godparents to my daughter. Mr. Alvarez is a business owner, not some drug-smuggling gang member. Of course not!"

Cruz held up his hands. "Ms. Palmer, I certainly didn't mean to offend you. But we have to explore all avenues of this tragedy. I'm sure you understand."

Lydia just gave them a cold look.

"OK, well, we have your statement as well as your prints and hair samples. Thank you for speaking with us, Ms. Palmer. We have no further questions at this time. You are free to go. And please, enjoy the rest of your stay here in San Antonio." Henderson said, as he stood indicating her dismissal.

Lydia left the station and headed back to the hotel.

"What was that all about? Why are they questioning you? Do they think you're involved in that murder?!" Evie asked when she returned.

"It is of no consequence," Lydia said. "But I guess I told them what they needed to know."

"Antonio always gave me the creeps when I was around him. I can't say I'm surprised someone knocked him off! I just feel terrible for Isabella. I hate that this has happened to such a lovely person," Evie said with a distaste to her tone.

Lydia hugged her tightly. "Darling, as I said, it is of no concern to us. Isabella will rise above this as she always does, and we will be here for her if she needs us to be. Let's go ahead and pack now. Then we can take half the day to go to the Riverwalk and revisit any of the shops you liked before heading home tonight. What happened in San Antonio will stay in San Antonio. I'm determined to end this trip on a good note."

Chapter 25

The morning was off to a very rocky start. Isabella had been at the police station until the early morning hours. The sun was now rising in the sky and the temperature followed suit. It would be a hot, miserable day with all the humidity due to the overcast sky. Isabella was headed to Enrique's room to discuss their next move and what might happen. As she was entering the courtyard, she ran into Mary Lou Anderson.

"Oh, hey, Belle," Mary Lou called out to Isabella as she waved her over.

Isabella nodded and continued through the lobby. This was not the day she wanted to spend listening to that woman chat. Unfortunately, Mary Lou caught up with her.

"Did you hear there was someone shot in this hotel last night? I tell you what, we just aren't safe anywhere," Mary Lou confided. "I wonder who it was? The police have been here all morning taking hair samples and fingerprints from all the hotel guests. They are really focused on finding the person."

Isabella was tired. She just wanted to go to Enrique's room and figure things out, but Mary Lou was relentless.

"The wedding guests are all being questioned in case you were wondering. My friends were just appalled that something like this would happen. Of course, we should all be cleared in the matter. We all have alibis. How about you? Have the police questioned you? Have you spoken to any of your people?" she inquired.

"I have not. I am trying to reach my brother, Enrique. I am on my way to find him. Have you seen him?" Isabella asked.

"Do you think your brother is involved? I've not seen any of your people around. Could some of them be involved? You know, some of those men have been seen lurking around." Now she was crossing the line. Isabella couldn't stand here any longer.

"Lurking around? My people? My people! What are you saying?" Isabella questioned.

"I just meant your wedding guests, I meant no disrespect to you, sweetheart. There just seemed to be a lot of men and not many women in your group. That's all. Are you alright?"

"NO! I am NOT alright! For your information, it was Antonio who was shot. The police are calling it a murder," Isabella blurted out. "Now, I must go and find my brother, Enrique. If you would excuse me."

"Antonio? Your Antonio? Oh. My. God." she said in a staccato tone as she clutched her pearls. We need to call Sam and Sofie and tell them what is happening! This is awful!"

"Please, Senora Anderson. Do not call our children on this matter while they are on their honeymoon. There will be time enough for the devastating news when they return." Isabella said. "The police are sending Antonio's body away for an autopsy and because it is a crime, and he is from another country, it will take some time before his body is returned to Mexico."

"My God, Belle! How are you so calm?" Mary Lou questioned. "I would be crying my eyes out if it were my husband, Buddy."

"I have seen much death in my life. There will be time to mourn when I return home. And, just to be clear, my name is Is-a-bella!" She stressed. "Now, if you will excuse me, there is much to be done."

With that, Isabella pushed past her and got into the elevator. The doors closed on the shocked face of Mary Lou Anderson.

"Well, I swear, I never thought this would happen at the wedding. What kind of family did Sam marry in to?" Mary Lou said to no one in particular as she wandered through the hotel in search of her husband.

Pablo was sitting in the lobby listening. He immediately contacted Victor. "Isabella has returned from the police station. She is searching for Enrique, and she looks panicked."

"I'm on my way."

Chapter 26

The police department crime division began processing all the evidence. There were fingerprints on the door that didn't match Isabella, Antonio or his girlfriend. It was doubtful that it would match that of any housekeeping individual either. When they ran the prints through the database, a teacher by the name of Sarah Lawson was a near perfect match. The investigation team wondered what kind of motive a teacher would have.

"We need to dig into information on Sarah Lawson. See who she is, what kind of person, etc. Find out if she is registered at the El Amado Hotel and what her business is in San Antonio during the school year. It might just be a coverup," Detective Cruz said. "Do we have a fingerprint match on the lipstick?"

"We got one good print off the lipstick, but it doesn't match Sarah Lawson. There isn't anyone in the database either. I'm still working on a possibility for that," the investigator replied.

Detective Cruz asked, "What about the hair fibers we recovered? Anything on that yet?"

"It's going to take more time on the hair. But at this point, we've determined that the fibers are from two different people. They took a sample of the girlfriend's hair, and it was a no-go. Lydia Palmer wasn't a match either. I think we are dealing with two different attackers at this point," commented Detective Henderson.

"Remind me where the hair fibers were found besides the ones in Antonio's hand."

"We found matching fibers on his jacket and also a couple caught on the inside of the door handle. But here's the really interesting part about those fibers," commented Henderson. "The crime lab was able to determine that the hair had come from two separate individuals, right? But they were also able to tell it came from two different females."

"I have an idea that Sarah was working closely with someone. Check with the hotel and see if anyone else was staying in her room. Find out all you can," Cruz said.

Luna Aguliar had an alibi. She had remained in the bar after the reception. The bartender confirmed her alibi, her hair wasn't a match to the fibers found on the jacket of Alvarez therefore she was cleared by the police. Antonio had lots of enemies, and their search was just beginning.

As Detective Cruz spoke with the forensic team, he realized that the DNA from the hair fibers was a tricky matter.

"To test a hair for nuclear DNA, the hair must have tissue attached to the root end. This was not the case for the crime scene evidence," explained William Smithson, the forensic expert.

"Then how can the hair samples help us?" Cruz questioned.

"If there is no root tissue, then the alternative is to test for mitochondrial DNA found within the shaft of the hair itself," Smithson said.

"Will that give us anything to go on?" questioned Cruz.

"Actually, it will. A researcher from the University of California, Santa Cruz, recently had a breakthrough in the way DNA could be extracted from hairs making it possible to match genotypes from hair with other DNA. Though hair samples tested in this way are not 100% accurate, it could support any other evidence collected," Smithson said.

"Let's start with that and see where it takes us."

The investigative team began to focus on Sarah Lawson. And after much digging, they hit upon something.

"Listen to this: it seems that Sarah Lawson had been a witness to a cartel hit in Austin several years ago. For some reason, she couldn't I.D. the men when called in by the police."

Cruz commented, "That's an interesting twist. Dig up all you can on that murder and find out exactly what happened with Sarah in the case."

"Detective, Sarah Lawson was staying in the same room at the Hotel with Ms. Emily Martin. Does that name mean anything to you?" questioned one of the other officers working on the case.

"It means we have our second suspect! I'm willing to bet the fingerprint on the lipstick matches Emily Martin. See what you can dig up on her. There must be another connection we haven't found."

The crime department had two suspects based on fingerprints and possibly hair strand samples. When they checked with the guests registered at the hotel, the investigators noted that the two sisters were on the same floor of the hotel as the victim, and right next door to the victim's wife. That fact also stood out to them as suspicious.

Now it was a matter of motive. The investigative team continued to work through the night to find some kind of connection. During the early morning hours, they finally hit on a connection.

Detective Henderson assembled the team. "This is what we know so far about our two suspects. Sarah Lawson had close ties to Libby Bercher who went into the witness protection program some 20 years ago. It seems that Libby's parents owned a chain of jewelry stores known as Luxe Loom Designers. Apparently, they were killed by the cartel when their money laundering scheme went wrong. Sarah was close to Libby and had to have had some knowledge of her parents' dealings. She worked for the family in their jewelry store chain. According to police records, she worked for them for several years while she attended college. She was a witness when the Berchers were gunned down, though that bit of information was kept from the media. She was unable to identify anyone and therefore, not a reliable witness."

"So why was her name kept from the media?"

"The report said she suffered from a condition known as the misinformation effect. I've actually seen this happen firsthand. The misinformation effect is the way false or misleading information distorts a person's understanding of an event, even if they have a factual understanding of the event. In other words, it's when our memory for past events is altered after exposure to misleading information. According to the report, Sarah was questioned and misled with false information after hours of questioning. Apparently, there were some dirty detectives working on the case. It can mess with your memory of what you actually witnessed. She wasn't able to identify the perpetrators and therefore considered an unreliable witness. No need to report her name if she couldn't testify."

"That's Sarah's connection. I'm wondering if she has some kind of vendetta after all these years. I'm sure it must have messed up her life in some way. Did you find anything on her sister, Emily?" Cruz asked.

"Yes, we did," another detective on the case spoke up. "Sarah Martin works in New York for J.T. Steele. You may recall that Steele is on the FBI watchlist for smuggling as well as money laundering. He is a part of the Acero family from Oaxaca, Mexico. Nothing proven, as of yet, but Antonio Alvarez was originally from Oaxaca before establishing his business in Culiacán. We also know that both women had recently completed an Ancestry.com kit, they would need the results of that. Have we gotten that info yet?"

"We certainly have. Check this out. In digging further into the ancestry test, it seems that the two sisters are somehow related to the Martinez family in El Salvador. Their great-great-grandfather was a

Martinez. He changed his name to Martin when he immigrated to the United States. But even more interesting, one of those connected relatives, though somewhat distant, is Enrique Martinez and his sister, Isabella Martinez-Alvarez," an investigator remarked.

"I've always thought those ancestry kits were bogus, but now they are giving us more to go on. Very interesting," remarked Detective Henderson.

Detective Cruz was piecing together all the information. "And what do we know about Enrique Martinez?"

Henderson responded, "He was possibly in partnership with Antonio Alvarez and ran one of the businesses in El Salvador. My guess is that he is also into the laundering business and part of the cartel."

"Henderson, you're right on the money. Martinez is on the FBI watch list," Cruz remarked. "Do you think this was a family hit?"

"Looking at the information from the hotel, it seems that Isabella's hotel room was next door to the Martin sisters. It's all coming together. Perhaps the Martins were "sicaria" or hit women. The FBI has been seeing more and more of that in recent years," Detective Henderson said.

"Let's put this all together. Assuming there are six degrees of separation, we can probably connect all the players together in some way. Let's get this on the evidence board and see if we can make a solid connection. In the meantime, Henderson and I will head back to the hotel and do a little more digging."

The concierge informed the detectives that Emily Martin had asked for an Uber the night of the crime. They were headed to *Rita's on the River*. He was quick to say both women were wearing cocktail dresses and were ready to party! He also overheard one of them mention *The Moon's Daughters*.

Detective Henderson headed to *Rita's on the River* and Cruz went straight to *The Moon's Daughters*. When they met back up, they compared notes over a cup of coffee.

"I don't really have much to report. I can confirm that the two women had been to *Rita's on the River* for drinks and a meal. They dined there and left at approximately 9:30 PM according to their credit card receipt. Nothing stood out to the hostess or the waiter, but they did confirm that the two sisters were there on the night of the murder."

"Well, listen to this," Detective Cruz said. He pulled his small notepad from his pocket. "It seems that the bartender at *The Moon's Daughters* remembers them both very well. He can verify they were at the bar from about 11:00-12:00 that night. They were partying it up at the bar. He said some guy at the bar was watching them and bought a couple of rounds of drinks. They drank and danced until close to midnight. He remembers that the dude seemed upset about something and rushed out."

"Do we have the identity of the guy?" Detective Henderson asked.

"That we do!" smiled Detective Cruz. "The bartender looked through the receipts and found the one for all their drinks. They were paid for with a credit card by none other than Enrique Martinez!"

"But where were the sisters between 10:00 and 11:00?" Henderson questioned.

"My guess is that they slipped back to the hotel, knocked off Antonio Alvarez and got to *The Moon's Daughters* in time to meet up with Enrique; a pay up of sorts. The bartender said that Martinez passed something to one of the girls before leaving and she slipped it into her handbag. He said she didn't even look at it."

"Bingo! Let's head back to the station and see if anything else has been discovered. Then I think it may be time to put out an APB for two crime sisters."

At the precinct, The CSI team had all the dots connected. They had a witness, evidence, suspects, and now they had a motive! The detectives were ready to make an arrest.

When they arrived back at the hotel, much to their dismay, the sisters had checked out. The desk clerk told the detectives that Sarah Lawson had taken the shuttle to the airport and Emily Martin had a vehicle brought to her from the valet. Henderson and Cruz were determined to make an arrest before the two left the city.

"This is Detective Cruz. We need all units in the vicinity of the airport to detain Mrs. Sarah Lawson. Do not let her get on a plane! She should be headed to North Carolina. Notify the airport that we are on our way."

"Alert all patrol cars. Looking for a 2024 gray Ford Bronco rental with a Louisiana license plate. The suspect is Ms. Emily Martin from New York. Do not let her leave Texas."

Chapter 27

"Sarah, this was the best week! I'm so thankful that you are always full of good ideas," Emily said as she hugged her sister. "Even if I did have to take care of a thug," she thought. "My little secret."

Sarah said, "You know you should never question me. Don't forget Michael and I are taking the kids to Denver at Christmas. Please reconsider going. We could invite Michael's friend Rick. You know, the attorney? It's always good to have an attorney on your side. Who knows what kind of mischief we could get into there. Just promise me you'll think about it." She gave Emily a big hug. "I love you. Safe travels, Emily. Call me when you get in. I worry about you driving."

"I can certainly take care of myself, but I'll call when I get to Dallas and again when I land in New York. I'll think about going to Denver," Emily said as her mind went to the image of Michael's friend, Rick. "Hmmm, maybe I should consider going," she thought as a smile spread on her face.

"Give my love to the kids and Michael. Have a safe flight," Emily said.

Sarah headed for the airport shuttle and Emily climbed into her SUV. The sun was just climbing up in the sky. It was going to be a glorious day, perfect weather for traveling.

When Sarah arrived at the airport, she checked her bags and then headed for the terminal. At the TSA Pre-Check, she was prepared to load her phone, iPad and purse into a tub. Being the teacher that she was, she was always prepared ahead of time. She slipped off her shoes and waited in line. She handed her ticket to the smiling TSA Agent. Withing seconds, the agent stopped smiling.

"Excuse me just a minute," she said looking away. "Hey, Bob!" She motioned a security guard over to the counter and pointed at her screen.

His expression became stern. "Ma'am, would you please step out of the line and come with me?"

"Excuse me . . . Officer Jones?" Sarah said as she leaned in close and read his badge.

"I need you to step out of the line, please ma'am."

"Did I do something wrong? Was I in the wrong line?" Sarah was starting to get anxious.

Two other TSA agents came over. Officer Bob Jones leaned over and muttered something to the other two. One got on either side of her, blocking her entry into the terminal.

"Ma'am, I'm going to ask you to put your shoes back on and come with me. You don't have a choice. Let's go!" Officer Jones instructed.

Sarah complied with his request. She was escorted from the line and taken to a small office. Once seated, the agents left her alone in the office and stood outside the door.

"I'm going to miss my flight!" she yelled through the door. "Is this because I have snacks in my bag?"

At that moment, a much older TSA agent stepped into the room. He was a pudgy man with droopy eyelids, and reader glasses perched at the end of his nose. He was balding with a fringe of gray hair around his head.

"I am so sorry Ms. Lawson," he said as he clasped his hands in front of his rotund belly. "I'm Frank Wilson, the agent in charge of this area of the airport. We have been asked to detain you for just a bit. I can assure you, if given the go-ahead, we will get you on a flight home in no time. We just ask for your patience in this matter. As soon as the detectives arrive, we'll get this cleared up in record time."

"Detectives? Because I had some snacks?" Sarah asked incredulously.

There was a knock at the door and Detective Henderson entered. He was accompanied by two uniformed officers.

"Sarah Lawson?" he asked. "May I see your ID, please."

Sarah reluctantly handed him her driver's license. "What, may I ask, um, sir, is going on? Is, um, i-is there a p-problem?" she stuttered.

Without answering her questions, Henderson turned to the two other officers with him. "Cuff her." Then he turned towards her. "Sarah Lawson, you are under arrest for the murder of Antonio Alvarez. You have a right to remain silent. Anything you say can and will be used against you in a court of law. You have the right to an attorney. If you cannot afford an attorney, one will be appointed to you. Do you understand your rights?"

Sarah was so stunned; she couldn't find her voice. The two officers lifted her from the chair and turned her around. She stumbled as she was cuffed. Tears welled up in her eyes and her heart began beating faster. Everything seemed to be moving in slow motion. They walked her out of the airport and into a waiting police car. All she could think about was **Michael** and the kids.

Emily was cruising along Interstate 37 when she noticed blue lights in her rearview mirror. "Just great!" she thought as she slowly merged and pulled to the side of the road.

A uniformed officer walked up and stood just behind her front window, hand on his weapon. "License and registration, please."

"I'm sorry," Emily pleaded. "Was I going over the limit? I was jamming to the music and wasn't paying attention." She adjusted her blouse to expose her cleavage and batted her eyes at the officer.

"Ma'am, license and registration," the officer repeated undeterred by her actions.

Emily turned back to her purse, rolling her eyes at his strict nature. She retrieved her license and handed it to him, smiling her sweetest smile.

"Emily Martin?"

She nodded.

"I'm going to have to ask you to step out of your vehicle for a moment, please ma'am."

When she complied, he said, "Please face your vehicle and place your hands above your head and on the vehicle."

"What is this all about?" She questioned, her voice nervously shaking.

"Ma'am, please face your vehicle and place your hands above your head." The officer took one hand at a time and cuffed them behind her back as Detective Cruz exited the police vehicle.

He looked at her license and then at her face. "Emily Martin, you are under arrest for the murder of Antonio Alvarez. You have a right to remain silent. Anything you say can and will be used against you in a court of law. You have the right to an attorney. If you cannot afford an attorney, one will be appointed to you. Do you understand your rights?"

"Seriously?! What do you think I did? I didn't kill anyone!"

The officers gave each other a knowing look.

"Where are you taking me?" she questioned as they moved her and placed her inside the patrol car.

Neither the officer nor the detective spoke another word. "But my rental! What about my rental?" She cried as she kicked against the back seat of the patrol car. "I have personal items in the back."

"Ms. Martin, the vehicle is the least of your worries," Detective Cruz said as he shut the door.

The police officer shoved a search warrant in her face and then searched her vehicle while she sat in the cruiser. She knew what they would find, and she knew it wouldn't be good. She had a 9mm Glock 43X in the glove compartment and two Dewar containers with liquid nitrogen in the back. She also had a huge set of Chef's carving knives. She had a concealed carry license for the gun in New York, but she was certain it wasn't valid in Texas. This was not good.

A second patrol car arrived, and an officer got out of the passenger side. The patrol car left and continued down the highway. The second officer got into her vehicle and drove off just as the detective returned to the cruiser.

He opened the front passenger door and leaned in. "Ms. Martin, you're in more trouble than we initially thought."

Emily leaned forward and rested her head on the back of the front seat as tears began to form.

Chapter 28

The police station buzzed with a quiet, methodical energy, a rhythm born of routine and necessity. Harsh fluorescent lights hummed overhead, casting their cold, unforgiving glare on the scuffed linoleum floors and metal desks cluttered with paperwork, half-empty coffee cups, and the glow of computer screens. Voices carried in low, clipped tones, punctuated by the crackle of radios and the steady tap of fingers on keyboards.

The booking area sat just beyond a heavy steel door, its stark design giving no hint of welcome. A single counter stood as the first point of contact, where officers behind thick panes of reinforced glass processed the new arrivals with clinical precision. To the left, a sleek fingerprinting machine blinked patiently, waiting to capture prints that would soon be entered into the endless labyrinth of records. To the right, a wall-mounted camera with height markers loomed, ready to preserve faces in the stark, unflattering permanence of mugshots.

A hard metal bench, bolted to the floor, lined one side of the room, its surface cool and unyielding. Those who sat there shifted uneasily, the clink of handcuffs a quiet reminder of the boundaries they now faced. The air was heavy with a mixture of stale coffee, the faint tang of disinfectant, body odor of those awaiting processing, and something less tangible, a tension that seemed to seep into the walls themselves.

Through it all, officers moved with practiced efficiency, their faces a blend of weariness and sharp focus. They had seen it all before; the defiant stares, the quiet tears, the cocky smirks. The station was a machine, grinding steadily forward, indifferent to the humanity it processed. It was a place where stories began and ended, where lives shifted irrevocably with the sound of a pen scratching across paper or the metallic clang of a cell door closing.

Sarah stood before the camera a disheveled mess. "Please face the front," the officer directed as the camera flashed. "Now to the left, thank you. And now the right."

Sarah had never had a mugshot taken and she felt violated. The officer led her to another area of the room and handed her a wet wipe.

"Please clean your fingers, ma'am."

Sarah did as she was told and then the officer took Sarah's right hand and, grabbing each finger, rolled the tip across the machine, then the fingers together. She did this with each hand. Sarah had gone through fingerprinting before because she was a teacher, but she hadn't been made to feel like a criminal. The officer handed her a lidded cup.

"I need you to step into this room and give me a urine sample," she instructed, "and leave the door open."

Sarah did as she was told, all the while feeling more and more humiliated and dehumanized. She was then led to an interrogation room, handcuffed. She had just been booked into the Bexar County jail for processing.

Moments later, Emily was brought in and put through the same process. Neither sister had any idea the other sister was also being charged.

Sarah was having a full-blown meltdown. She hadn't stopped crying since her mugshot. Her hair was a mess, mascara running down her face in streaks and snot dripping from her nose, she tried to wipe her face on her sleeve, but it was difficult for her to do since she was in handcuffs. She was supposed to be in class on Monday and here she was, still in Texas. She hadn't even been able to call Michael. She sat in the interrogation room wondering why she was there and what she was going to tell her administration when the detectives entered the room. Sarah straightened, panic evident in her eyes.

"Good afternoon, Ms. Lawson. I'm Detective Cruz and I believe you have already met my partner, Detective Henderson." Looking back towards the door he called, "Guard, could you please bring some Kleenex in here for Ms. Lawson so she can wipe her nose? And, if you would, remove the handcuffs."

"Ms. Lawson, may we call you Sarah?"

She nodded as she wiped her eyes and then blew her nose.

"Thank you, Sarah," he began as he took a seat across from her. "We would like to ask you some questions regarding the recent murder of Antonio Alvarez. You have been booked and fingerprinted because all the evidence we have so far points to you. I would like to give you a chance to tell your side of the story. Would you be willing to do that? You can talk now, or you can wave your right until you have an attorney."

"I didn't kill anyone!" Sarah cried as she sniffed, and a hiccup escaped. "I want to call my husband. I want my attorney here." She began crying uncontrollably and sobbing, "I just want to call Michael. Can I do that?"

She blew her nose several times, but it didn't stop her crying. She remembered thinking that all the tissues she went through looked like white flowers crumpled on the table. What a time to be thinking creatively. "I want... my... phone call," she sniffled.

"Yes ma'am. We'll make the arrangements. In the meantime, you'll have to remain in a cell until such time when an attorney can speak with you." Detective Cruz and Henderson left the room, and the guard came back, handcuffed her and led her away to a holding cell.

After being processed, Emily was pissed. She thought it all came down to the fact that she had a concealed weapon in her car. She carried the gun because she lived in New York, and it made her feel safe. She had carried the gun for the past four years after being mugged on the subway. She hadn't even thought about it being an issue until the police searched her car. The officer said she was being arrested for some guy's murder. God, she wished she could call her attorney or better yet, Sarah's husband, Michael. She depended on Michael whenever she was in a bind. He would be the one to tell Sarah about her arrest and calm her down when she fell apart with worry. Emily couldn't imagine why she would be suspected of murder unless it had something to do with the guy she coldcocked in the alley. As she was considering all the possibilities, the detectives entered the room. She braced herself, anger evident in her eyes.

Detective Cruz entered the interrogation room, his face bathed in the harsh glow of the overhead light. A single table separated him from the woman seated on the other side. A woman who looked tense but determined. Emily certainly had a different demeanor than her sister. "She must be the mastermind," he thought as he sat across from her.

"Good afternoon, Ms. Martin," he began as he took a seat across from her. "As you know, I'm Detective Cruz and this is my partner, Detective Henderson." He motioned to the man standing at the door. "I know you have already been booked and fingerprinted. I'm sure you're concerned, and I can understand if you're a bit upset."

"If it's about the gun in my glove compartment, I can explain. I live in New York, and I have a 'conceal to carry' license for my own protection. I tried to explain that, but no one seemed to care," Emily blurted out.

"We have lots of questions for you, Ms. Martin, some are about the things found in your car, but our main reason for arresting you is for the murder of Antonio Alvarez. All the evidence we have collected points to you. So, you can answer our questions now, or wave that right and answer the questions when you have an attorney present," Detective Cruz explained.

"I want an attorney," Emily stated matter-of-factly.

"I thought you might. You'll be given a chance to make a call to arrange for an attorney, unless you want a court appointed attorney. I would assume you want your own attorney present."

"I want to call my brother-in-law, Michael. He knows plenty of lawyers and he will arrange to have someone represent me."

"Very well."

Nothing else was said. Emily was escorted from the interrogation room in handcuffs and left alone in a cell to await her one call.

"Ms. Lawson, please stand and put your hands out in front of you," instructed the officer. She did as she was told; what else was there to do.

As the officer placed her in handcuffs once again, he said, "I'm taking you down for your phone call. I would really appreciate your cooperation."

She entered a hallway with a row of phones. "You have three minutes to make your call," she was instructed. He uncuffed her and she immediately rushed to a phone and quickly dialed Michael's number.

He picked up on the second ring. "Hello?"

Sarah began sobbing the moment she heard his voice. "Oh, Michael! I think I am in some kind of trouble, and I need your help. I don't really know what's happening!"

"Sarah? Sarah, what's wrong? I'm at the airport waiting for your plane. Where are you?" Michael questioned.

"I'm still in San Antonio. Please Michael, I've been arrested for **MURDER**! What am I supposed to do? Michael, please..." Sarah cried.

"Murder? What are you talking about? You're in San Antonio? Is Emily with you?" Michael was firing questions at her so fast she didn't have time to answer.

"I'm alone in here. The police arrested me at the airport. I don't know where Emily is, she headed back to Dallas in her rental car and then on to New York when I left for the airport. Michael, they're saying I killed a man, and they have evidence. I need a lawyer!"

"Oh my gosh! OK, sweetheart. Calm down. You're being charged with murder, but you don't know who, and you're being held where? Is this guy connected to the cartel!?"

"Alvarez or somebody. I don't know. I don't know anything about him. I'm at Bexar County something or other. My mind is a mess. Please just come help me," she said between sobs.

"Hold tight, baby. I'll call Rick and see what he can find out. Then I'm on a plane to Texas. Everything will be ok; it's probably just a huge mix-up. I love you and I'll get to you as soon as I possibly can." Michael comforted her.

"Michael, call Mrs. Williams and tell her I need another week of personal leave. Surely, I'll only be a week. I love you. What are you going to tell the kids? Do you really think this could have anything to do with the cartel?!"

Before Michael could answer, the officer declared her time was up and the phone line was disconnected. Sarah was led back to her cell to sit and wait. It was anybody's guess how long she would be there.

Michael's mind was reeling. Arrested for murder? His sweet Sarah? As he was scanning through the contacts in his phone for the number to call Rick Spencer, their attorney, his phone rang again.

"Sarah?" he anxiously said into the phone.

"Michael, no this isn't Sarah. It's Emily. I'm in all kinds of trouble in Texas and I'm going to need your help."

Chapter 29

Rick Spencer and Michael Lawson had been friends about as far back as any friendship goes. They had grown up living next door to each other and considered themselves brothers. Michael was from a large family and there was always something going on at his house. Rick enjoyed the excitement. He was an only child and thought he was missing out on something. Michael's home provided him with what his own home lacked. Michael, on the other hand, enjoyed the quiet solitude that Rick's house afforded him. It was a win-win situation for both boys.

Whenever they were seen together, which was pretty much always, their friends called them the dynamic duo. There was rarely one without the other; a regular tag team, a force to be reckoned with.

As a kid, Rick was always the mediator in any fight that broke out at Michael's house. He would call the accused and the accuser together and sort things out. He had known from a very early age that he wanted to be a lawyer and maybe someday, even a judge. His grandfather had been an attorney and taught Rick to love the law.

During one particular fight at Michael's house, Rick insisted on holding court in the storage shed out back. They set up crates for the judge and the attorneys. It seemed that Michael's little sister, Vivy, accused their brother, Matt, of pulling the head off her doll. Rick determined which sibling would represent Vivian and who would represent Matt. The rest of the siblings and neighbor kids would be the jury. It was a compelling case, and one that received a lot of attention in the neighborhood. For you see, Vivy was guilty of always crying and tattling on the others. No one thought she should have her day in court. Rick saw it otherwise.

"The law is the law," he had told everyone. "Now let's have court." He put his robe on and signaled the bailiff to begin.

Bailey was just seven years old and always got to be the bailiff. He thought it was his right since his name sounded like his position. In his high-pitched voice, he began.

"Everyone, stand up! The court of General Sessions, Sunnyside Drive is now starting. The honorable Judge Richard Spencer is in charge!"

Rick walked in wearing a white choir robe smuggled from the First Baptist Church children's department. Rick thought God would understand his need for a robe and hopefully forgive him for taking it. Of course he would have preferred a black robe, but sometimes you just had to make do.

"Everybody, sit back down," instructed the bailiff. He looked over at Rick and grinned a snaggle-toothed grin. "Matthew verses Vivian is why we're here."

The trial began and witnesses were called to the makeshift stand. When a neighbor kid testified that she witnessed Vivy breaking off the head of her doll in an attempt to clothe it, the evidence was clear, and the case came to an abrupt halt.

Rick banged his gavel, a small wooden mallet they had found in the shed. "Ladies and gentlemen of the jury, you are free to go play. I'm sorry you didn't get to decide a verdict today."

After the jury stood, Rick turned his attention to Vivian. "You are sentenced to sit on the porch until dinnertime and watch the other kids play."

After closing the courtroom, Rick took Vivy's doll and worked at putting the head back on. It just required a little more muscle than Vivy could manage. While he worked on the doll, he talked to her about her tattling.

"Kiddo, you need to stop tattling all the time. No one likes that you do it and everyone always thinks you're lying. Someday, you're going to need someone to believe you. Do you hear what I'm telling you?" Rick asked her.

Vivian nodded her understanding.

"From now on, I want you to come to me. I will always be around to help you out. Michael is my best friend, and you are his little sister. That makes you kind of like my little sister, too. Here's your doll. Now go sit on the porch and play with her." Rick gave her a little hug and sent her off.

It amazed Michael that his siblings and the other neighborhood kids always listened and obeyed Rick. He just had that power over them, and he expected everyone to follow the rules.

After their undergraduate studies, Michael and Rick had gone their separate ways, though they remained in touch as often as they could. Rick headed to law school and Michael continued beyond his undergraduate studies to earn a doctorate in chemistry and engineering at the University of North Carolina.

It was in grad school that Michael met Sarah in the library on campus. She was working on her master's degree in education. He soon figured out her schedule and tried to be present whenever she was in the library or on her way to a class. She was smitten the first time she laid eyes on him.

When Michael proposed to Sarah, it was natural that he asked Rick to be his best man. Though Michael had several brothers, his strongest bond was Rick. Sarah grew to love Rick as much as Michael did.

Over the years, Rick and Michael maintained a close bond. And Michael always reached out to Rick whenever there was a legal matter. The two had discussed Sarah and her experience witnessing a murder and suffering from the misinformation effect. As an attorney, it was intriguing to Rick. He had studied it but had never actually known anyone who suffered from the effects.

Therefore, it was no surprise that Michael should call Rick when he received word that his wife and sister-in-law had been charged with murder. Rick was his go-to attorney whenever he had a question about the law. This was more than that. He would need Rick to do the impossible; defend his wife on a murder charge.

Chapter 30

Michael paced the floor, as panic began setting in. How in the world could Sarah and Emily have been arrested for murder? What evidence could the police possibly have to hold them, much less convict them? His mind was racing! The first thing he needed to do was call his good buddy and attorney, Rick Spencer. He didn't know if Rick handled criminal cases or not, but he was about to find out.

"Hello? Rick? Thank God you're there. I really need your help in a major way. Please tell me that you handle criminal cases," Michael said pacing the floor.

Rick Spencer was a smooth-talking, charismatic, and razor-sharp legal virtuoso. His southern charm and accent might lead you to believe that he was very laid back. But don't be fooled. Rick was the kind of lawyer who could walk into a courtroom, exuding confidence and charisma. He had a way with words that could turn the tide in any case, and he was not afraid to take risks and bend the rules when necessary to get the job done. Rick was not your typical lawyer in a stuffy suit type; he had a more casual, stylish look in his well-tailored blazer and jeans with just the right amount of stubble on his face. Some would say a real Matthew McConaughey vibe.

"Well hello stranger. What can I do you for?" he asked with his southern drawl.

Michael sighed. "I know you're going to think this is crazy, but my wife, Sarah, and my sister-in-law, Emily, are being held in the Bexar County Detention Center in San Antonio, Texas for murder! It's just the craziest thing!"

"For murder, you say. Who are they suspected of killing?"

"Rick, I really don't know any of the details. The best I can tell was some guy named Antonio Alvarez. I've tried calling San Antonio police and they're no help. I've got to get down there and I really need to have a lawyer with me."

"By all means! That falls right within my wheelhouse, Michael. I would be more than glad help to you out," Rick said as he jotted some notes onto a legal pad. "I've got a college buddy of mine that practices law in San Antonio. I can give him a call, get him over there to counsel the girls and see what's what. You said Antonio Alvarez murdered ... Bexar County Detention Center ... Sarah Lawson .... Emily, what is Emily's last name?"

"Martin. It's Emily Martin," Michael said.

"Martin, right, your sister-in-law. I recognize the name now. And what were they doing in San Antonio in the first place?"

Michael was getting impatient. "Sarah was at a gifted conference and Emily was showcasing a new product she developed for an entrepreneurial cooking show or something like that. Is that important? Rick, my wife is in jail, and I need to get down there."

"Just one more thing. Did either of them say anything to the police, did they give a statement or ask for a court appointed attorney?" Rick asked.

"I don't think so. I think they're both in shock, but they were smart enough to ask for a phone call. And I don't think either of them realized that the other had been arrested. I told Emily when she called, but I don't think Sarah knows unless the police have told her at this point. I called you as soon as I spoke with them. And one more thing, Emily had a Glock 43X in the glove compartment of her car."

"I see. And why is that?" Rick asked.

"She lives in New York. It's just for protection. Do you think that will cause added trouble for her?"

"In a case like this, it could cause more trouble than not, we'll just have to get down there and see what's going on. One more thing, brother. Do you think this is in any way connected to the cartel based on Sarah's past experience? I know she has always been concerned her memory would return and she was afraid of the consequences."

"I don't know any of the details. I certainly hope not but she's been having those night tremors again. It makes me worry that her memory is returning. This whole thing is crazy! Rick, I'm jumping in the car and heading to San Antonio once I get the kids settled with friends. What did you say your buddy's name was?" Michael asked.

"It's Brian Sisco. You'll really like him. But right now, I need you to just sit tight until I can get Brian on board. Get your kids settled, notify Sarah's employer that she'll not be at work next week and then we can head to Texas together. I'll talk to you in a bit. And Michael, don't worry. With Brian and me working together, we'll beat this thing, whatever it is."

Michael made the necessary arrangements for the kids to stay with friends, giving the excuse of spending the weekend together with Sarah alone, he called Sarah's supervisor for an extended leave, packed a bag for a few days in San Antonio, and then he sat by the phone waiting for Rick's call. This would be the longest wait of his entire life.

Rick logged onto the FBI database and pulled up the name, Antonio Alvarez. As he sat reading the blurb, he slowly began shaking his head. This was unbelievable.

There has been a breakdown in the conglomerate of the Guadalajara cartel as a new Dom takes control. Antonio Alvarez, age 45, known as "El Mas Loco"- the craziest one – was found shot to death in his hotel room at the El Amado Hotel and Resort in San Antonio, Texas. While attending the wedding of his daughter, Sofia Alvarez, it is believed that Alvarez was overtaken by two sicaria (hit women) working for Enrique Martinez. Sources say Martinez, the brother-in-law of Alvarez, was also in San Antonio.

"Well, alright, we've got ourselves a case," Rick thought as he reached for the phone to call Brian.

Chapter 31

Victor lingered in the shadows beneath the trees at the edge of the El Amado estate, his figure barely discernible in the dim light. Antonio's men encircled him once more, their faces taut with unease as their eyes darted nervously through the darkness.

"We have word of two arrests for the murder of Dom Alvarez. Two women are being held at the Bexar County Detention Center. If the case goes to trial, they will be transported to a prison in Gatesville, Texas."

"How will we handle this? We have no contacts in this prison." Jorge questioned.

"We are meeting with the Los Urbanos today. They also have a presence in Texas and will help to eradicate the problem," Victor responded. "Let's finish this and return to Mexico better and stronger."

"Sí, Dom Sanchez," the men responded.

"How do we know we can trust them?" questioned Rameriz.

"We are loyal to Los Urbanos in Mexico. Their point man in Texas is Dom Chavez, a longtime friend of

Antonio's. He can be trusted as well as his men," Victor explained.

Jorge was concerned. "What will we do about Isabella? She shows no interest in keeping our business thriving."

"She will do as I ask or she will be eliminated," Victor smiled. "I will go to her myself and see where she stands. But mark my words, we *will* take over the business and continue with our work."

"And Enrique, what of him?"

"Enrique has no desire to be a part of our operation. He will be an easy elimination. A hit has already been ordered upon his return to El Salvador," Victor said with an evil smile playing on his lips. "Now let's move. Time is wasting."

They left the El Amado Hotel, each man packing a gun, and loaded into four black Cadillac Escalades, Dom Sanchez in the front vehicle. Enrique observed them leaving and immediately went to Isabella's room. They needed to formulate their own plan.

Dom Victor Sanchez and his men drove to an industrial park in San Antonio where they met with the members of Los Urbanos in a deserted building.

"We believe the women who murdered Dom Alvarez are sicaras working for the Los Cali cartel. They are currently being held at the Bexar County Detention

195

Center. I have been informed that they will soon be transferred to the Linda Woodman State Jail in Gatesville where they will be held until their trial." Victor had been given detailed information from an informant working for the court system.

"Their names are Sarah Lawson and Emily Martin. We have it on good authority that these women are actually from the Martinez family of El Salvador and have changed their names in order to go undercover."

"Sí, we know of Woodman in Gatesville. We have some of our people imprisoned there. It is just a matter of me giving the word, and your problems will be over." Dom Chavez was a powerful man with interests in the U.S. as well as parts of Mexico, Guatemala and Belize. "We just ask for your alliances in Mexico."

"Consider it done," Victor responded. "With Dom Alvarez out of the picture, we are looking for new alliances. There is one more matter we need to discuss. Isabella Alvarez may be a problem. It would be nice to leave her here in the U.S."

"Sí, we can make her disappear along with the rest of her familia." Dom Chavez then turned to his top lieutenant. "Send word to our informant at the prison. Let her know about the elimination of the Martinez sisters. It must be done quickly, within the week."

Handshakes were given all around, loyalties sworn, and then Victor and his men headed back to the El Amado Hotel to prepare for their departure. Everything was falling into place.

Meanwhile, Enrique headed to the room of his sister, Isabella. She had been moved to a room on the third floor as the entire sixth floor was under police investigation and considered part of the crime scene.

"We need to talk," he said as he pushed his way into her room.

"Enrique, what is it, que?" Isabella asked. She was alone and had already sent Antonio Jr. back to school, telling him she would contact him when a funeral was held. Her plan was for him to never return to Mexico.

"Victor is on the move. He left with Antonio's men, armed. I fear for our lives."

"What are we to do? I have been told by the authorities that I cannot leave Texas until after the trial. I must see this to the end," Isabella said.

"I knew it was dangerous coming here! Sofía should have married at your home where it was safe. This place is unprotected and insecure. We need to leave this resort and find a secluded place to wait it out until the trial is held." Enrique was agitated as he paced her room.

"And then what? Victor will try to take over. What am I to do?" Isabella questioned.

"You will return to my home in El Salvador where I can keep you safe. I will make plans to have the guest house prepared for your arrival. There, Victor cannot harm you."

"No! I will not just walk away from my life. I have a home in Culiacán, and I am not going to move three thousand kilometers away because of someone like Victor. Antonio's men are loyal to me."

"You think that is true? You believe they are loyal? You are a fool! The only one loyal to you is ME," Enrique spat. "Antonio said as much just this week."

Isabella fell into a chair and cried. "But I have nothing left. I will lose my home, I have lost my daughter in a marriage, my son denies his heritage, and now the elimination of my husband."

"Que? Did YOU kill Antonio?" Enrique was in a rage. "Tell me!" he yelled at Isabella.

"No," she said in a whisper.

"What do you know? Who killed Antonio?"

Isabella shook her head. "I am not certain. But I am glad he's gone. I went to his room to clear things up and he had a gun. I think he was going to kill me...."

"Why are you just speaking of this to me? You could have been a suspect!" Enrique yelled.

"The authorities did not suspect me. He was going to kill me; do you not understand that?" Isabella replied. "I went to his room that night and he held a gun to my head, but I am alive. It could have been my death you were dealing with."

Enrique paced the room. "Pack your things. You are not safe here. NOW! PACK!"

Though Dom Chavez had given his word to Antonio's men, Victor trusted no one. He made a phone call to his cousin Louis, who happened to have a girlfriend in the prison.

"I need you to get a message to Marysol."

Chapter 32

Brian Sisco was an ambitious lawyer who always strived for success. He had a strong desire to win and was known among his peers to have a competitive nature. Brian was very loyal to those he cared about and would go to great lengths to protect and support them. Standing at six foot six inches, and weighing 250 pounds, Brian had a commanding presence, making him a formidable lawyer.

"Hey Sisco, Rick Spencer here.... Good as I ever was...You? ... That's good, that's good... Hey, I have a favor to ask you."

 As he entered the Bexar County Detention Center, Brian Sisco needed no introduction. He was known throughout the area and well respected.

"Good afternoon, Officer Turner," Brian said as he entered the office.

Wilma Turner was an older woman with thinning gray hair cut close to her head. She wore her iconic purple glasses perched at the end of her nose.

"Hey, Sisco. What brings you here today?" Officer Turner asked, a big smile spreading across her face.

"I'm here to see a couple of my clients, Sarah Lawson and Emily Martin. I'd like to have both women brought in together so that I might hear both of their stories at the same time, since they've been charged for the same crime," he said, showing her his identification. He had done this so many times, it was routine for him.

"No problem, Sisco." She handed him a basket for his keys, phone, and anything else in his pockets. She passed a clipboard across the counter. "Sign here and I'll get someone to take them both to room 3. I'll have an officer up here in no time to take you down."

Sisco walked through the metal detector and retrieved his messenger bag and personal items. The officer on duty inspected his bag and waved him on by. Doors buzzed and another officer appeared to lead Sisco to the empty meeting room.

Brian stood as Sarah was brought in and seated at the table. "Get those handcuffs off her," he insisted.

Sarah mouthed, "Thank you."

As he was about to introduce himself, Emily was also brought in. The officer uncuffed her immediately before leaving. Sarah leaped out of her chair and rushed to her sister. "Oh my God, Emily. I'm so glad you're here. How did you know to come?"

Emily looked incredulous. "Don't be so excited. Apparently, I have been arrested for murder."

"They think I murdered someone, too," Sarah replied.

"Yes, when I spoke to Michael on the phone – my one phone call – he told me they had arrested you at the airport."

"You talked to Michael? What did he say? Has he talked to the kids yet? What about my boss, did he say anything about that?"

"OK ladies, just hold on a minute. Before we go any further, let's take a step back. First things first; I'm Brian Sisco," he said as he shook their hands. "Most people just call me Sisco. My buddy, Rick Spencer, asked me to come down and get things rolling so we can get you two out of here."

"You talked to Rick?" Sarah asked as she started to tear up. "Rick's going to help us?"

"Something like that. I'm an attorney in San Antonio so the case will be filed under my name in this jurisdiction, but Rick will be second chair for your defense. He and your husband, Michael, are in route to Texas as we speak. They should be here first thing tomorrow."

Sarah began sobbing. "Will I be able to see Michael? I miss him so much!"

"As I said, first things first. Let's start there and see where we end up. Ladies, if you would, please take a seat, and we can get started," Sisco said as he indicated the two chairs opposite him.

Sarah cast her eyes up at the security camera.

"Don't worry about the camera. They can see us, but they can't hear anything you say. Our conversation is secure. So, what brought you to Texas?" He pulled a legal pad from his satchel and prepared to take notes.

Sarah began, "I was attending the National Talented and Gifted Conference. I presented my unit on accidental discoveries and led the teachers in making their own dippin' dots. I convinced Emily to come along. She's a chef and ..."

Emily interrupted. "Sarah, I can speak for myself. And that's way too much information. I don't think he cares that you were a presenter." She patted Sarah's hand and continued. "I was attending an entrepreneurial cooking week hosted by the convention center showcasing my invention called the

Nitro-Chill. We stayed in the same hotel but attended different conferences."

"Interesting," Brian said as he scribbled on his tablet. "I see you both have a clean record which is in your favor. Have either of you ever heard the name Antonio Alvarez before you were arrested?"

"NO!" they both said in unison.

Brian continued, "What about Enrique Martinez. Ever hear of him before?"

They both shook their heads, then Emily said, "Not really. We did have drinks with some guy named Enrique Martinez at the bar called *The Moon's Daughters*. He gave me his card, but I put it in my purse without paying much attention to it."

"Could he have possibly been Enrique Martinez with ties to Antonio Alvarez or the cartel?"

Emily shrugged. "I don't know."

Brian asked, "Where is that handbag now? Is it in police custody?"

"I would assume so. They arrested me on the interstate and some cop came and drove my SUV away. My purse was in the vehicle," Emily answered.

"The detectives have your fingerprints at the scene. They also say they have some hair samples. But you have no idea how your fingerprints or hair could have been found in the victim's room? You never went into any other hotel room but your own, is that correct?"

"Correct," they both said.

Sisco looked at his notes. "Let me see if I have this straight. You were both in town for separate conventions. Sarah, you're a teacher and Emily, you're a chef. You've never heard of Antonio Alvarez. You were in a bar called *The Moon's Daughters* at the time of the murder and a guy named Enrique Martinez bought you both a couple of drinks in the bar, but you don't know if he is connected to Antonio Alvarez. You have his business card of some sort, but you aren't sure where it is. You weren't even aware that a murder had taken place. And you don't know how the police department has your fingerprints or DNA which they found at the crime scene. Does that pretty much sum it all up?" They both nodded.

"Ladies, we have some digging to do. Oh wait, one more thing; Emily, you had a Glock 43X in your vehicle and a couple of Dewar containers of liquid nitrogen along with some serious knives? I definitely need to hear more about that."

Emily dropped her head on the table and groaned as Sarah looked at her in surprise. "You have a gun? Why would you have a gun?"

Sisco interrupted, "You have more charges against you than Sarah, though you're both being charged with murder. The prosecution will have that in their discovery, so I need to know all the details before they question you. I want to know everything there is to know, everything they will dig up before hearing it from the prosecution at the pre-trial hearing. Girls, Let's start spilling the tea, so to speak."

Emily confessed, "I keep a gun in my possession. I live in New York and sometimes things can get scary. I was mugged on the subway a few years ago and ..."

"You were mugged? Oh my God! Why didn't you tell me that?" Sarah practically screamed at her sister.

"I didn't tell you because I knew you would react this way. Yes, I have a gun, and I do have a license to carry the gun but only in New York. I completely forgot about it before heading out for my trip, but it is a registered gun. When I got to the airport, they allowed me to place it in my checked baggage unloaded. When I was leaving the hotel, I stuck it in the glove compartment. Seriously, it's just a small, little gun. As far as the Dewer containers are concerned, that's a simple explanation. I use liquid nitrogen with my Nitro-Chill so I had the containers on hand should I need them. There was no malicious intent AT ALL. And let's be real; I am a chef, and I prefer to use my own cutlery."

"That all makes sense, but I know the prosecutor and he can take information like that and twist it in such a way that you are guilty before you ever go to court. And no gun is just a small, little weapon if it can take the life of someone. The victim was shot so the prosecution will definitely use that against you. You know how to use a gun. We will need to plan out our defense for whatever he may decide to throw our way."

"If you are working with Rick, I can put my complete trust in you," Sarah said, holding her hand up as if swearing the truth.

"I appreciate your trust," Sisco smiled. "Is there anything else, anything at all that you may have seen or heard that could shed some light on this murder? You were on the same floor as the victim. Think back over the past week."

"Now that I think about it, I do remember on the day of my presentation, when I was walking to the exhibit hall at the convention center, I was startled by a couple of guys that looked like gang members. They were having a heated argument about some guy. One of them said, he will kill you if he finds out you are seeing some girl. I seem to think the name was Lina or Lana. Something like that. They just glared at me as I walked past, and it scared me. I remember thinking what girl would be worth killing for, but I was so nervous about my presentation, that I pushed it from my mind. Do you think that has anything to do with what happened?" Sarah questioned.

"I'm not sure, but it is certainly something to check into. I'm making a note of that name. We will look to see if it is in any of their discovery files. You never know what is related to a case until you discover that it is."

Sarah mused, "I guess that's why it's called discovery. Makes sense to me now."

"Anything else that might connect either of you to the crime? I heard a rumor that the detectives are trying to connect it to the cartel."

Emily and Sarah looked at each other and then at Sisco.

"The cartel?" Sarah asked, bringing her hand to her neck.

Sisco raised calming hands. "I don't think either of you have to worry about that."

"Sarah, you need to tell him everything. Don't leave a single thing out," Emily urged.

Sarah sighed, closed her eyes for a moment and then went into detail about working with her college friend's family and the hit on their jewelry store. She explained that she couldn't identify anyone and was not listed as a witness. But her friend was in the witness protection program, and she hasn't seen her since.

"Alright, there may or may not be any connection here, but good to know. At this point, sit tight. After the pretrial motion, we will be able to have access to everything they have. Then we will be able to build our defense. It may not be easy, but we will get it done. Is there anything you need before that time?"

Neither sister knew what to ask other than when they could get out of the detention center and go home but Sisco didn't have an answer to that.

Chapter 33

The plane descended through a sea of cotton-like clouds, the sunlight breaking through in radiant beams as the San Antonio skyline came into view. Below, the vibrant sprawl of Texas' seventh-largest city stretched out in all directions, a tapestry of sun-bleached roads, modest neighborhoods, and gleaming glass towers.

The plane touched down with a jolt, the tires skimming the tarmac before settling with a gentle roar. The familiar ding of the seatbelt sign being turned off signaled a collective sigh of relief among the passengers. Some immediately stood, stretching cramped limbs, while others fumbled with carry-on luggage and mobile phones.

Rick and Michael exchanged a quick glance. "We've got to move," Rick whispered urgently, unbuckling his seatbelt in one swift motion.

Michael followed suit; his movements were quick but deliberate. "No kidding."

They stood and maneuvered through the narrow aisle; their bags already slung over their shoulders as they edged past slower passengers still wrestling with their belongings.

"Excuse us," Rick said as politely as he could manage, though his eyes remained locked on the exit.

"Watch your elbow," Michael muttered as a fellow passenger nearly clipped him.

"Just keep going," Rick replied.

They stepped into the jet bridge, the heavy Texas air hitting them like a wave. Rick paused only briefly before pressing forward. "Stick with me," he said over his shoulder.

"I'm right behind you," Michael assured, quickening his pace as they navigated the labyrinthine terminal.

The terminal buzzed with activity; businessmen, families, soldiers, all there for different reasons, and all headed in different directions. Rick weaved through the throng with practiced ease, his eyes scanning for the fastest route.

"There," he said, pointing to a less crowded corridor.

"Got it," Michael replied, falling into step as they surged forward. The iconic teal and white mural displaying "Welcome to San Antonio" flashed by in a blur.

"Let's go," Rick urged, already moving toward the exit.

Michael motioned for Rick to keep going. "Just keep leading the way."

The automatic glass doors parted, and they stepped into the dazzling Texas sun. The parking lot shimmered in the heat, and the unmistakable hum of cicadas filled the air.

"Damn," Michael said, wiping his brow. "That sun is bright."

"Welcome to South Texas," Rick replied, heading directly towards the car rental lot. "Wait here, this won't take long," he said as he headed into the rental office.

Moments later, he emerged with keys in hand. "We're in the Red F-150 truck," he said tossing his duffel into the bed of a pickup truck. He climbed into the driver's seat, the leather hot to the touch from the sun. "It'll cool off. Eventually."

Michael climbed in beside him, the seat creaking under his weight. "Eventually? That's comforting. Nice choice of vehicles, I think?"

"When in Rome, do as the Romans do. This is Texas, so we've got to have a truck!" Rick turned the key, and the truck roared to life with a satisfying growl. The smell of sunbaked vinyl and gasoline filled the cab.

Rick pulled up the GPS on his phone. They had just enough time to get to the Bexar County Detention Center before the pretrial motion.

After signing in and going through the metal detector, they were escorted to a questioning room, their steps echoing down the long hall. Sisco was already there and waiting with the sisters. Sisco nodded to Rick and offered his hand to Michael, an apologetic smile on his face that showed his perfect teeth.

"Sisco, always good to have you on my side," Rick said as he entered the room. "Sarah, Emily, we're going to try and make this thing go away."

Michael shook Sisco's hand, his lips pursed, determined not to lose it in front of Sarah and Emily. "Hey, Sarah, honey, I made it and I'm here for you."

Sarah couldn't stop crying when she saw them. She wanted to put this crazy mistake behind her and go home. "I love you. I'm so sorry for whatever this thing is. I'm just so sorry..." she trailed off.

"You've done nothing wrong. Rick and Sisco are going to prove that. I love you too, baby." Michael just wanted to hold her, but that wasn't possible.

An officer entered and informed them it was time to head to the courthouse. Emily and Sarah were escorted out and loaded into a secure van. They would meet their attorneys and Michael there.

Standing before the judge was unnerving. Both women were in orange jumpsuits and neither had been given an opportunity for a shower or even a brush for their hair. They looked like wrecks and, in Emily's mind, guilty.

"Can we not wear our street clothes for this?" Emily had complained.

Sarah also chimed in. "Orange isn't a good color. It screams guilty when you're in court wearing a prison jumpsuit and handcuffs!"

Rick assured them. "It's just a pretrial motion to plead guilty or not guilty. He can't judge you today. He is just determining whether or not to continue with the legal process."

The hearing was quick and to the point.

Judge Connelly asked, "How do you plea?"

And they both had responded, "Not guilty."

Connelly banged his gavel, declared that their trials would be combined as one, had them returned to the county detention center and then determined a date for the preliminary hearing. At that point, it would be determined if their case would go to court.

Rick had told them it would be that way but not to worry. He and Sisco were working on their defense.

They would have their day in court. They gave the sisters one last goodbye before they were loaded into the van and escorted them back to the detention center.

Chapter 34

The pretrial meeting was set with the prosecution. It was an all or nothing situation as the evidence stacked against them. After dropping Michael off at the hotel, they headed to Sisco's office to prepare for their meeting.

"Let's review our list of things we want to cover today," Sisco said as he pulled out his notebook. They're going to try and bulldoze us, but stand firm and stick with this list," he told Rick. "I've been up against these guys before and they are stone cold and heartless."

They looked over their list together to solidify it in their minds.

- Evidence collection procedures
- Chain of Custody
- Laboratory Analysis
- Expert Witness Qualifications
- Reliability of the evidence
- Exclusionary evidence: Are there any arguments or evidence suggesting that the hair samples do not belong to the

defendants? Is there any basis for challenging the admissibility of the evidence in court?
- Discovery and disclosure: Has the prosecution provided all relevant information?
- Constitutional issues: Were Emily's rights violated during the search and seizure of her vehicle?
- Witness statements

Rick and Sisco arrived at the Cadena-Reeves Justice Center which stood like a stone sentinel in the heart of downtown San Antonio. The building wasn't beautiful, not in the way the nearby historic courthouse boasted its Spanish colonial architecture, or the River Walk meandered with romance, but it was formidable. Inside, the air was cool with the faint scent of stale coffee. The sound of hushed voices and footsteps across the tile floors echoed throughout the entry.

The reception area was unassuming with no frills. Several clerks were busy typing as people waited for assistance at the counter. Just beyond the reception area, the district attorneys' offices spread out like a beehive, separating each assistant DA with tan cubicles. To the right were the conference rooms and the DA's office. William Bain and his team were squeezed into the largest conference room around the oak conference table sitting in their cracked vinyl chairs when the lawyers for the defense arrived. The back wall had a large whiteboard being prepped for the murder trial. Sarah Lawson and Emily Martin's names were written at the top in bold letters along with their pictures. The number of attorneys attending the meeting, and the names of the two defendants were meant to intimidate Rick Spencer and Brian Sisco. They may have been nonplussed, but they didn't show it. They had both seen this kind of tactic before and they were determined to maintain their coolness.

Bain took the lead. "Good morning, Counsel. I hope you are well today. I'm William Bain and these are my co-counsel."

"We are indeed well. As you know, I am Brian Sisco and this is the other attorney in the case, Rick Spencer. Now let's cut the small talk and get down to business," Sisco responded.

"Very well. We have provided you with all the forensic reports on the hair samples and the fingerprints. Have you had a chance to review them?" Bain questioned.

Rick was quick to respond, "Yes, we have reviewed the reports. But we do have some concerns about the chain of custody for the evidence. Can you provide more details on how the evidence was handled from the crime scene to the laboratory?"

"Certainly. Officer Speakman, a trained forensic technician, collected the evidence at the crime scene. It was properly sealed, signed, and transferred to the police evidence locker. The samples were sent to the state crime lab via a secure chain of custody process," one of Bain's people responded.

Sisco commented, "Fine, but we'd like more information on Officer Speakman's qualifications and training. It is crucial given the significance of the evidence in this case. We have two women being charged with murder based on a handprint found on the outside of a door."

"I assure you; Officer Speakman has a solid track record with ten years of experience in forensic analysis, including specialized training in evidence collection. We're confident in his abilities," Bain responded.

Sisco was unrelentless in his questioning. "We may need to verify those details independently. Moving on, we're considering a motion to challenge the admissibility of the DNA evidence based on the lab's testing procedures and also on the fact that it wasn't hair from the root of the head. You can't prove DNA without it. Can you shed a little light on the methodologies used?"

"The lab employed standard DNA test procedures, including PCR and gel electrophoresis. The protocols strictly adhere to industry standards, and the analysts performing the tests are certified experts," Bain responded.

"Um-hmm. I see," Sisco responded, not fully understanding what he had just heard. He jotted a few notes on his legal pad as if he did understand. He would have to contact his own specialist for a detailed explanation.

"It seems that Emily Martin's rights may have been violated with the search and seizure of her car and its contents. Care to comment on that?" Sisco asked.

Bain responded coolly, "I can assure you that her rights were not violated. We had a search warrant along with the warrant for her arrest. Protocol was followed to the letter of the law. That woman had a Glock 43X in her car! Raises some suspicion, don't you think?"

Rick pressed on. "We'll be reviewing those procedures and warrants closely. Additionally, we're interested in any exculpatory evidence you may have. Have all relevant materials been disclosed?"

"In accordance with our obligations, all discovery materials, including any exculpatory evidence has been provided. Is there anything else from either of you?" Bain questioned.

"We just want to be certain that we have all evidence in this case. We don't want to be surprised in court. I'm sure you understand," Rick said in an even tone.

Bain quickly responded, "Oh, if there is any other discovery material, we will be sure to send it all over to your offices by the end of the day." He gave his people a knowing look to indicate that there would be boxes of information the two attorneys would receive that would bury them in paperwork.

With that, the meeting ended, and the two attorneys left. When they reached Sisco's office, Sisco was concerned about all the evidence. He felt like it would hold up in court. They were due to appear before the judge in less than a week.

"What do you know about Judge Connelly? Have you ever appeared before him in court?" Rick questioned.

Sisco thought for a moment. "I haven't been in his court before, but I have heard he is fair. He doesn't put up with much, though, so we will have to tread carefully. He is going to want a speedy trial since he is ready to retire. My only concern at this point is how we are going to defend these two ladies. I don't see a way out of it." Sisco said.

Rick leaned back in his chair; the wheels visibly turning in his head. "Don't worry too much. The trial hasn't even started. There is always a way out when you're innocent. We're just going to have to work harder to find it going up against the prosecution. Bain has an army of people on his team, but we have innocence and the law."

"There is one thing that concerns me a great deal and that's the involvement with the Mexican cartel that Alvarez was mixed up in. Along with the fact that Sarah may have witnessed a hit by the cartel when she was in college. Those guys NEVER forget. I'm concerned for the welfare of our girls and for Michael. I think we need to get the U.S. Marshals involved in this and get some witness protection for them until this thing is over," Sisco said.

"You may be one hundred percent correct on that, my friend, definitely something to consider."

Chapter 35

The following week, the two women were in court for a preliminary hearing to determine if they would go to trial and if they would receive bail if a trial were forthcoming. Paying bail for one accused of murder would be a hardship for Michael, but for two accused of murder? He would have to use his house, cars and business as collateral and even that might not be sufficient.

"ALL RISE! The Court of General Sessions Ninth Judicial Circuit is now in session. The Honorable Wilfred M. Connelly presiding," the bailiff loudly announced.

As the heavy wooden door of the courtroom chamber swung open, a hush fell over the courtroom as anticipation intensified. All eyes turned toward the judge's bench. Judge Connelly strode into the courtroom with a measured and deliberate pace. His presence commanded respect, and the mere sight of him invoked a sense of importance that only decades on the bench could bestow. He was a portly man with a distinguished face etched with lines of countless decisions. Judge Connelly carried himself with the grace and authority of a man who had seen it all, from high-profile trials to complex legal disputes.

"Be seated. The State of Texas versus Emily Martin and Sarah Lawson is now in session."

The judge banged his gavel and cleared his voice. "As you know, today we are here to determine if there is sufficient evidence to hold a case for a murder trial. The purpose of this hearing is to determine whether or not the defendants, who are before the court, may have committed that crime. We will begin by hearing from the prosecution. Mr. Bain?"

Bain stood and buttoned his suit jacket, ever the professional. "Your honor we have evidence that shows the Sarah Lawson and Emily Martin were in collusion with Enrique Martinez, a person of interest with the FBI, suspected to be in alliance with the Mexican cartel. And that Ms. Lawson and Ms. Martin entered the deceased's room at the El Amado Hotel and Resort, overpowered him in his drunken state, and committed murder, shooting him with his own gun. We have a witness that saw a blonde woman entering and exiting his room around the time of the murder, we have fingerprints and DNA evidence to back that up. It is our hope that you recognize that we have enough evidence to go to trial."

"Defense, any statements you'd like to make?" Judge Connelly motioned for them to speak.

Sisco stood before the judge, "Yes, your honor. Based on the evidence presented to us, we believe that it is all circumstantial. The prosecution is grasping to get a conviction. We have witnesses that place Ms. Lawson and Ms. Martin at a restaurant and a bar away from the El Amado Hotel and Resort at the time of the murder. We will also speak to the charge of fingerprints being at the scene."

"Very well," Judge Connelly said. "The prosecution may continue by calling their first witness."

Bain stood again. "We call Ms. Clara Underwood to the stand."

Ms. Underwood stood and smoothed her Mexican embroidered dress or huipil. Its vibrant colors contrasted with her silver hair. Her ears were adorned with turquoise earrings, and she had a handsewn leather bag across her shoulder. The perfect picture of someone who had vacationed in San Antonio.

Mrs. Underwood knew what she had seen, and she was willing to tell it. She was sworn in and seated in the witness box.

"Please state your name."

"My name is Clara Jane Underwood."

"Ms. Underwood, could you tell the court your business at the El Amado Hotel?"

"I took my grandchildren there. They're sitting right there," she said as she pointed them out, a look of pride on her face. "I was tired after a full day of shopping, so I stayed on the premises and let them venture out on their own to enjoy the sights."

"Thank you. Ms. Underwood, were you registered at the El Amado Hotel the night that Mr. Alvarez was killed?"

"Yes, I was. Such a terrible thing to have happened."

"And can you tell the court what you witnessed in your own words?"

She began her long narrative. "I kept looking out the peephole in the door waiting for my grandkids. I thought it was time for them to get back. I saw a blonde woman at the door across the hall. She was fumbling with her shoe and cussing. She kept calling to someone. When I looked again, she was knocking on the door and listening to see if she could hear someone. Wheel came back on, so I stopped looking through the door."

"Wheel? Bain questioned.

"You know, Wheel of Fortune. It was a good one too. The final puzzle was so easy, I was yelling the answer, but the guy didn't guess in time."

"I'm sure it was a good show. But let's get back to what you saw," Bain redirected her.

"Oh, yes. Much later, the guy across the hall came back. He had a wine bottle and glasses in his hands, and he was mad because he couldn't get the door open, and no one inside would come to the door. I thought he was drunk. It wasn't long after that, the blonde came back and knocked again. He opened the door and started cursing at her. At least I think he was, it was all in Spanish, but he sounded really angry. He pulled her into the room. When he slammed the door shut, I went back to watch TV. The news was on, and I wanted to see what the weather was going to be the next day. I was hoping it wasn't going to rain," she said.

"Then what happened?"

"When Jimmy Kimble or is it Kimmel, I can't remember. Anyway, when he was doing his monologue, I heard what I thought was a gun, but there were lots of fireworks going off too. I looked and saw the blonde leaving in a hurry. The next thing you know, the little skinny girl was back, and she was screaming about the guy being shot. That's when I called the front desk, and all the police and Mexican mafia showed up!"

"Thank you, Ms. Underwood," Bain said as he sat back down but before yielding to the defense, he stood again and showed Ms. Underwood a picture of Antonio Alvarez.

"Ms. Underwood, is it your testimony that this is the man who was staying in the room across the hall from you?"

"Yes, that's the one."

"Thank you, no further questions."

Sisco stood before Mrs. Underwood. "You seemed to be very busy that night. It sounds like you gave a good account of all the goings on. You mentioned the Mexican Mafia. What does that mean? Could you please explain it?"

"Oh, I saw those Mexican men everywhere that week lurking around spying on people. Several of them had been to that room before that night. Made me nervous and all."

"Did you happen to see them enter the room the night of the murder?"

Mrs. Underwood responded, "I saw them early in the day, but that night I didn't notice them."

"Thank you, Mrs. Underwood, no further questions for this witness, your honor." Sisco returned to the defense table.

"Mr. Bain," the judge directed.

"Thank you, Mrs. Underwood, you may step down. Your Honor, we would like to call William Smithson to the stand."

After Smithson was sworn in, Bain continued with his questions. He called several people to the stand to testify about the fingerprints, DNA evidence and so forth. Things were not looking good.

Rick Spencer called on a few of his expert witnesses, but it didn't add much to the argument.

The judge concluded that there was probable cause to believe that the crime was committed by the defendants, and a trial date was set as well as a time to select jury members. He denied bail based solely on the fact that neither woman was a resident of Texas and therefore, could be considered potential flight risks. Both women would be placed into the custody of the Texas prison system.

Their attorneys assured them that it should be a quick trial. They would figure everything out. However, the evidence was compelling.

As they were being handcuffed, Sarah saw the picture of Antonio Alvarez on the prosecution's table. Her face turned white, and she fainted.

The defense was escorted to a side room as Sarah was slowly gaining her senses. "It's going to be fine, Sarah. We'll try to make this a quick trial," Rick said as he patted her hand.

Sarah came to with a start. "That's not it. It's not! I saw the picture of the Alvarez man. It's him! I remember now. It's him. The man who murdered Libby's parents!"

Chapter 36

The news that Antonio Alvarez was the one who may have gunned down John and Mindy Burcher in Austin was absolutely unnerving. Sarah was shaking uncontrollably as memories began to resurface.

"It's all coming back to me. My therapist said it would. I know for sure it's him. I can see him clearly in my mind, I tell you." Sarah was completely unnerved.

"Not a word, Sarah. Do not breathe a word of this to anyone. Your life may be in danger. And we certainly can't have the prosecution hearing this. It would just be another thing that could convict you," Rick warned.

"I need to see my therapist. I can't handle this alone in jail. I'll lose my mind. Michael, please. I'm scared!" Sarah cried. "My brain is in overdrive!"

Michael was holding her and trying to get her to do her breathing exercises she had learned. "Just breathe, baby."

There was a knock at the door and an officer entered, cuffed the two sisters and led them away.

"I love you, Sarah. We're going to fix this!" Michael yelled, as the two sisters were being led to the van.

"Rick, get her out of there. She can't deal with this. I'm worried about her mental health. Do something to help her," Michael pleaded.

Rick was obviously out of his wheelhouse with this. He had never had this situation occur in all his years as an attorney. "Sisco, any thoughts?"

Sisco replied, "Everyone just take a minute to calm down. I'll head down to the prison when we leave here and check on the girls. In the meantime, I think it would be in their best interest to speak with the judge and ask for protection for the girls and Michael's family. If Sarah remembers, chances are someone associated with Alvarez will recognize her."

"Sisco, we can't just go to the judge and tell him that Sarah just identified Alvarez as a murderer. That information would need to be handed over to the prosecution!" Michael hissed.

"Guys, we need to figure this out NOW!" Michael was in a panic.

Sisco was calm and cool. "We will simply go to the judge and ask for additional protection based on the fact that Antonio Alvarez was a suspected cartel member and therefore, lives need protection – just in case."

Within the hour, Rick and Sisco, along with William Bain, stood before the judge in his private chambers.

"We're concerned about the well-being of Sarah Lawson and Emily Martin. Whether they are guilty or innocent, there is involvement with several cartel groups; Guadalajara, Los Urbanos, Los Zeta, maybe even more," Sisco explained.

"What are you asking from me?" questioned the judge.

"The victim was on the FBI watch list, for God's sake! These ladies and their family need some kind of protection," Rick protested.

"Very well. I suppose I see your point. Bain, do you have an objection to protective custody for the defense?" Judge Connelly asked.

"I do not, your honor. But let the record show that I don't see the relevance," Bain replied, his arms crossed across his body.

"Duly noted. I will place both women in protective custody at the prison, keep them away from the general population for their safety. And what are you suggesting for the family?" Connelly questioned the two defense attorneys.

Sisco was quick to respond. "Sarah Lawson's husband, Michael, is here in San Antonio awaiting the

233

trial. We'd like some kind of police protection for him."

"I see no need for him to stay in San Antonio until the trial. It's more than a month away. Let's get him to a safe house for the time being. Anything else, gentlemen?"

"We just want our defendants and their family protected. That's all we can ask," said Sisco.

"I understand your concern; I'll get the ball rolling. Now, if there is nothing else, I'll see you all in court."

They were dismissed without another word.

Chapter 37

As soon as the judge made his ruling for a trial, and the girls were promised protection by the judge, Michael returned home to face his children. This would be a difficult task explaining that their mom and favorite aunt had been arrested for murder and were awaiting a trial. How do you even begin to tell your kids? And what about friends, people at work, the church? How would he explain police protection? This was going to be the hardest thing Michael had ever faced. At least he had his best friend, Rick, to confide in.

The kids walked through the front door excited to see their parents.

"Mom, Dad, we're home," Zach called as he threw his backpack onto the hallway floor.

"Where's mom?" Jordan asked when she entered the living room. "I thought she'd be here."

Zach was also surprised that their dad was the only one there and waiting for them. No lights were on, but the family room was lit by the slowly setting sun. Michael was sitting on the couch, deep in thought.

"Kids, come sit with me. We have some things we need to discuss about your mom and Aunt Emily," Michael began. "I'm not sure how to start, so I'll just start at the beginning. I told you Mom hadn't left San Antonio, and I was going to spend a few days away with her, but I didn't tell you the entire story. Mom and Aunt Emily have been arrested for a murder that took place in the hotel, and they are going to be there until their trial."

"What? Murder? Are you serious? Why? How?" Jordan powered questions his way.

Michael threw up his hands to express his confusion and continued with his explanation. "Most of the evidence is circumstantial, but there are a few things the lawyers are trying to work out."

As Michael began to unfold the story of the murder and arrest, someone knocked on their front door.

"Let me see who that is, just sit tight," Michael said as he rose to answer the door.

He looked through the peephole in the door and saw two men in suits standing on his front porch. "I hope these guys aren't Jehovah's Witnesses, not today," he thought as he opened the door.

"How can I help you gentlemen today?" Michael asked.

The first guy was much older than Michael with a thick mustache and glasses and a stout build. He held up a bifold wallet with a golden badge that read U.S. Marshal. "Mr. Lawson?"

"Yes, what is this about?" asked Michael.

"We're with the U.S. Marshal's Office," the second man, much younger and in better shape, said as he also held up his badge. "I'm Deputy U.S. Marshal Bentley Pierce and this is my partner, Deputy U.S. Marshal Jim Morrow. May we come in?"

"OK," Michael said, stepping aside and letting them enter. "What is this all about?"

"Mr. Lawson let me start by saying, we're sorry about your wife's impending trial," said Morrow. "A murder trial is never easy on the perpetrator's family."

"My wife didn't kill anyone, let's get that straight right from the start," Michael said defensively. "Why, exactly, is the U.S. Marshal's Office involved and what could you possibly want from me? I'm not the one on trial and I wasn't even in San Antonio with my wife when the crime was committed."

"May we speak with you and your children?" Pierce asked.

"Please, by all means, come in and make yourselves comfortable. Can I get you anything?" Michael said, remembering his manners. "I'm guessing you guys are the ones that are going to be watching our house and keeping an eye on things."

Morrow responded, "Sir, time is of the essence. Your wife is involved in more than just a murder. Antonio Alvarez was involved heavily with several cartels in Mexico. We believe you and your family are in danger."

"How does that involve us?" We don't even know Alvarez or anyone else with the cartel," Michael said.

"Alvarez was on the FBI watch list as was his brother-in-law, Enrique Martinez. Your wife and sister-in-law met up with Martinez at a local bar the night of the murder. The cartel is aware of the meeting, and more than likely, they will seek revenge for the murder of a kingpin. A murder that wasn't ordered by them. As we said before, we believe your lives are in danger," explained Pierce.

"There will be time to discuss all of this later, once we have you in a safehouse," Morrow said.

"What? A safehouse? You just want us to pick up and leave now? Like right now without a second thought? That's just crazy!" Michael exclaimed.

"Yes. Now."

"Dad, do we have to go? I don't want to leave here. We have school and I have baseball practice," fretted Zach.

"I have plans tonight with my friends," said Jordan. "I'm not going anywhere."

"And what about my job?" questioned Michael. "I have a job, you know."

Deputy Pierce said, "I know this seems like a lot to take in, but I'm telling you, baseball and your friends won't be important if the cartel gets to you first. And, if necessary, if your wife is found guilty, you can get another job under an assumed name. At this point, the agency will take care of your job and school as well as your personal needs."

Jordan began to get anxious. "We don't have to go with you, do we? What if we just say no?"

Pierce tried to remain calm. "We can't force you to go, but I strongly advise you to leave and when I say leave, I mean now."

"But what about Sarah's trial? I need to be there to support her. She can't go through all this alone. I won't abandon her," Michael said. "What about that?"

"The trial is a month away. Today, we need to secure your safety. There will be time to discuss the trial and your support at another time," Morrow said.

Pierce interjected, "Keep in mind that if your wife is found guilty, your life, as you know it now, will be over. You'll assume new identities and be moved to a new location."

"I told you; Sarah didn't do this!" Michael was beginning to break down.

"Until she is proven innocent, and the perpetrator is found, we need to keep you safe. It's important to go now, before it's too late," Morrow explained.

"I guess it's something we need to do because I don't want to get involved with the Mexican cartel. But I'm feeling overwhelmed by all of this. I just need to make a few phone calls to let friends and business associates know what is happening." Michael stood and pulled his phone from his pocket.

"Sir, you can't do that. If you agree to witness protection, you'll have to surrender your phones as well as your laptops immediately. No outside communication," explained Pierce. "That's protocol."

"Dad, I'm not giving my phone or laptop to anyone! My life is on that phone," Jordan cried.

"I appreciate what you're trying to do here, but I'm going to need a minute to discuss this with my kids – alone, if you don't mind," Michael said.

"Certainly, but you need to be quick. We don't know how quickly word will spread and the cartel will move," Morrow said.

"Can I call my lawyer and let him know what's going on and where we're going?"

Pierce replied, "I'm sorry. But no phone calls. Your attorney knows you're going into protection. He's the one that requested it. Now please, Mr. Lawson, time is of the essence."

Michael went to the master bedroom at the back of the house with his children. The bed was un-made and clothes were strewn everywhere. He had left in a hurry to get to Texas. There wasn't time to tidy the room. "Sarah would be so upset with me," he thought. "But I can't think about that right now."

"Dad, we can't leave all our friends," Jordan began with her pleads to stay. "There is too much going on right now. And nobody is taking my phone away." Tears filled her eyes, and she began crying. "We weren't witnesses, so why do we need protection?"

Jordan was a junior in high school, just hitting her stride with friends and boys. She favored her mom with her long blonde hair and green eyes. He saw more and more of Sarah in her every day; the way she moved, laughed, and worried about unnecessary things. Michael knew it was an important time in her life. But so was keeping her alive!

He didn't even need to hear Zach's concerns. He was a freshman in high school and had just made the varsity baseball team. He had a powerful left-hand pitch that could strike out almost any batter, and the coach was very impressed with him. He had his future already mapped out.

No parent should have to make this decision and certainly not without their partner. What would Sarah do? She would put the kids' safety first and foremost above everything else. He knew that and he knew what he needed to do.

"Kids, look. I know this is going to be hard, but it's just until Mom's trial is over. We can look at it as if it were a vacation. I really don't think it will be permanent. Mom didn't do this. When she's proven innocent, we will be free of this and we can go back to our lives," Michael pleaded with his kids.

"But Da-a-a-a-d," Jordan started to complain. "What about Thanksgiving? My God, Dad. What about Christmas? Are we going to have to spend the holidays in hiding? I don't want to do that. Da-a-d!"

"I don't want to hear it. I get it, you don't want to leave, and I don't want to leave our home either. It's just temporary. What do you say? Look at it as a holiday get-away. It could be an adventure. Are you with me?

For Mom and Aunt Em?" Michael was practically pleading with his own children.

Both of his kids were crying now but Zach was the first to succumb to Michael's pleas. "I'll do it for Mom."

Jordan took a big, shaky breath and sighed. "OK, Dad, for Mom," she said.

They had fifteen minutes to gather all that they would need for the duration of the trial; clothes, treasures, baseball gloves and bats, anything that was important for day-to-day life. Without a look back, the Lawsons were loaded into a white, unmarked van and were whisked away to an unknown location to begin a new life, at least for a few months.

Chapter 38

Sarah didn't even have a chance to say goodbye to Michael before she and Emily were escorted to a waiting van that would take them to prison to await their trial. She had just had a revelation about the murder she had witnessed and was in complete shock. Riding to the prison, she could only cry. Emily was angry. Angry for all they were going through, but deep down, she was glad that Antonio Alvarez was dead.

Facing a murder charge, Emily and Sarah had found themselves in a predicament they had never imagined. But things were going to take an even more sinister turn. They were being transported to the Linda Woodman State Jail in Gatesville, Texas and placed on pretrial intervention until their trial date. The county jail was shocking enough, but this would break them.

The ride to the institution was sheer misery. They boarded the bus where another woman was already seated. The guard handcuffed Sarah and Emily to their bus seats so sitting was uncomfortable. They were not allowed to speak, and the guard was ruthless.

"Sit in your assigned seat, and keep your traps shut!" he yelled. He kept his rifle aimed in their direction through the duration of the ride. The drive lasted almost two hours. Emily wanted to comfort Sarah, but she could only look sympathetically at her.

A guard met the bus and escorted the three women inside to be processed. He was built like a weightlifter, his arms as big around as Sarah's head. He wore a heavy black belt strapped around his waist with a radio that crackled as they walked inside. He didn't seem to have a care in the world and showed no interest in the new inmates.

They were led down a long corridor, still handcuffed. They stopped at a steel gate that blocked their way. The guard used his radio to signal his arrival. The gate opened and the three women ushered past. The gate slammed shut with an earsplitting sound. Each woman had their handcuffs removed and then placed in a holding cell and handed a packet of forms along with a dull, stubby pencil.

"Fill all these forms out," the guard grunted as he started walking away.

The forms consisted of medical history and medicines taken. There were questions about needing counseling and whether you had any enemies that posed a danger. It also asked what level of education you had completed, former jobs, etc. And finally, who to contact in case of an emergency.

Before Emily or Sarah had been given enough time to complete the forms, a female guard came to the cell. "Which one of you is Lawson?"

Sarah stood, and looking back at Emily with fear in her eyes, said, "That's me. I'm Sarah Lawson."

The guard stepped to the cell door and unlocked it. "Let's go, Lawson," she said.

Sarah followed her down the corridor to another room.

"Strip," the guard commanded.

Sarah just stood there dumbfounded.

"Are you deaf? I said strip and leave your clothes there on the table. Let's go lady, I don't have all day!"

The guard held a clipboard and made checks as she inspected Sarah closely. "Raise your arms. Show me your palms. Lift one foot at a time and show me the bottoms. Spread your feet apart and bend over. Spread your butt cheeks."

Each direction was more humiliating than the one before. Sarah did as she was ordered and then she was given a pair of orange pants with an elastic waistband and an orange shirt.

"Grab one pair of panties, a sport bra and a pair of socks from that shelf. What size shoe do you wear?" the guard asked.

"Eight, I uh, I wear an eight," Sarah was barely able to speak.

When she was dressed, the guard took her back to the holding cell. Emily and the other woman were gone, leaving Sarah alone.

Another guard came and took her to an exam room where a nurse was waiting. She never looked Sarah in the eye but focused on her own clipboard. After reviewing Sarah's paperwork, she took Sarah's temperature, blood pressure and pulse. Then it was back to the holding tank.

An older woman came to the cell and asked if she was Sarah. She unlocked the cell and took her to a small office.

"Please have a seat," she said as she pointed to a chair across from her desk. "I'm Ms. Corrigan, and I'll be your counselor while you're here. I just have a few questions to ask you before you go to your cell."

She went through her list asking questions and making marks on her paperwork. "Have you ever worked for law enforcement? Have you ever testified in court against someone? Are you affiliated with any gangs or other criminal organizations? Are you afraid for your life at this time?"

It was overwhelming to Sarah. Before she had time to gather her thoughts, she was escorted back to the holding cell. Different staff members interrupted her every fifteen minutes. She had to be fingerprinted again, mug shots taken again, and she was given an inmate identification card and told to remember her number. She was no longer Sarah Lawson; she was inmate number 697238.

Finally, the last interruption was a guard asking if she wanted to donate her personal clothing or have it stored for her release. She had no idea how long she'd have to wait for trial, so she donated her personal clothing. She only asked that her locket be saved.

In another part of the prison, inmate number 342212 had a visitor and was given a directive: three knee deep on the new cellmate. "No problem," thought Marysol. She spoke to the prison bug and asked for one of the new prisoners to be moved into her cell.

Emily and the other woman were finally returned to the same holding cell dressed in similar prison scrubs. Before the sisters had a chance to speak, the huge guard was back. "Come with me." He handed each of them a bedroll and a simple care package. This was not how they thought their lives would go.

As the three women were being escorted to their individual cells, they caught bits and pieces of conversation from some of the inmates. Words like new meat, pretty girl, cartel, murder and revenge echoed around the prison. If they had ever feared for their lives, this was the worst time of all.

Emily was placed in a cell on the second level of the prison and Sarah on the third. They would be kept from each other with their only communication through other inmates. Fear crept into their hearts as they realized they were not only battling the justice system, but also a force that was far more menacing, the cartel.

The first day was a nightmare. As usual, Sarah couldn't control her crying.

"Girl, that's enough crying. You'll run outta tears before you're outta here. Save it for another day!" Martha yelled. Sarah's cellmate, a large woman approximately 60 years old, with a buzz cut and tats on her arms and neck, had reached her limit and had threatened Sarah within an inch of her life. She cried softly into her pillow that night until finally falling asleep.

During her sleep, Sarah's nightmares returned. She heard the pop of a gun. Her breathing quickened.

This time, she tried to focus on the faces of the shooters. They shifted in her vision, warping and swirling like smoke but when she reached out to pull the mask away, she saw the face of Antonio Alvarez and another man. She screamed!

Emily seemed to have had a better start than Sarah. At least she wasn't crying uncontrollably. She would be sharing a cell with a sweet Hispanic girl named Marysol. She appeared to be in her twenties and wore her black hair in a long braid down the middle of her back. She had a scar along her left cheek and had a notch cut from the middle of each eyebrow. She was very sweet to Emily and even offered her some of her snacks and a magazine to read. However, Emily had seen enough crime movies to feel very wary of her cellmate's intentions. But after the day of processing she had gone through, she accepted Marysol's kindness.

Rumors spread like wildfire through the prison cells about an ordered hit on Sarah and Emily. The cartel, believing that the two women had killed Antonio Alvarez, wanted to have them taken out and had ordered the hit.

When Emily awoke the next morning, Marysol was sitting on her bed staring at her, a menacing smile spreading across her face.

"Good morning?" Emily hesitantly said.

"Ya think?" Marysol said, one eyebrow raised, a smirk on her face.

Emily quickly rose and self-consciously readied herself for the day. She felt as though something might be off and she would need to be on high alert. Marysol watched her every move, never looking away, the half-smile never leaving her face.

The cell doors automatically opened with a loud clang. As women began emerging from their cells, bits and pieces of conversation could be heard traveling through the air as the inmates began heading to the dining hall for breakfast. Emily was hesitant to follow Marysol for fear of where she'd lead her. She spotted a group of decent looking women headed in a singular direction and she followed them, Marysol following in her stead.

Sarah had a fitful night full of nightmares and waking terrors. Could she really be found guilty of murdering the man who murdered her friend's parents? Life was crazy like that. She had to wrap her mind around the fact that she was in prison and basically on her own. She rose from her bunk full of fear and trepidation.

"Good morning to you, dear teacher," Martha said in a sing-song manner like a little schoolgirl. "You sure had a doozy of a dream last night. It scared the shit outta me when you screamed. But I see you survived."

Sarah was in fear for her life as she spoke. "Uh, right. G-g-good morning," she said hesitantly.

"Girl, stop shaking in your shoes. I ain't gonna hurt cha," Martha said laughing.

Sarah just looked at her and blinked several times in disbelief.

"I guess we might have gotten off to a rocky start." Martha extended her hand. "Hey, I'm Martha. I'm your cellmate. Nice ta meet cha."

Sarah hesitantly shook her hand. "I'm Sarah."

"Girl, I know who ya are. We all know. You took out a kingpin, money-laundering, filthy spic."

"I didn't kill anyone. I don't know what you think you know, but I'm innocent," Sarah stammered.

"Ain't we all innocent, sweetheart, ain't we all! Hey, you're welcome to ride with my group. Just stick with me and you won't dance on the blacktop."

"Ride? I'm not sure I ...."

"Ride, honey! I take care of you, keep you safe, watch out for you. I do you the favor," Martha explained.

"Why?"

"Someday, I'll need to be paid back with a favor from you."

"What kind of favor!?" Sarah was terrified.

"Just don't you worry none about that. I'll let cha know when I'm needing something," Martha smiled.

"W-what did you mean by ...uh... dance... on the... on the blacktop?" Sarah asked, feeling more intimidated.

"Stabbed girl! There's already a hit on you! Don't worry. I'm here all day!"

"With me all day?"

"Miss Sarah, you've got a lot ta learn in here. That means I have a life sentence. I ain't going nowhere."

Sarah felt like she would faint or throw up, but she was too afraid to do either. She didn't want to get stabbed, but 'riding' with Martha might be more dangerous. She needed to find Emily.

She prayed she would be found innocent. Being here 'all day' felt like it might be a short day for her.

The sisters made it through the first day without any more problems, but it was just one day. They might have a lifetime to worry. Martha didn't call up any favors and Marysol just watched and waited.

On the second day, after hearing from the judge about an imminent threat, the prison authorities took immediate action. Unfortunately for Emily, the guard sent to retrieve her was a bug. He called her to the door of the cell and then turned his back. She was confused. Why would he turn his back on her? It was only a matter of seconds before she knew. Marysol grabbed her in a chokehold and jabbed a small knife into her back. Emily tried to scream, but she was also being choked.

"This is just a friendly warning. The next time you won't be so lucky!" Then Marysol released her, slipped the knife into the hand of the guard and simply walked away.

The 'bug' called another guard on his walky-talky and the two of them lifted Emily up under her armpits and dragged her to the infirmary.

"What happened to her?" questioned the nurse.

"I have no idea. I just found her this way," said the guard as he laughed and walked out.

Emily wanted to tell the nurse. She knew it had been Marysol. If she told, she might be killed the next time. She prayed to God it was just a threat.

"What happened to you? Who did this?"

"I-I-I don't know. I was... attacked from behind." Emily could scarcely believe that this was happening to her. "Surely the guard saw."

"Him?" the nurse spat. "Not him. I don't trust him."

After Emily was stitched and resting in an infirmary bed, the prisoner next to her spoke.

"Watch your back. The guard that brought you in is a bug!" she hissed.

"Bug? Did... you say...bug?"

"Yeah, he's a bug; a prison staffer that can't be trusted. I've heard the rumors. He's probably getting paid on the outside to deliver messages to the inside," confided the girl. "Just be very careful, always."

Emily nodded a thank you to her.

"Hey," she spoke again. "Who's your cellmate?"

"Marysol. I didn't catch a last name."

The inmate looked terrified. "She was sending you a warning. She will not stop until she kills you. She runs this place."

Emily turned away from her and softly cried. She was innocent, but would she make it out alive?

As Sarah was placed in a single-occupant cell in the highly guarded section of the prison away from the general population she asked about Emily.

"Where's my sister? Is she being moved here too?"

"Not today. She's in the infirmary."

"What? What happened to her?" Sarah cried.

Nothing else was said as the door to her cell shut with a loud clang. She was alone; alone is solitary confinement with no one to answer her questions.

By the end of the week, she thought she heard Emily's name spoken by one of the guards. She rushed to her cell door just as Emily passed by in handcuffs, a guard on each side of her.

"Emily! Emily are you alright?"

She tried to look at Sarah, but the guards pulled her along. "I was stabbed, but I lived!" she yelled.

Could they breathe a sigh of relief? Maybe for the time being. They couldn't begin to imagine what fate may have befallen them had they not been moved. Now the waiting and worrying really began.

Sarah needed to talk to Rick and Sisco soon!

Chapter 39

Twilight washed the sky in purples and pinks as the unmarked van headed out of town on its way to the safe house. An hour into the drive, a light drizzle began to fall. The headlights of oncoming cars reflected off the wet highway. Deputy Pierce drove the van with Deputy Morrow in the front passenger seat.

Michael sat in the second row of seats with Zach on one side and Jordan on the other. The kids were scared and worried about what the future held. He could sense their nervous trepidation as they both seemed to cling to him. He had no idea where they were headed or how long they would have to stay. The U.S. Marshals assured him that his job was secure and would be waiting for him if he was able to return.

They drove through the night leaving North Carolina on Interstate 40. Michael recalled driving through Charlotte sometime around midnight. They remained on interstate 40 headed towards Nashville. He was thankful that the kids slept most of the way. Neither deputy spoke a word making the drive a quiet one.

From Nashville, the van headed toward Memphis, Tennessee. At some point during the night, the stress of it all was more than Michael could bear. He gave up the fight and fell asleep.

Michael suddenly awoke, sitting up with a jerk. The van was idling in a long line of traffic. Everything was at a standstill.

"What's going on?" he asked as he leaned forward in his seat to get a better look.

"Not sure at this point. Maybe a wreck ahead of us but it's hard to tell. We've been sitting here for more than half an hour," Deputy Pierce said.

At that point, a police officer drove the opposite way along the shoulder of the highway with his loudspeaker on. "Stay in your vehicles. Do not attempt to leave your cars. Repeat, stay in your vehicles."

Pierce and Marrow made eye contact. An entire conversation transpired in one look.

"I'm on it," Morrow said, as he unbuckled his seatbelt.

"What's going on?" Zach asked as he woke from sleep.

"Just sit tight, we're about to find out," Pierce said.

Morrow left the vehicle, flashed his badge and flagged down the police officer. Michael could see the two of them talking but couldn't tell much of what was being said. The officer was animated, arms moving as he spoke. He pointed to the direction they were heading, and Michael thought he saw the officer say 'explosion' as his arms flailed into an arch pattern.

When Morrow returned to the van, he opened the back and grabbed a small duffle. Coming around to the side, he opened the sliding passenger door and dropped the duffle inside before going to the front and getting back into the passenger seat.

"What's this?" Michael asked.

Deputy Morrow was all business. "Sir, I'm going to need you to open the duffle and grab the bullet-proof vests, one for each of you. Make certain that they are secure on your children. Then I will need the three of you to move to the next row of seats. Be prepared to duck and cover if given the signal."

Adrenaline began to pump through Michael's veins. Something was going down. With shaky hands, he retrieved the vests, handing one to each child. "Can you tell us anything more?"

Deputy Morrow responded, "Just do as I have instructed."

"Dad, I'm scared!" Jordan whispered, as tears begin to fill her eyes.

Zach nodded in agreement, his eyes wide with fear.

"Me too," Michael admitted. "Me too."

Morrow then leaned across the van head-to-head with Pierce speaking in whispers. Both deputies had their handguns in their hands and resting on their laps, prepared. They remained in the van, stationary for another hour, no traffic moving in either direction. Morrow was on the phone speaking in short, one-word responses.

Without warning, the highway opened back up and the flow of traffic continued. Michael looked out the window for any sign or indication of what had happened. He saw nothing. Neither deputy spoke but returned their handguns to their holsters. Morrow instructed them to remove the vests and relax. It was an extremely tense hour and a half. But nothing more was said about it.

As the sun was coming up, the van was headed north along highway 23.

It was a beautiful, tree-lined drive through the mountains of Arkansas. They passed by several small camper parks and general stores as well as places to launch canoes to float the Buffalo and Mulberry Rivers.

Michael began to relax a bit feeling the remoteness of their location. "This is a beautiful stretch of highway," he commented, trying to ease the tension.

"It is indeed. It's known to the locals as the pig trail," Deputy Pierce pointed out.

"Pig trail?" laughed Zach. He was waking up and taking notice of the surroundings.

"It's a nineteen-mile stretch of highway that runs through the heart of the Boston Mountains which is a part of the Ozark National Forest." Pierce told them.

"But why the name pig trail?" asked Jordan, finally coming alive.

"That's an interesting question. Because this road is a major travel way for students, fans and others visiting the University of Arkansas Razorbacks, folks believe it got its name that way."

Hey, the Tarheels have played the Razorbacks before," Zach commented.

Deputy Pierce turned and gave him a knowing nod.

"It sounds like you know quite a bit about the area," Michael commented.

Pierce responded, "As a kid, I grew up along the Mulberry River before leaving home for college. I know this area like the back of my hand."

261

They passed through the small towns of Turner Bend, St. Paul and Huntsville. In Huntsville, Deputy Pierce stopped at a small dive and bought breakfast for everyone. He pulled off the highway at Withrow Springs Park where they had a picnic secluded from the world.

After traveling through Eureka Springs, they soon found themselves on a dead-end road in the middle of nowhere, Arkansas. Two cabins on stilts stood before them.

"You guys will get the treehouse in front, and we will be in the smaller treehouse behind it," Deputy Pierce instructed.

"A treehouse? That's funny. It's not in a tree, it's just a house on stilts," Zach observed.

Well, buddy, up in these parts, it's called a treehouse," laughed Deputy Morrow. "Now let's get you all inside and settled. Make sure our groceries have been delivered as promised."

The treehouse was spacious and yet quaint. The living room was surrounded by an enormous rock fireplace with a large television mounted above. A huge sofa sat directly across from the fireplace with a cushy chair on either side. There was a selection of movies on the coffee table and games on the shelf.

The place had a huge master bedroom downstairs next to the kitchen boasting a four-poster bed. The bathroom had a standup shower and a large jacuzzi tub. Upstairs was a sleeping loft with two twin beds and a smaller bathroom.

Michael knew it would be difficult for his children, and especially for Jordan so he compromised. "Jordan, you take the master bedroom with the lovely view, and Zach and I will bunk together upstairs." He hoped that would earn him some points with Jordan since she was struggling.

There was an expansive deck at the back of the treehouse with a walkway that led across to the other treehouse. No other home of any kind could be seen in any direction. Below the house, Michael noticed a trail that led through the woods to a small lake. It wasn't home, but it wasn't a bad place to be, if it meant their safety.

"Welcome home, kids," Michael mused.

Just at that moment, Jordan fell onto the king-size bed spread eagle, Zach dropped onto the sofa and they both let out a miserable groan.

Before Deputy Pierce left, he spoke to Michael. "I'll bring you guys secure computers tomorrow for any schoolwork the kids will have and research you may want to do. But remember, NO social media, no emails, nothing that would give away your location."

"Are we really safe here in the middle of nowhere, Arkansas?" Michael questioned.

"Don't worry about anything. We have security cameras at the beginning of the road, several in the trees and one at each point of entrance into your house. If anyone gets past all of that, then they also must get past Morrow and me. Trust me, you're safe."

"I assume you have access to view all the security cameras."

"Absolutely. The second treehouse has a screen showing each of the cameras. If anyone enters the premises, we will know."

"Pierce? What happened on the interstate, can you tell me anything about it?"

Pierce responded, "I can tell you this much: An unmarked van was targeted and forced off the highway. It exploded on impact with a concrete retaining wall. We are still investigating the matter."

"An unmarked van like the one we were in? Do you think we were being targeted?" Michael questioned, obvious fear in his eyes.

"That remains to be seen. It is under an FBI investigation at this time."

"Thank you for your quick response and for taking care of my kids."

"No problem, man, it's my job. Now relax. You're definitely safe here. I'll come back around 12:30 with pizza for your first meal. Try to enjoy your morning. And just to be sure, you are all welcome to walk down to the lake or explore the woods, under our supervision, of course."

At that point, Pierce left through the back door, heading to the smaller treehouse, leaving the Lawson family alone to deal with their thoughts.

Chapter 40

The sharp clang of a prison cell door echoed through the cold, dimly lit hallway. Sarah Lawson and Emily Martin had been behind bars for weeks now, and while they had adjusted to the routine, the arrival of Thanksgiving only served as a stark reminder of everything they had lost.

Sarah sat on the edge of her cot, staring at the gray concrete wall, trying not to think about the smell of roasted turkey and warm pumpkin pie that would be filling her mother's kitchen back home. She could almost hear the laughter of her children, Jordan and Zach, the clinking of silverware, and the hum of the football game playing in the background, as Michael and her father coached from the couch. But here, in this place, the only sounds were the occasional cough from another inmate and the distant buzz of fluorescent lights.

Thanksgiving in prison was an unremarkable day. Afterall, what was there to even be thankful for? Another day behind bars?

Sarah had hoped she would be given a decent meal on this day, and it gave her hope for something good. What she got was completely different than she had imagined. Lunch was the same as the day before, except for a wiggly slice of turkey, instant mashed potatoes and watered-down gravy. For supper that night she could expect a cold bologna sandwich. Afterall, the kitchen supervisors wanted to go home and have a real Thanksgiving feast with their families.

She sat alone in her cell, with her meal before her. She poked at the turkey with her plastic fork. "Not exactly a home-cooked meal, but I guess it's better than nothing." But then a thought came to her. It's not the food I've always been thankful for; it's the people.

She hurried to the door of her cell and yelled through the bars down the corridor to Emily. "Here's to another day survived, and to the people who keep us going."

Emily, alone in her own cell, lifted her cup of water as a toast to her sister. "Happy Thanksgiving, sister!" she shouted aloud.

It wasn't the Thanksgiving they wanted, but it was the one they had. And in that moment, though they were separated by a few cells, they found a small sliver of gratitude in the midst of this horrible tragedy.

Chapter 41

"**D**ad, I love you, but I can't do this anymore. I need to talk to people my age. Zach just isn't cutting it," Jordan complained. "I'm living in a nightmare!"

"You think I like hanging out with you? How's my hair, do these pants make me look fat, what shade of polish do you like best? You're killing me, Smalls!" Zach complained using a high voice to imitate his sister.

"That's enough you two. I know you want to get home and get back to your life with your friends but that just isn't possible. Besides, staying in the Ozark mountains has been refreshing. In case you forgot, today is Thanksgiving, so let's be thankful for each other," Michael commented.

"Right Dad, mountains, and trees and ... nothing. There is nothing else here. What am I supposed to be thankful for? Solitary confinement?" said Jordan.

"You have us, and you have a computer to do your schoolwork with, that's something at least," Michael pointed out.

"What use is a computer when you can't access social media? I need to know what's happening at school with my friends!"

"I need my social media," Zach mimicked his sister.

Jordan gave him a death stare.

"Mom's trial will start soon. Rick said he felt like it would move quickly. It's just a matter of time," Michael explained.

"Well, that's time I don't have, Dad! Baseball season is about to start. I need to be on the field practicing with the team, not in a cabin in the woods," said Zach. "How long does that even mean, a matter of time?"

"We've been over this before. When the trial begins, the prosecution will present their case and then the defense will be given their chance. Rick doesn't know how long the prosecution will drag this out. I can't give you a date if that's what you're asking," Michael told them. "Just be thankful that we're safe."

"I think we would have been safe at home," Jordan pointed out. "There has been zero problem for us since we got here. I wanted to spend Thanksgiving break with my friends. We were planning so much to do! I am missing ALL of that."

Michael was hesitant to tell them all the details, but he allowed for one. "Deputy Pierce said that there had been some activity at our house, people snooping around, asking questions. Since no one knows what happened to us, no one was able to say anything. And ... I might as well tell you. There was actually a break-in at the house."

"What? Was our stuff stolen? Who broke into our house?" Jordan was beside herself.

"It doesn't appear that anything was taken, but the detectives found a noose hanging from the upstairs banister. They believe it's a warning from the cartel. Just suffice it to say, had we been home, there might have been trouble."

He would never tell his kids that a van like theirs had exploded on the interstate and that the cartel was suspected of the accident. There was also the incident with Emily being stabbed at the Prison.

"Oh my God, dad. That's so scary," Jordan cried. "I just want this nightmare to end and Mom back home with us."

"Me too, honey," Michael said as he hugged his daughter close. "That's all any of us want. Now, who's up for a hike to help release all this pent-up energy? Let's take a hike before Deputy Pierce returns. He promised us a real Thanksgiving feast. Let's work up a good appetite."

Michael needed the distraction more than his kids. Their lives were truly in danger. Sarah and Emily were alone in the prison, and he could do nothing to protect them. At least his kids had two U.S. Deputy Marshals watching their every move.

They headed down the trail in the warm, early morning sun with Deputy Morrow close behind them. Michael was thankful to have him nearby. The cartel was looking for them and he didn't believe they wanted to chat.

When they were nearing the lake, a gunshot rang out. Everyone hit the ground as Deputy Morrow signaled them to do. Deputy Pierce was quickly on the trail and rushing everyone up to the safe room as Morrow carefully picked his way through the woods on high alert.

He spotted a man and a young boy just across the way, rifles in hand. They had shot a deer and were trying to carry it to their truck. Morrow tucked his weapon into the back of his waistband and jogged over to offer his assistance.

"Hey man. Sorry we crossed over onto your property. My son here just shot his first buck. He didn't get a clean hit, and the deer jumped your fence before dropping. I hope you don't mind," the man said.

"Congratulations on the hit, young man," Morrow said shaking the boy's hand. Let me help you with that."

He helped them load the buck into the back of their truck then headed back through the woods to the safe house.

Deputy Pierce greeted him at the door. "Morrow, that was a close one! I heard the shot and saw the man with a rifle on the monitor. I was running out the door before I realized it was a deer hunter."

"Nothing like a little action before lunch. Let's get these folks up to their cabin and thank the good Lord it was just that and nothing else."

When they returned, the treehouse dining table boasted a real Thanksgiving feast. Pierce had a huge turkey, and all the fixings spread out on the table, with two kinds of pie in the kitchen. The smells were intoxicating.

Michael insisted that they each express something for which they were thankful. It wasn't a Thanksgiving they were accustomed to with Sarah and her mother cooking and Emily laughing and joking, but it was something. They were safe.

"I am thankful for our safety today. Morrow, Pierce, your fast action was appreciated. That is more important than possessions," Michael said.

Jordan spoke next. "I guess I could say I am thankful for all of you, even though you drive me crazy most of the time." She gave Zach a little shove. "I wouldn't want to go through all of this without you."

"Well, I'm thankful for all this food! Let's eat," Zach said laughing.

After dinner, they sat around the fireplace with a football game playing on the television in the background. They talked about better times and memories of Thanksgivings past. Zach got into a conversation with Deputy Jim Morrow.

"I hear you're a baseball player. You any good?" Morrow asked.

"I'm alright, I guess."

"Oh yeah? What position do you play?"

Zach responded, "Pitcher mostly, sometimes shortstop."

"Pitcher, huh? Is your knuckleball any good?"

Zach rolled his eyes. "I only have one pitch. It's the dad special, straight down the gut across the plate."

"Funny, I've never heard of that one before," Morrow said with a smile.

Michael interjected, "In case you haven't noticed, I'm not very athletic. I have worked with Zach the best I can, but I'm out of my league when it comes to different ways to throw a ball. I did my best just getting him through little league!"

Zach frowned, "Yeah, I was supposed to start pitching lessons, then you guys showed up and changed everything. Coach is going to be disappointed when I get back and I haven't learned anything. He was counting on me being the best left-handed pitcher on the team."

"If you have your glove and a ball, I could go outside and show you a thing or two. I keep my baseball glove in my bag just in case. I've been known to pitch a few back in the day," Morrow suggested.

"Don't let him fool you, kid. Jim Morrow was set to be one of the greatest pitchers in the history of baseball before he was injured. Was it the Cardinals you pitched for, Jim?" Deputy Pierce said.

"Now, don't go bringing up my past," Morrow responded meekly.

"You pitched for the Cardinals?" Zach asked incredulously.

"Just for a couple of seasons in their minor league. I was doing pretty well and about to be called up until I got smacked by a foul ball right in the shoulder of my pitching arm. It did more damage than the doctor could fix. That's when I had to change career paths," Morrow explained.

274

"Oh man! That sucks!" Zach said. "But you can still teach me to throw?"

"Sure kid, I can still throw a ball, just not as hard as I once could."

"Dad, did you hear that? Morrow was a Cardinal baseball player. He's going to show me how to throw the heat!" Zach cried.

Zach grabbed his ball and glove and headed outside. "Let's go, man," he called back to Morrow.

When they were outside, Zach asked, "What kind of pitch can you show me?"

"That depends," said Morrow. "What kind of pitch do you want to learn? I can show you how to throw a fastball; four-seam or two-seam. And I could probably even help you with a knuckleball, curveball and a changeup if you're really interested. Throwing left-handed? I could help you with pretty much whatever you are willing to learn. I'm a lefty, too."

Michael looked out the window and smiled. This was just what Zach needed to distract him. Now all he needed was a distraction for Jordan, something to be excited about. She would be a challenge. He spoke with Deputy Pierce about an idea he had, and Pierce was all in.

An hour later, Deputy Pierce returned to the treehouse with a large, brown paper bag. "Hey Jordan, guess what's in the sack?"

Jordan just shrugged, uninterested.

"You might want to come over and take a look," he urged.

She pushed up from her seat and walked into the kitchen with an indignant look on her face. "What?" she uttered.

Pierce handed her the bag. When she looked inside, a huge grin began to spread across her face. "You got this for me?" she asked.

Pierce nodded. "My job is to keep you safe, but it's also to keep you happy."

Jordan began taking things from the bag; new cosmetics, nail polish, fuzzy slippers, a facemask and all the latest issues of Seventeen Magazine and Cosmopolitan. Things to make a teenage girl happy, if at least for a day.

"Sorry I've been so rude. This is really nice." She thanked him and started to head to her room for a makeover.

"Wait, Jordan. I have an even bigger surprise for you. I hope your dad doesn't mind that I took the liberty to get you something a little extra. But I expect you to share it with Zach."

Michael perked up as Jordan gave him a pointed look. "What could you possibly give me that I'd want to share?"

Pierce went back to the door and retrieved a small box with holes poked in the top. "This was last minute, but it caught my eye."

When Jordan opened the lid, a small black and white kitten poked it's head out. Jordan's heart melted on the spot. "Oh, my goodness. Hello, sweet baby!" She pulled the fluffball from the box and cradled the kitten in her arms.

Michael looked at Pierce. "A kitten? I asked you to get her something for a little distraction. This is huge!"

Pierce just shrugged and grinned. "What girl doesn't love a kitten? It will give her something to focus on, don't you think?"

Jordan squealed with delight when the kitten yawned then curled up against her, purring. "I'm going to name you Nova because you are a bright light during a sad time." She cuddled the kitten and headed to the back door to show Zach.

Deputy Pierce turned his attention to Michael. "I hope you don't mind that I got the kitten. That was the best I could do on Thanksgiving at the convenience store, but it seemed to do the trick."

"No, I think it's wonderful. The kids have been begging for a pet since we lost their dog last year. You did good," Michael said, though his eyes were full of sadness.

"What can we do to give you a bit of joy?"

"Just get my wife out of prison and send us home. That's all I want," Michael responded as he went upstairs to his room and closed the door.

Chapter 42

The sisters were handcuffed and escorted to a consultation room at the prison. Their lawyers were there and waiting. When the guards left the room, Sarah rushed to Emily and encased her with a huge hug. At least she tried. With the handcuffs attached to her ankles it was quite difficult. "I love you. I'm so thankful you're alive!"

"I was worried for my life! Being in the infirmary was just as terrifying as my cell. Inmates handcuffed to hospital beds?"

"How are you girls holding up? Are you healing up ok, Emily?" Rick asked after the two released each other from their embrace.

"We're still alive, thanks to your fast action in getting us moved to protective custody," Sarah said as she slipped into a chair across from Rick and Sisco.

"We could have been killed! This is all so surreal. Did you find out anything about that girl, Marysol? Why would she stab me?"

"The FBI believes the Alvarez family, or their associated cartel may have put out the hit. The prison authorities believe it was a 'three knee deep' hit. That means to stab someone for injury to serve as a warning," Rick explained.

"Do you think they'll try to kill us?" Sarah was terrified.

Rick reassured them both. "The authorities don't think so at this time. But if you are found guilty, there will be some problems."

"I'm just ready to put it all behind us. We need to get out of this place," Emily commented.

"I'm absolutely terrified that they'll find out I have my memory of the Bercher murders. I promise you it was Antonio Alvarez. There was another man, and I'm sure if I saw a picture, I could identify him too. I have recuring nightmares but now I am seeing the faces of the two men. I'm really freaking out about all of this. If the prosecution knows my connection, they'll pin it on me for sure! You have to do something, Rick," Sarah pleaded.

"Unfortunately, they know of the connection. The detectives on the case discovered it early on in their investigation. The only thing they don't know is that you have recovered your memory of the incident."

Sisco chimed in, "That's what our goal is today. We need to come up with a solid defense."

As Rick went over the evidence with the two women, Emily told him about dropping her lipstick. Maybe that would be a defense, but not likely. She didn't have proof. A woman across the hall was a hot witness. She would testify seeing a blonde woman. Her description fit.

"My shoe was too loose, and I was adjusting the strap. Just because I may have stopped outside her room, doesn't mean I committed murder. She didn't even see my face," Sarah complained. "I was bent over to make an adjustment."

Rick scribbled something into his notebook, a contemplating look on his face. "Good point," he mused.

"The witness said you knocked on the victim's door. Did you do that? Did you knock?" questioned Sisco.

"I remember holding on to a door handle so I wouldn't fall. Perhaps it was outside the victim's door? And yes, I knocked. Emily dropped her lipstick; we told you that."

Sisco shook his head. "Again, a poor defense." The most compelling evidence was the hair found in the victim's hand. It matched them both! There was no explanation. Sisco began his line of questioning.

"How do you know Enrique Martinez and his brother-in-law, Antonio Alvarez?"

"We all know how I know Antonio Alvarez, don't we! I witnessed him gunning down my best friend's parents. What do I say when the prosecution asks me that?" Sarah pressed.

"We won't call you to the stand if we can avoid it. Back to the question at hand. How do you know Enrique Martinez?" Sisco asked again.

"We don't know them! Why would we know drug kingpins?!" Emily fussed. "Look. One guy shot up Sarah's employers and the other guy hit on me in a bar, doesn't mean I have a knowledge of him or have a relationship."

"Let's not forget the fact that you had Enrique Martinez's business card in your purse! That's incriminating evidence that the prosecution will use, to be sure. Did he pay you off that night for taking out his brother-in-law? Was that what it was?" Sisco pressed.

"You're insane!" Emily shouted.

"And as a sidenote, it seems that your boss, T.J. Steele is evidently on the FBI watchlist as a money launderer. Any thoughts about that? He grew up in the same city as Antonio. Hell, they're probably friends. Did he order the hit?"

Emily just shook her head. "What? That's absolutely ridiculous! It just keeps getting worse and worse. How is this even happening?"

Sisco continued, "And you had a gun in your possession. Was it the gun that killed Antonio Alvarez?"

"That's enough! I will not sit here and listen to this shit! I have a mind to ..."

"To what? Kill me?" Sisco asked. "You have a temper, and the prosecution is going to use it to their advantage."

"Sisco is right. They will try to crucify you, get you to squirm, explode in the courtroom. Then they'll drive the final nail in your coffin. Let's get our heads on straight and figure this thing out. We have to get to a solution in court without having to put the two of you on the stand," Rick said.

Sarah sat in stoned silence for several minutes when she suddenly had a thought.

"Wait a minute... remember when we did the ancestry test? There were some connections to some people that we questioned. We laughed because one match was from El Salvador, and we thought it was crazy. The last name was Martinez. Martin is a shortened version of that name. Our crazy uncle told me it was true, that our great-great-grandfather actually came from El Salvador. We thought he was making it up because he's senile. Neither of us knew that we had any El Salvadoran in us! Could that be the connection the prosecution has? Could it possibly be Enrique?"

"Right," Emily pipped up. "We even joked about it at the bar when the guy, Enrique, said he was from El Salvador."

"It's a starting place at any rate," Rick said, wondering what he had gotten himself in to. "So, we might have your connection to Antonio Alvarez with the fingerprints at the scene according to the prosecution, and you seem to have a reason for the fingerprints, but what really stumps me are the hair samples. You can't refute that. Your hair was in the victim's hand and that's where the prosecution will nail us! And to make matters worse, we still have to explain the gun in your car, Emily."

"I carry that gun for protection and I'm not ashamed to say I know how to use it. It doesn't mean I murdered a guy. I live in New York after all. There is nothing to explain about that," Emily stated matter-of-factly.

"I like a woman who packs the heat," Rick teased to lighten the mood.

"And the Dewer tanks filled with liquid nitrogen? Do all women in New York carry lethal gas with them too?" Sisco was getting frustrated with Emily's attitude.

"I already told you; those tanks were for my Nitro-Chills. I had them for backup in case I needed more," Emily explained.

"That doesn't refute the fact that liquid nitrogen can cause asphyxiation. This doesn't bode well for you," Sisco stated.

"Nothing about this charge bodes well for me. But it's all circumstantial evidence."

Rick grinned his most charming grin. "You know, you would make a good defense attorney if you ever decided to give up your day job."

Emily just rolled her eyes and flashed a sarcastic smile his way.

In the files that the prosecution had sent over, it was confirmed that the business card found in Emily's purse when her car was impounded by the police, was, in fact, the business card belonging to Enrique Martinez.

"So, explain the meeting you had with Enrique Martinez at the bar, *The Moon's Daughters*," Sisco questioned.

"As I told you before, we didn't have a meeting with him. We were there. He was there. He saw us, thought I was hot," she flashed a smile at Rick, "and he bought us a couple of drinks," Emily spouted.

"And then?"

"And then I danced with him one time. He got a phone call, bid us goodbye, rushed out. End of story."

"How long were you with him?"

"Somewhere from about 11:00 to 12:00. That's when he left. We left the bar not too long after that. That's it."

"The bartender from *The Moon's Daughters* is on the witness list. Care to let us in on what he witnessed?"

"Drinks and a dance. That's it!"

Sisco shook his head and reviewed his notes. "You left the hotel and headed to Rita's sometime between 7:00-7:30. You had drinks and then a meal. You left the restaurant around 9:30 and headed to *The Moon's Daughters*. That would place you at the bar at approximately 10:00. If you met up with Martinez at 11:00, what were you doing from 10:00-11:00?"

"We were at the bar, we told you that," Emily chided.

"The bartender doesn't remember seeing you until 11:00 when he brought you drinks from Enrique," Sisco said, his eyebrows forced into a frown.

"But we were there," Sarah said. "We did take a little stroll down the Riverwalk to help me sober up a bit from the margaritas I had at *Rita's on the River*, but we didn't walk for very long. I was in high heels for goodness sake! Oh yeah, we also stopped for some coffee in that little shop then went into the bar."

"The problem is, we don't have a witness that can confirm the time. And that's where you two are caught by the prosecution. The coroner said Alvarez was shot sometime between 10:00 and 10:30 **PM**."

"And unfortunately, your word just isn't good enough," said Rick.

Without a witness, they had a problem. Using Enrique for an alibi was out of the question. He was part of the problem. The bartender wasn't much help either.

Emily was right, it was all circumstantial evidence but so was their defense. They needed hard proof that they didn't commit this crime. Without a witness, that was going to prove very difficult.

However, neither of them had a record and had never heard of Antonio Alvarez, that is until Sarah recognized his picture after the fact. That was a moot point. An elementary teacher and a chef, two sisters, would never do this.

"Times up," the guard warned. Both girls stood and prepared to be cuffed and escorted out.

"We'll be in touch," Rick said.

"I have a quick request," Sarah said as she handed two envelopes to Rick on her way out.

The attorneys continued to dig, going over all the information. They would have to do a lot of work to make a strong defense.

Chapter 43

Snow began to descend upon the mountains of Arkansas casting a serene and enchanting spell over the peaks and valleys, painting the landscape in a pristine cloak of white. The mountains, once adorned with the vibrant hues of autumn, now wore a tranquil mantle of snow. The snowflakes began to cling to tree branches creating a delicate covering. The world outside the treehouse seemed to hush, as if nature itself was taking a collective breath, preparing for Christmas.

The Lawsons were nestled inside their treehouse sitting before the glowing fire, the kitten curled in Jordan's lap. The world seemed to be at peace. The silence was broken by a loud knocking at the door. Everyone jumped at once.

Michael cautiously opened the door to a young Santa Claus carrying a Christmas tree on his shoulder. And behind the tree, one of Santa's helpers in the form of Deputy Morrow. He had a huge box in his hands.

"Me-e-e-r-r-r-y Christmas!" Deputy 'Claus' called as he entered the cabin. "Ho, ho, ho!"

Jordan and Zach groaned in unison thinking they were too old for this nonsense, but each secretly excited.

Deputy Pierce, aka Santa, brought in a huge blue spruce, already on a stand. He plunked it in the corner next to the fireplace. Deputy Morrow followed behind with a box of assorted ornaments.

"It is time to decorate this tree," Morrow said. "If you've been good, Santa might come tonight and leave you some presents."

Halfheartedly, Jordan and Zach came forward and began digging into the ornaments. Within minutes, laughter and excitement began to fill the emptiness of the room. It did Michael wonders seeing his children enjoying themselves. Maybe they could find solace in the true meaning of Christmas. Just maybe.

Deputy Pierce heated a pan of hot chocolate and then popped some popcorn to string. He and Morrow were determined to give this family the best Christmas away from family and friends that was humanly possible.

Later that evening, as the daylight faded, the mountains came alive with the soft glow of moonlight reflecting off the snow. It was a beautiful reminder of God's creation. Everyone stood on the deck in awe and wonder, the twinkling lights of the tree reflecting behind them.

That night, as Michael and the kids were preparing for bed, Morrow and Pierce stashed a few gifts under the tree before heading to their own cabin. Christmas morning would come with surprises.

Jordan slowly began to wake as the sun glistened off the snow casting a brightness into her room. Suddenly, it occurred to her that it was Christmas morning. She didn't know why she was excited, except she was. It was human nature to be excited on Christmas morning. She sprang from her bed with a shout. "Wake up! Merry Christmas, everyone."

Michael and Zach were down the stairs in record time laughing and hugging all around. They knew there would be no presents but somehow that didn't really matter.

"Let's try to remember that Christmas really isn't about the lights and trees, shopping and giving gifts," Jordan said.

"You are right. It's about honoring the people we love and those that love us. I am proud of you two for loving the season for what it is really meant to be," Michael said hugging his kids. He was so proud of them during this hard season of their lives.

Zach suddenly let out a whoop! "LOOK! There are presents under the tree! Dad!"

They rushed as one to the tree. Nestled underneath were three boxes, one for each of them. Jordan carefully lifted each box and distributed them. Together, they sat on the sofa.

"Zach, you go first," Michael directed.

Zach tore into his box. His eyes lit up with excitement. "Oh. My. Gosh! Look!"

Inside was an official Cardinals baseball glove, autographed by Deputy Jim Morrow. It was a priceless gift, and one Zach would treasure for years to come. "Thanks Deputy Morrow. This is awesome!"

"Jordan? You're next," Michael said.

Jordan slipped the ribbon off her package and opened the gift, careful not to tear the wrapping. Inside was a delicate gold locket. The outside of the locket had two little diamonds and was engraved with the words, 'Always in your heart'. Jordan immediately recognized the locket. It was the one her mother never took off. She carefully opened the locket. Inside, it held a picture of her mom and Aunt Emily. Jordan wiped a tear away and held it close to her own heart. "I don't know how this found its way here, but it is the perfect gift."

Zach spoke up, "Dad, you are up next. Open your present." Carefully, Michael opened the small package that had been labeled with his name. Inside, tucked within tissue paper, were two letters.

"What does it say? Is it a letter from Mom? Read it," both kids said at once.

Michael recognized Sarah's handwriting, and his heart leapt. It contained two letters, one addressed simply 'To my kids' and the other, 'To my best guy'. "I am going to save my letter for later, but this one is addressed to both of you. We can read it now."

Dear Jordan and Zach,

As I sit here writing this letter, my heart is filled with love and pride, as I consider what you both have brought to my life.

Although I am physically separated from you this year, please know that my love transcends these prison walls and reaches out to embrace you both.

Please know that you are always in my thoughts and prayers. I hope that the spirit of Christmas brings you comfort, joy and strength to face what comes our way.

Cherish your time together and know that I am counting the days until I can be home with you again.

I love you, a lot, a lot, a lot,

Merry Christmas!

Mom

Everyone sat in silence after Jordan struggled to read the letter, the weight of the situation, heavy on their hearts. Suddenly, their sadness was disrupted by the jingling of bells. In front of their treehouse sat Santa and his Deputy elf in a horse drawn sleigh. What a great distraction. Michael hurried his kids to get into their winter coats, gave them each a warm blanket and sent them outside for a sleighride. He would steal this time to read Sarah's letter. He knew he needed to be alone.

As he sat down, kitten curled in his lap, he carefully read the letter:

My Darling Michael,

Merry Christmas to you, sweetheart. I want you to know my love for you is immense! You know I love you more than my heart can hold.

Please remember the warmth of our hugs, the shared times together, and the simple joy of being married. That, and your unwavering support and understanding mean the world to me and keep me going.

Though my heart is heavy with the weight of the circumstances that led me to this place, I know you are safe and waiting for me. So, for this holiday season, I cling to the love I know you have for me.

I hope my words convey the depth of my love for you and the immense regret I feel for not being able to share this Christmas with you in person.

Until I hold you in my arms again, I love you always and forever,

Sarah

Michael held the letter close to his heart as tears began to fall uncontrolled. "Oh, Sarah, I love you so very much."

Christmas came and went as the short days and long nights dragged on. The trial was scheduled to start in January. The Lawsons were looking forward to a new year and a new beginning.

Chapter 44

What could possibly be worse than spending Christmas in solitary confinement in the Linda Woodman State Jail in Gatesville, Texas? Nothing. Absolutely nothing.

Sarah sat in her cell, the weight of sadness consuming her. She was not only away from her classroom and her home in North Carolina, she was also away from the three things in life that made it worth living: her two children and her husband. And today was Christmas.

Occasionally, Sarah heard bits and pieces of songs as the other inmates began singing Christmas carols, their voices drifting down the corridors. If she was still in the general population, she could be singing along and even attending church. But that wasn't a possibility in solitary.

Making her misery even worse, she heard a guard shout 'Merry F-ing Christmas!' as he banged on her cell door, meal in hand. She reached for her meal, and at the same time, the guard grabbed her wrist.

"Have you been a good little girl? Santa can come back later when you're nestled all snug in your bed," he said laughing wickedly.

Sarah wrenched herself free and admonished him. The guard continued down the corridor. "Merry F-ing Christmas," he said again as he banged on the cell of the inmate next to her.

Her meal was meager for such a holiday, dry turkey, stuffing, cranberry sauce and a slice of pumpkin pie. Not much better than the Thanksgiving meal. She wondered what her family was having. Were they celebrating? Were her kids happy? She had asked Rick to get her precious locket from the prison and send it to Jordan. She wondered if he had been able to do that for her. She had also given him a couple of letters; one for the kids and one for Michael. It was the best she could do.

Today, on Christmas day, her heart felt heavy. She was missing out on the traditional celebration she shared with her family. A precious time just beyond her reach. It was the most miserable and desperate she had ever been. No, she decided, it couldn't get much worse.

As she sat staring at her meager meal, a verse suddenly came to mind. 'I always remember you in my prayers, day and night. And in these prayers, I thank God for you.'

"God, thank you for my family. Please keep them safe," Sarah prayed.

She lifted the spoon to her mouth when she suddenly stopped. Emily was down the corridor in a similar cell, in the same situation. Sarah could hear Emily softly singing.

"Silent night. Holy night. All is calm, all is bright ..."

Sarah joined in singing. "Round yon virgin mother and child. Holy infant so tender and mild..."

The other inmates in solitary confinement also joined in. 'Sleep in heavenly peace, sleep in heavenly peace.'

Sarah felt at peace. She felt the spirit of Christmas right there in her lonely cell. God was going to get her through this. She felt it deep within her heart.

"I love you, Emily! Merry Christmas!" Sarah yelled, as she clung to the cell bars.

"I love you too, Sarah. Merry Christmas."

Chapter 45

The smell of incense was strong in the tiny chapel. The pews were adorned with Christmas wreaths and candles burned at the altar. There was no heat inside the building so a chill hung in the air. Outside, the sky was dark and dreary with light rain falling. Antonio's body had finally been released and cremated. It was a perfect day to hold a small memorial for a wicked person. Isabella gathered with her son, Antonio Jr., her daughter and new son-in-law, Sofía and Samuel, and finally, her brother, Enrique. Father Joseph from the local diocese was also present.

Isabella walked to the front of the chapel, her footsteps echoing throughout.

"I know this is a somber occasion, but I am truly grateful to have you all here with me. Your father loved you dearly and I know you will miss him."

Isabella continued, "Though we do not know all the details of his death," she looked directly at Enrique, "he died a proud man and father."

The priest, an aging man with little hair, walked to the altar with a slow, determined shuffle. He spoke a few words about death, delivered the eulogy and spoke a few words about the life of Antonio, though he had never met him.

They bowed their heads as the priest prayed the rosary and sprinkled holy water on the cremation vessel. "In the name of the Father, and of the Son, and of the holy spirit..."

"Amen," they all said in unison.

"Dios ayúdame," Isabella said as she crossed herself. "God help me."

After the priest departed, Isabella instructed her children not to return to Mexico. There were dangers there far greater than they could imagine. She would have Antonio's cremated remains sent to Mexico. Victor could deal with that. He could toss them into the ocean for all she cared.

Thankfully, Antonio had followed her wishes last year when she asked him to establish a trust fund for each child. They were aware of threats from the cartel even then. Antonio Jr. and Sofía would never have a need unmet.

Sofía was concerned. "Mamá, what will you do after the trial?"

"I do not know. I will figure it out, I'm sure. Enrique wants me to return to El Salvador and my old life before your father."

"Come to Texas. You can stay with us. I want you with me," Sofía pleaded.

Isabella patted her hand. "Take good care of yourself and let Samuel continue to treat you like a queen. But that is not to be. I will not be moving to your home. I love you, mi amore."

"I love you, too."

"A.J., my beloved son, finish your studies and make a life for yourself here in the states. And please, if you will, stay close to your sister. She needs you in her life. I love you as well, mi amore."

They all embraced and then Sofía left with Samuel, along with Antonio Jr. Isabella felt deep in her heart that she would never see her children again.

She was left alone with Enrique to figure out what they would do.

"Not such a Feliz Navidad, is it?" Isabella said as she and Enrique left the chapel and headed to their vehicle. "I feel as though my life is already over."

On the drive back to their hotel, they each felt the guilt of the situation in their hearts.

Chapter 46

The courtroom was somber and heavy with anticipation as District Attorney William Bain sat across from defense attorneys Brian Sisco and Rick Spencer. Jury selection was often the most tedious part of a trial, but everyone in that room knew it was also one of the most crucial.

Forty-five potential jurors were escorted into the courtroom, each curious about the upcoming trial. Both sides trained their eyes on the group looking for potential people to cut. Both the defense and the prosecution were given ten peremptory strikes or strikes that the lawyers got to exercise for really any reason whatsoever so long as it wasn't for purposes of race or religion or anything of that nature. After excusing the twenty selected, the judge allowed the remaining twenty-five to be questioned by both sides.

Bain straightened his tie and addressed the jury pool. "Ladies and gentlemen, thank you for being here today. This process is vital to ensuring a fair trial for both the state and the defendants. I will be asking some questions to better understand if you can fairly and impartially evaluate the evidence."

He turned to the first prospective juror, juror number four, a middle-aged man with salt-and-pepper hair. "Sir, do you have any personal beliefs that would make it difficult for you to judge this case based on the evidence alone?"

The man shifted in his seat. "I believe in the justice system, but I also think sometimes innocent people get caught up in things. I'd have to be absolutely sure before convicting someone."

Bain nodded, making a note. "That's exactly the kind of careful consideration we need. Thank you."

Rick Spencer leaned forward. "If I may, Mr. Harper, you mentioned innocent people getting caught up in things. Have you or anyone close to you ever been wrongly accused of something?"

Harper hesitated before answering. "My nephew was arrested once. Turned out to be mistaken identity."

Spencer smiled reassuringly. "That must've been tough on your family. Do you think that experience might make you skeptical of law enforcement?"

Harper sighed. "Maybe a little. I mean, mistakes happen. But I'd still listen to the facts."

Brian Sisco exchanged a glance with Spencer before making a mark on his legal pad.

The process continued, with Bain questioning potential jurors about their backgrounds, beliefs, and any biases they might hold. A young woman expressed concerns about being impartial due to a past experience as a victim of crime, while an older man proudly stated his belief in the absolute authority of law enforcement. Both sides took mental notes, evaluating which individuals might help or hinder their case. Then they followed up with their own line of questioning. Have you ever been a victim, witness, plaintiff or defendant in a criminal or civil suit? Have you ever been convicted of a misdemeanor other than traffic violations? Are there any special accommodations the court would need to make if you were selected?

After a short recess, Bain and the defense team huddled together, comparing notes.

"We need to strike Harper," Bain said, tapping his pen against his pad. "He's skeptical of law enforcement, and that's going to work against us."

"Against you, yes. But he has firsthand experience with someone being accused of something based on mistaken identity. That's what we feel this case is-mistaken identity," Sisco pointed out.

"Look, I'm trying to work with you on this. I want a fair trial. You let me strike Harper, and I'll give you one," Bain countered.

"We can agree to that," Sisco said. "Then we want to keep that retired teacher, Ms. Ellison. She's analytical and won't be easily swayed by emotion."

Spencer smirked. "And she's got a son who's a public defender. She'll likely be sympathetic to our side."

Bain sighed. "Fine. We'll keep Ellison, but that young woman who was a victim of a violent crime, she's too emotionally invested. We need to strike her."

The defense team exchanged a glance before Spencer shrugged. "We won't fight you on that one."

One by one, jurors were eliminated from the group, and others were selected. The final cut was given to the judge for his approval.

Judge Connelly reviewed the list and then spoke to the members of the jury selection. "I would like for jury members 5, 7, 9, 11, 18, 18, 19, 27, 32, 34, 36, and 43 to remain. All the rest of you are dismissed. Thank you for your time.

When the courtroom cleared of all but the twelve, Judge Connelly addressed them. "You will report to this court Monday morning at 8:00 AM where you will be given instructions by the bailiff. After that, the trial of the State of Texas VS Sarah Lawson and Emily Martin will begin promptly at 9:00 AM. If you have any questions, please address them to the court secretary. You are dismissed until then."

The final panel consisted of a mix of ages, backgrounds, and professions. As Bain sat back, he studied the faces before him. This jury would decide the fate of Sarah Lawson and Emily Martin. He felt most of the jury selections had gone in his favor.

When Sisco and Rick Spencer left the courtroom, they both had smug smiles on their faces as they high fived each other. They believed the majority of jury selections had gone their way. And now, the real battle was about to begin.

Chapter 47

The prosecution was working diligently to achieve a conviction in the upcoming case: The State of Texas VS Sarah Lawson and Emily Martin. The detectives had provided William Bain with enough material to convict Sarah Lawson and her sister, Emily Martin. In fact, he had enough evidence to convict the entire family if he wanted to do so!

"Alright, people. I need everyone focused on this case. It is our job to get to an ending; one we can all live with. Where are we with the evidence at the crime scene?" Bain questioned his staff.

Meridith perked up. "The evidence is all there. We have hair samples and fingerprints from the crime scene matching the defendants. We also have Emily Martin's Glock. We know it wasn't the weapon used, but it was in her possession."

"Good," Bain responded. "What about the witnesses?"

"Witnesses are prepped to provide clear and consistent testimony. We will be calling Ms. Clara Jane Underwood, who saw a blonde woman entering and leaving the deceased's room. Officer Speakman will testify concerning the validity of the hair samples. We also have the bartender, Duane 'Crash' Hankins, from *The Moon's Daughters* who saw the defendants conversing with the deceased's brother-in-law where some sort of exchange took place. And of course, testimony from the deceased's associate giving an account of the grievance between Alvarez and his brother-in-law," Jake Burns, a first-year intern said with a smirk. "Oh yeah, we also have the medical examiner prepared to give crucial details about the cause and manner of death."

"Excellent," Bain said. "Moving right along. I'm assuming every piece of physical evidence is cataloged to ensure it is admissible in court. A clear record of who handled the evidence to prevent tampering claims? Yes?"

"Um, yes. Yes, we have that covered."

"Perfect. It seems that you have followed through with your assignments. Now we need to shift our focus to establishing the motive, the means, and the opportunity. We need to connect the defendant to the crime by demonstrating their reason for committing it, their capability to carry it out, and their chance to act. Then we can link the evidence to the defendants. And don't forget to anticipate the defense tactics. We must consider possible defense arguments and have rebuttals prepared. I need the entire team on this.

Meridith, I need you to prepare all the exhibits. I want to show the jury, beyond a reasonable doubt, that these two sisters killed Antonio Alvarez."

Chapter 48

With just days to go before the trial, Sisco and Rick were working frantically to build their defense. Sisco had a topnotch investigator working for him at his law firm who simply went by Mare. He had asked her if it was short for anything. No, just Mare. She had also told him there was no need for unnecessary details like last names. Mare was good enough to go by, and she only worked part-time for him. She had insisted from the beginning that he pay her in cash or through Venmo. Sisco didn't know her background and he didn't want to know. Mare could have been short for Mary, Marilyn, Maryann? It didn't matter. She was good at what she did and somehow, always came through for him. He immediately put her on the case. If there was any evidence that would help their case, she would find it.

Looking at Mare, no one would suspect that she was a private investigator. She had a tiny build, standing at only five foot two. She wore short skirts, tight shirts and high heeled boots; a dress code she found beneficial when questioning men. She kept her dark hair in a twisted topknot. Though she was small, she was mighty and strong. Nothing seemed to keep her from the truth.

Two days before the trial, Mare struck gold. She had searched through the mounds of discovery the district attorney had sent over. The name Lydia Palmer just kept needling her.

Mare traveled to Austin and spoke with Lydia. She had attended the wedding at the El Amado Hotel. She told Mare that her best friend, Isabella, was the mother of the bride. She stayed on the fourth floor of the main tower with her daughter, Evie. She had nothing else to add to what Mare already knew.

Amazingly enough, among all the documents and information that the district attorney sent over was a report from the detectives. Lydia's daughter, Evie, was bald. She questioned Lydia about her daughter but got nowhere; only that she suffered from alopecia. As Mare was leaving, she noticed a picture of Evie on the mantle. She had beautiful blonde hair. She hesitated for a moment.

"Is Evie here? May I speak with her?" Mare asked.

"Oh honey, she just left to go back to school after the break. She's in her first semester at the university," Lydia explained. "Was there something you needed to ask her? She was cleared by the police."

"Oh, no. I was just going to corroborate your story. Thanks, anyway," Mare said. She would do more digging and then look for Evie.

Mare had a friend who wore an assortment of wigs for her job as a nightclub dancer. Kara didn't want to be recognized by any johns she might run into on the street. The wigs were a great disguise. She gave Kara a visit to discuss wig hair.

"I'm curious about your wigs. Tell me, is there any difference in kinds of wigs?" Mare asked.

Kara began an explanation. "Oh sure! There are two different kinds of wigs made; some are synthetic, and some are made from human hair. Human hair wigs tend to be more durable and can even have a longer lifespan compared to synthetic hair if you maintain proper care of them."

"Interesting."

"Also, with human hair, you can style the hair with straighteners and curling irons. If you used them on synthetic wigs, it could damage them because they are not heat resistant. They can also frizz and become unmanageable. They're cheaper, but you get what you pay for."

"What about the way they look?"

"Let me show you. See this wig? It's synthetic and it kind of looks like doll hair. It's shiny and brassy looking. Now, look at this one. It is made from human hair, so it looks soft and natural."

"You're the best, Kara. Thanks for your help!" Mare left and headed over to the university to get a loc on Evie.

After locating her, Mare followed Evie that afternoon and when she stopped in at a coffee shop, Mare stood in line behind Evie and commented to her about her hair.

"You have the most beautiful blonde hair," Mare mused.

"Oh, thank you," Evie said smiling.

"I just love the cut. Is it difficult to style it that way? It's so bouncy and shiny."

Evie looked a bit embarrassed. "Actually, to tell you the truth, it's not my real hair. It's a wig."

Mare played up the role of impressed woman. "Oh my God! I couldn't tell at all. Where did you get the wig? I might need one like that for a backup on bad hair days, you know what I mean?"

"You can't really purchase a wig like this anywhere. I have alopecia and because of my condition, I qualified for the wig. It's made from real hair, that's why it looks so natural." Evie played right into Mare's hands.

"You certainly can't tell. What company did you say provided you with the wig?" Mare asked.

"It's a non-profit organization called Strands of Hope. You should check it out. They take donations of real hair from all over the United States. It's a great organization," Evie explained.

"Thanks, I'll do that," Mare said. As Evie turned around to place her order, Mare retrieved a few loose strands of hair from the back of Evie's jacket. She tucked them into a small Ziplock bag. Evie turned to speak to her again, but she had simply disappeared.

Could it possibly be? Sisco was impressed with Mare's work yet again. He immediately contacted Rick and gave him the information. Rick made a trip to the prison to speak with the sisters.

"I know this is really a long shot, but I have to ask, have either of you ever donated your hair?"

"Actually, we have. It was Sarah's crazy idea. She's always thinking of ways to help kids in need. It's just her nature," Emily said.

"Do you think there is a connection?" Sarah asked, the wheels turning in her mind.

Rick said, "I'm not sure yet, but I'm working on a possibility of a connection. It might be our answer. I'll keep you posted."

"We're not going anywhere," Emily said with half a laugh.

Rick learned that Sarah and Emily had both donated their hair just a month before their trip to San Antonio. Hopefully, he now had a defense. He would place Lydia and Evie Palmer on his list of witnesses.

The hair samples were sent to a crime lab that Sisco chose. "We don't want to use the same lab as the prosecution. No need to mix up the samples or give the prosecution a heads up. Besides, we need our own expert testimony when it comes to hair DNA."

Everything was falling into place. All the evidence the prosecution would present could be refuted. All they needed to figure out was who committed the crime. If they could do that, the girls would be safe to live their lives and Sarah's family could return home.

Sisco headed back to the hotel. The prosecution had footage from the front of the sixth-floor elevator, but it didn't show Sarah or Emily in the footage at the door of Alveraz. His room was too far from the camera. It merely showed them getting on the elevator at the approximate time they stated.

But a thought occurred to him. He requested the footage from the fourth-floor camera. That was not part of the evidence from the prosecution. Perhaps it would shed some light on their suspicions.

Chapter 49

"ALL RISE! The Court of General Sessions Ninth Judicial Circuit is now in session. The Honorable Wilfred M. Connelly presiding."

Judge Connelly entered with steady, purposeful steps. He moved with the precision of a man accustomed to the weight of justice resting on his shoulders. The courtroom fell silent, tension tightening like a drawn bowstring. Members of the press were seated between the columns and on the left behind the public gallery, each one hoping for a story. Connelly's steel-gray eyes, sharp and discerning, seemed to pierce through pretense, as he looked around the courtroom. Clad in his flowing black robe, he carried an aura of quiet power, the kind forged by years of navigating the complexities of the law and humanity behind it.

During pretrial hearings, he had determined that the cases of the two defendants would be combined into one case to streamline his calendar and resolve the case more efficiently.

"Be seated. The State of Texas versus Sarah Lawson and Emily Martin is now in session."

Judge Connelly banged his gavel and cleared his throat. "Members of the jury, your duty today will be to determine whether the defendants are guilty or not guilty of the murder of Antonio Alvarez based only on the facts and evidence provided in this case. The prosecution must prove that a crime was committed and that the defendants are the ones who committed the crime. At this time, we will hear opening statements from the State's attorney and the defendants."

The suits, as Emily viewed them, were Texas State's district attorney for Bexar County, William Bain, and his entourage. They were gathered at the Plaintiff's table; three seated at the table and two directly behind. The defendants had their own personal lawyer, Rick Spencer from North Carolina as well as Rick's college buddy, Brian Sisco who practiced law in Texas. They were all seated at the defendant's table. Brian also had his assistant, and an investigator present in the courtroom.

"This is it, gentlemen. Life without parole for both women," whispered William Bain, the state district attorney, just moments before he stood before the jury.

"Good morning, ladies and gentlemen of the jury. My name is William Bain, the district attorney for Bexar County. It is my pleasure to represent the state of Texas and to serve as a prosecutor on this very important case."

Mr. Bain was a figure of authority and experience. His countenance was etched with wisdom from his years spent in the pursuit of justice. Standing at 6 feet two inches, he towered over the jury box. His presence and demeanor, as he presented the case, resembled an intricate dance within the courtroom. It was a delicate balance between the law, ethics and the pursuit of truth. William Bain had prosecuted a wide array of cases, from petty theft to high-profile murder trials, providing him with the experience he would need to try this case.

Bain continued, "On October 12, 2024, the defendants in this matter, Sarah Lawson and Emily Martin entered Mr. Antonio Alvarez's hotel room and after overtaking him, murdered him with his own gun. The State will call five witnesses to the stand to testify. The first witness will be Mrs. Clara Underwood. Mrs. Underwood was directly across the hall from Mr. Alvarez, and she will give testimony of seeing the two defendants outside his room and later entering that same room where a scuffle ensued. We will call the defendant's girlfriend, Luna Aguliar, to the stand who will testify that when she returned to their hotel room, she found Mr. Alvarez's body and hotel security was called. Our forensics specialist, William Smithson, will explain how their fingerprints and DNA were present in the room. We will also call members of Mr. Alvarez's staff who will testify to a grievance between Mr. Alvarez and Mr. Enrique Martinez, a relative of the two defendants, which provides a motive. And finally, a witness who places the two women in a bar conspiring with Mr. Martinez.

At the conclusion of the case, and after you have heard all the evidence, we are confident that you will return a verdict of guilty."

Bain was very eloquent in his opening statement. He pointed out the two defendants as if he had witnessed the murder himself. Bain yielded the floor to the defense.

"Good morning, ladies and gentlemen. My name is Rick Spencer, and I, along with my colleague, Brian Sisco, represent the defendants, Ms. Emily Martin and Mrs. Sarah Lawson."

Rick was a small-town criminal defense lawyer. Most cases he handled involved drugs, domestic violence, assault and battery and the occasional disorderly conduct. He had only tried one murder case in all his years as a lawyer. But the Lawsons trusted him, and he was affordable. He certainly didn't command the attention that Willam Bain received. He stood before the jury in his pressed jeans and tailored jacket, his tie loosely around his collar. His partner, Brian Sisco, saw a few more high-profile cases and had the experience of several murder cases. He sat at the defense table with a look of concern on his face after hearing the opening statement of the prosecution. Hopefully, together, they made a decent team.

Rick Spencer cleared his voice, adjusted his tie, and continued with his opening statement to the jury. "Mrs. Lawson is an elementary gifted and talented teacher who happened to be staying at the El Amado Hotel for a teacher conference. She is highly regarded by her faculty, parents, and students. Her sister, Ms. Martin, is a chef and an entrepreneur. She owns the company *Savory Bytes* and is known across the country for her invention of the Nitro-Chill. She was in Texas presenting her new cooking gadget, at The International Food and Wine Festival. The defendants stand here today, wrongly accused of the crime of murder, a very serious offense. There is simply no motive and the evidence is flimsy at best."

Mr. Spencer continued, "We will call our own witnesses who will testify about the reliability of the DNA found at the scene, and the likelihood that this crime was committed by someone other than these two women. At the conclusion of this trial, the defense will ask that you find our clients not guilty of murder, the only appropriate verdict in this case. The prosecution will not meet their burden of proof. There is simply no motive for this crime. A verdict of guilty would be a travesty. Thank you."

It was now happening. Sarah just wished she had Michael seated in the courtroom to support her.

William Bain stood before the court and called his first witness, Mrs. Clara Underwood. She gave the same testimony she had given at the pre-trial hearing. She had seen a blonde woman in a cocktail dress several times outside the door of Antonio Alvarez. She had heard an apparent gunshot and called the front desk.

It was Sisco's turn to cross examine.

"Good morning, Ms. Underwood," he began.

She smiled with her lips pursed and gave him a slight courtesy nod.

Sisco continued, "On the night in question, is it your testimony that you witnessed the comings and goings of a blonde woman in the room across the hall from you?"

"That's right."

"And could you describe that woman?"

"Well, she was blonde, I know that much," Ms. Underwood said.

"So, it was just one blonde woman, correct?"

"At one point it was two that I saw."

Sisco was on point. "Was it one or two?"

"Two total. I saw two and then I saw the one again after the gun shot."

"You didn't notice any facial features or scars or anything that would distinguish her from any number of other blonde women?"

"She had on a cocktail dress and high heels," Mrs. Underwood crossed her arms.

"I see. So, your answer would be no to my question."

"Objection," Bain said. "Testifying."

"I'll restate that, your honor. What is your answer to the question? Did you notice any physical features that stood out to you?"

"Well, no."

"And tell me, Mrs. Underwood, when you stated that you saw this blonde woman, was your hotel door open so you could see her clearly?" Sisco questioned.

"I already told them," She said, gesturing to the prosecution, "that I was looking through the peep hole."

"That's it? You are able to identify a murderer looking through a peep hole? Ms. Underwood, do you wear prescription glasses?"

"Yes, I do."

"Do you know what your prescription is for those glasses?" Sisco asked.

"Heavens! I don't know. I just know I need my glasses to see. I can't see a thing without them."

"Ms. Underwood, I spoke with your ophthalmologist, and he said your vision was 20/200. Does that sound about right?"

"If that's what he said," Ms. Underwood said, crossing her arms.

"So, you don't see well at all, you were looking though a tiny peep hole, yet you were able to identify my clients? Are you sure about that Ms. Underwood?"

"Well, I um, I ... thought..."

At that point, Sisco turned to the judge. "I present exhibit one to the court." He had the bailiff bring over a door with a peep hole.

"Mrs. Underwood, could you please stand and look through the peep hole of this door?"

She looked at him like he was crazy. "Mrs. Underwood?" Sisco carefully escorted her to the door. Sarah and Emily stood up along with two other blonde women similarly dressed.

"Now if you'll notice, there are four blonde women standing at the defense table. Could you tell me which two you saw that night?"

"I can't do that! It's too hard to see through this door," Mrs. Underwood said, clearly irritated.

"Thank you, Mrs. Underwood. No further questions for the witness, your honor." Sisco walked back to the defense table with the smallest hint of a smile. The bailiff escorted her back to the gallery.

Bain cast a glance towards the defense, shaking his head in disbelief before speaking. "Your honor, we call Ms. Luna Aguliar.

"Ms. Aguliar, do you swear to tell the truth, the whole truth and nothing but the truth?"

"I do," she said looking around the courtroom for Victor.

"Ms. Aguliar, please state your relationship to the Mr. Alvarez?"

"Um... we were friends." she said.

"And Ms. Aguliar, could you tell us what happened the night of the murder?" Bain questioned.

"Yes. I was in the bar most of the night and then I went up to my room. When I went in, I found Antonio's body. He had been shot." She dabbed her eyes with a tissue and let out a tiny sniffle.

Bain adjusted his tie. "No further questions."

Sisco approached the bench. "Ms. Aguliar, you stated that you were friends, but it was more than that wasn't it? You were sharing a room, correct?"

"We were. He loved me!" she cried.

"Did his wife know you and Alvarez were lovers?" Sisco questioned.

"Objection, your honor," Bain interjected.

Judge Connelly said, "I'll allow it. Ms. Aguliar, you will answer the question."

"I guess she knew. Most everyone did. But I'm sure she wasn't happy about it," Luna said with confidence.

"Ms. Aguliar, were you also having relations with Mr. Victor Sanchez?"

"Objection, your honor. Relevance?"

"I'll withdraw that. No further questions." Sisco dismissed her and took his seat next to Rick.

Bain stood again. "Your honor, we call William Smithson to testify."

After Smithson was sworn in, Bain began his line of questioning. "Mr. Smithson, please tell the court what your field of expertise is."

"I'm a DNA forensic biologist," Smithson said. "I work for an independent lab in Dallas."

"Mr. Smithson, as you know, hair follicles were found at the scene of the murder," said Bain. "As most people know, you can't extract DNA unless the hair follicle contains the hair root. Isn't that correct?"

Smithson said, "Correct."

"Then how, exactly, could we determine that the hair found at the scene belonged to the defendants?" Bain questioned.

"In recent years, a breakthrough in the way DNA can be extracted from hairs has been discovered. By using a technique that was originally used to extract DNA from fossilized bones, we have been able to create our own genotype. We applied our findings to a DNA database and were able to find a match. It's not 100% accurate, more like 80%, but once you have a suspect, you can make an extremely accurate comparison of the hair follicles," Smithson stated.

Bain continued, "And what was your conclusion, based on the hair shafts found at the scene compared to the hair shafts of the defendants?"

"In my opinion, it was a near perfect match," Smithson stated.

"No further questions for this witness, your honor," Bain stated.

"Any questions from the defense?" asked the judge.

"Yes, your honor," Sisco said as he stood and buttoned his jacket.

"Good afternoon, Mr. Smithson. I just have one question for you. In your research, how long can a human hair, not attached to the root, maintain that person's DNA? In your personal opinion, of course."

William Smithson looked aggravated. "I would have to say, in my opinion, based on all the information available at this time, it would last about three months."

"No further questions," Sisco said as he sat back down.

"Call your next witness," prompted the judge.

Bain was prepared to show probable cause. "We call Mr. Victor Sanchez."

As he was being sworn in, Sarah grabbed Rick's arm. She was quite shaken. All she could utter was, "Number two." Rick gave her a knowing look. He had a plan.

"Mr. Sanchez, please state your relationship to the deceased." Bain had a smug look on his face.

"Si, he was my boss."

"And what line of work were you in?"

"Mr. Alvarez owned Botella de Agua International in Mexico. We distribute bottled water and other drinks," Victor said with an air of confidence.

"And did Mr. Alvarez have any enemies?"

Victor straightened in his seat. "He have enemies. His biggest enemy was his brother-in-law, Enrique Martinez. I heard him threaten him in the bar the night he was murdered."

"No further questions, your honor."

"I just have one question," Rick said standing. "Would you do anything for your boss?"

"Oh, Si, yes. I am very loyal," Victor said smugly.

Rick waved him off. "No further questions." He looked at Sarah and gave her a wink. Rick was definitely on to something.

"The prosecution calls our last witness, Duane Hankins to the stand."

"Please state your name and your occupation as well as where you work?"

"My name is Crash. I'm a bartender at *The Moon's Daughters.*"

Bain cleared his voice. "State your legal name for the court."

"Right, um, my real name is Duane Hankins, but people call me Crash," he said with a dumb grin on his face.

"Ok, Crash, I just have a couple of questions for you," Bain said. "First of all, have you ever seen the two defendants in your bar?"

Duane nodded.

"Sorry, Duane, please answer verbally."

"Oh, sorry. Yeah, I've seen them before," said Duane.

"And could you tell us what you witnessed when you saw these ladies?" Bain questioned.

"Sure. They were at the bar and some guy comes over and buys drinks for them and I take 'em over."

"Do you know who the guy was? The one buying the drinks for the defendants?"

"Yeah. The dude paid with plastic. The name on the card was Enrique Martinez. Real smooth guy. He bought them Nineteen Twenties. Those drinks will knock you off your ass. Ha, can I say ass on TV?"

The judge interrupted. "You are in a court of law and as such will conduct yourself with respect. To answer your question, NO."

"Huh. Ok, um, well, like I said, those drinks will knock you off your... um... your barstool. Yeah, barstool," he said with a laugh.

"Did you witness anything else take place between them, anything of importance?" Bain questioned.

"Well, the two of them, the dude and the tall one over there danced and got real cozy, then the dude slipped her something that she put in her purse, and he left. The two of them left right after he did."

"No further questions," Bain responded.

"Defense?"

Sisco stood. "Hey, Crash. Just a couple of questions. Did you hear their conversation at all? Did Mr. Martinez ask them to kill his brother-in-law? Did he make a deal and pay them money?"

"Dude, I make the drinks, not the deals." Crash sputtered.

"Objection, your honor!" Bain was on his feet.

"I'll withdraw," Sisco said and returned to the defense table.

Bain called several other witnesses that had seen the sisters that night colluding with Enrique Martinez but nothing condemning. There was testimony about the women wearing cocktail dresses and strappy high heel shoes corroborating what Mrs. Underwood had seen.

"The prosecution rests, your honor," William Bain said, a smug smile on his face.

Judge Connelly was satisfied. "Do you have witnesses to call?" he asked the defense.

Rick Spencer stood and pondered that for a moment. "Yes, your honor. We have a few witnesses we'd like to call."

"Very well," the judge said. "We will continue tomorrow morning at 9:00." Then he banged his gavel, and the court was dismissed for the day.

"How do you think we're doing? I'm getting really nervous," Emily said.

Rick reassured her. "Don't you worry your pretty little head. As you said, it's all circumstantial evidence. Tomorrow will tell a different story."

Sarah grabbed Rick's arm. "That Victor guy, he's the other shooter in the murder of the Berchers. He and Antonio Alvarez. I'm certain."

"Oh, I got that from the look on your face. I'll keep that tucked in my pocket for now," Rick assured her.

"You girls try to get some rest and let us worry about tomorrow," Sisco said.

Emily and Sarah were handcuffed and escorted out of the courtroom, loaded into an unmarked van, and returned to the prison.

Chapter 50

The morning came bright and early. The courtroom was filled to capacity. The news media wanted to report the verdict in this trial since it had received national coverage. When the cartel is involved, everyone is curious.

The judge entered the courtroom with the usual pomp and circumstance. He was ready to get to the end of this trial. His fishing boat was calling him.

"Today we will hear from the defense," Connelly said as he banged the gavel.

Rick Spencer stood with confidence and authority as he said, "We'd like to call Miss Evie Palmer to the stand."

"Objection, your honor. This witness wasn't on our discovery list," Bain was immediately out of his seat.

The judge placed his hand over his microphone and instructed the lawyers to approach the bench.

"Your honor, her name was listed in one of the twenty boxes of discovery the prosecution sent over to Sisco's office," Rick said as he gave a cocky smile towards the prosecution. Bain threw up his hands in resignation.

"Very well. You may proceed," said the judge.

Rick restated his request. "Your honor, we call Evie Palmer to the stand."

Evie stood somewhat cautiously and moved to the witness stand where she was sworn in before being seated.

"Hello Miss Palmer. May I call you Evie?" Spencer asked.

"Yes," she replied.

"Alright, Evie. Would you please tell the court what condition you suffer from?"

"Objection, your honor. What does this have to do with murder?" Bain was getting agitated.

"I'll allow it. You may answer the question, Miss Palmer."

"I suffer from a condition called alopecia. Due to my immune system deficiency, all my hair fell out," Evie explained.

Rick continued, "You have lovely hair. Can you tell us about your wig?"

Evie smiled. "Yes, I just received my wig a few months ago from a company called Strands of Hope. It's actually made from real human hair, so it looks and feels completely natural."

"Isn't it true that it takes two or three hair donations to make just one wig?"

"Yes, I've heard that," Evie said.

Rick continued, "And Evie, would you be surprised to know that the hair on your wig was actually hair donated to Strands of Hope by the defendants?"

"Objection! Testifying," Bain said.

"Strike that," said Spencer. "That's all I have for this witness."

"Does the prosecution have any questions for this witness?" Conelly asked.

"No, your honor." Bain was angry.

"Very well. Counsel, you may call your next witness."

Rick couldn't help but smile because he knew what was coming. "We call Kevin Donavan to the stand."

"Please state your name and occupation."

"Um, my name is Kevin Donavan. I'm a DNA forensic specialist. I work in the district crime lab in San Antonio."

"Thank you, Mr. Donavan. Sir, we asked you to conduct a little research for us, didn't we?"

"Yes, you did," Donavan stated.

"Could you tell the court what we asked of you and what your findings were?" Rick asked.

"Yes. You asked me to take hair samples from Evie's wig and samples from both of the defendants and compare them. I conducted an analysis of the three samples and found that they were a 100% accurate match. I then matched them with the strands found at the scene of the crime, and again, it was a perfect match."

"Mr. Donavan, did those hair samples show you who committed the crime?" Rick asked, a grin forming at the corners of his mouth.

"No sir, they did not. Anyone could have worn Evie's wig and committed that crime."

"Objection!" Bain complained.

"Overruled," Judge Connelly said.

"I have no further questions, your honor," Rick said.

Bain responded without being asked, "We have no questions, your honor."

Judge Connelly said, "Anyone else you think you'd like to call?"

"Yes, your honor. The defense would like to call Ms. Isabella Martinez-Alvarez to the stand," Rick said feeling his confidence kicking in.

Isabella stood, and with shaking legs, walked to the front of the court. "I must stay strong," she told herself as she was being sworn in.

"Mrs. Martinez-Alvarez, was it your testimony that you spent the evening of the murder visiting with your friend, Lydia Palmer?" Rick asked.

"Yes."

"And were you there the entire evening?"

"Yes. We are friends and I wanted to spend some time with her. I stayed in her room until close to midnight. Then I went to my room and to bed."

"You say you were there until midnight? You are aware that lying in court is perjury?" Rick questioned.

"Yes."

"Mrs. Martinez-Alvarez, we did a little investigation of our own. Would you like to know what we found? Perhaps you can explain it to the court," Rick was really getting wound up now.

"Objection!"

"Sustained. Get to the point."

"Mrs. Martinez-Alvarez, if you will direct your attention to the screen. This is the security video from the fourth floor of the hotel filmed in front of the elevator. But if you'll notice, the camera angle allows for one room to be caught on the video tape. Can you see that hotel door?"

Isabella merely nodded.

"Let the record show that she is indicating yes with a head nod. Now, keep watching the video. Look, right there." Rick looked toward his defense table and asked that the video be paused. "Can you tell me who you see in that video?"

"I don't know what you're talking about," Isabella said, tension rising in her voice.

"Oh, but I think you do. I think you know exactly what I'm talking about. Isn't that you in the video, Ms. Alvarez?"

Objection! Your Honor. He's testifying!" Bain was angry now.

Rick continued, "And look right there. I believe that's a blonde wig in your hand. Isn't that right, Isabella? Did you borrow Evie's wig, Mrs. Alvarez?"

"Objection!" Bain was on his feet, his face flushed with anger.

Isabella was broken. "I didn't kill him. I borrowed the wig to trick him. That's all. He was angry with me, and we struggled. I knocked the wine over and then he threw me out. I went back to Lydia's room to return the wig."

"Mrs. Martinez-Alvarez, I do believe you're telling the truth. The time stamp on that security film shows the time to be 8:00. I believe earlier testimony stated that your husband's approximate time of death to be around 10:00 P.M. Did you lie to the court when you stated that you left Lydia Palmer's room around midnight?"

Isabella simply hung her head and sighed heavily.

"Ms. Martinez-Alvarez, please answer the question," Rick prompted.

"Yes," she admitted.

"No further questions."

Judge Connelly was unmoved. "Prosecution?"

"No questions, your honor," Bain said, confusion on his face.

Rick was really warming up. "Your honor, we Call Ms. Lydia Palmer to the stand."

Lydia was sworn in, worry and trepidation showing on her face. The courtroom was still as Rick Spencer moved toward the witness stand. His movements were deliberate, his eyes locked on Lydia Palmer. Her petite frame seemed even smaller under the scrutiny of hundreds of curious eyes, but her chin was lifted with resolve. The air in the room crackled with tension.

Rick adjusted his tie as he approached the witness box, his voice calm but edged with steel. "Miss Palmer, would you please state your relationship to Mrs. Isabella Martinez-Alvarez?"

Lydia clasped her hands tightly in her lap. "Isabella is my closest friend." Her voice was steady, but her eyes darted to where the sisters sat; Emily with her jaw clenched, Sarah pale and trembling.

Rick nodded. He paced slowly in front of her, each step echoing in the cavernous room. "Yes, and is it fair to say, you would do anything for each other? Within reason, of course."

"Of course."

"And you were with her the night of the incident in question?"

"Yes," she replied.

"Tell the court what happened that night. In your own words."

Lydia hesitated, a flicker of something unreadable crossing her face. "I was at the wedding of her daughter... and afterwards, we went to my room to catch up."

"And then?" Rick prompted her gently.

Her breath caught. She closed her eyes, as if trying to block out the memory, but when she opened them again, they were sharp with determination. "And then Isabella went to her room, and I went to bed."

Rick was ready for the home run hit. "Ms. Palmer you were the one to provide an alibi for your friend, Ms. Martinez-Alvarez, isn't that correct?"

Lydia could barely be heard. "That is correct."

"Ms. Palmer have you ever provided an alibi for her in the past, say 20-some-odd years ago?"

Bain was on his feet. "Objection your honor. Relevance?"

Rick flashed his famous grin. "I'll withdraw that question for now. Ms. Palmer, we will continue playing the film from the fourth-floor security camera."

Lydia turned pale.

"Look closely, Ms. Palmer. Someone else has that wig on and they are leaving your room after Ms. Martinez-Alvarez left. They pushed the 'up' button on the elevator. Can you see that? That person looks to be about your height and build, wouldn't you say?"

342

Bain stood. "Objection, your honor."

"Overruled."

"Was that you, Ms. Palmer? We have a housekeeper on the fourth floor with some very interesting things to say."

Lydia sat unmoving in her seat. She could only shake her head in defeat.

"Did you go up to Antonio's room and then a short time later return to your room with blood on your hands? The video clearly shows you with the wig in one hand and what appears to be blood on the other."

"OBJECTION! Testifying!"

"Did you go to the room of Antonio Alvarez, Lydia? Did you find him in a drunken state?"

Lydia was shaken. She looked down at her hands. "He was drunk. Angry. He didn't love Isabella anymore and he threw her out of his room. He brought his buchona to the wedding of his daughter!" Her voice grew firmer now, her words quickening.

The courtroom held its collective breath as Rick leaned forward. "What happened next, Ms. Palmer?"

Lydia's chest rose and fell as if she were struggling for air. "I told him to stop torturing her. He wouldn't listen. He laughed in my face and pushed me back.

And then..." Her voice cracked. "I grabbed the gun on the nightstand. I didn't think... I just reacted."

Gasps rippled through the gallery. Rick remained unmoved, his eyes never leaving hers. "You... grabbed the gun?" he repeated.

Tears streamed down her face now. "Yes. I—I shot him. I didn't mean to. I just wanted him to let her live her own life." Her voice broke into a sob. "It was me. I shot Antonio."

The silence that followed was deafening. Rick straightened, his expression composed, though his grip on the edge of the witness box betrayed his tension. He turned to face the judge.

"Your Honor, in light of this testimony, it is clear that my clients are not responsible for the charges against them. I move to dismiss all charges against Sarah Lawson and Emily Martin."

Sarah and Emily sat in suspended silence, both holding their breath in anticipation of what would happen next.

Judge Connelly, who had remained impassive through the dramatic revelation, lifted his gaze from his notes. His sharp eyes fixed on Lydia for a long moment before turning to the defense table.

"This court acknowledges the witness's sworn confession." His deep voice resonated through the

344

room. "The charges against Sarah Lawson and Emily Martin are hereby dismissed. They are free to go."

A collective exhale swept the courtroom. Emily reached for Sarah's hand, squeezing it tightly as tears filled her eyes. Relief and disbelief mingled as the weight of their ordeal began to lift.

The gavel struck once, a sharp crack that signaled the end of the trial. But as Lydia was escorted from the witness stand, her shoulders trembling with quiet sobs, the true consequences of her confession had only just begun.

He motioned to the bailiff. "Please escort Ms. Palmer from the courtroom and place her into custody. Jury, I apologize for taking up your valuable time in this case. It seems that we have a confession. Mrs. Lawson, Ms. Martin, our apologies. He banged his gavel once again and court was adjourned. He rose and quietly left the courtroom for the last time. What a way to end his career. Thank God it was over.

Rick practically skipped back to the defense table. Sarah and Emily were in tears.

Sisco said, "Rick, I just have one question. When did we talk to a housekeeper that saw Lydia?"

Rick grinned. "I didn't say a housekeeper saw her. I just said the housekeeper had some interesting things to say."

Sisco slapped Rick on the back. "You're brilliant, man. Just brilliant! I'm still not sure how you got her to confess to murder."

"Is it really over? That's it?" Emily practically jumped into Rick's arms.

Rick hugged her back and said under his breath, "To be honest with you, it might just be getting started with the two of us."

"When can I see Michael and the kids? I'm ready to go home!" Sarah said through her tears. "I can't believe you did it." She threw her arms around Rick and hugged him with all her might.

Then she moved on to Sisco. "You did an amazing job with our defense, even if we frustrated you. I'm so thankful that Rick has you as a friend. Any friend of his is definitely a friend of mine."

Sisco extended his hand to shake hers, but she pushed it away. "I don't think this is a handshake moment," Sarah said. Then she grabbed him into a bear hug.

Meanwhile, Emily was having a moment with Rick. They just stood there; eyes locked on each other. "I really don't know how I can properly thank you, counselor," Emily said.

"Well, I have some ideas," Rick said as a big smile played across his face.

Chapter 51

The courtroom atmosphere had been somber. Victor sat quietly in the corner of the courtroom taking in all the testimony as things were coming to an end. But then Isabella was called to testify. He wondered what she could possibly know. She wasn't even sharing a room at the hotel with Antonio. He was ready for the hit on these two women to take place.

When it was discovered that Isabella's goddaughter had a wig made of human hair, he had begun to worry. He could hear those around him whispering their doubt about the murder. Could the two women actually be innocent as they had said?

When Isabella made her way to the stand, he wondered why she seemed so nervous. She kept looking around the courtroom and every time her eyes fell on Enrique, she seemed to become even more worried and depressed. Sure, her husband was killed, but they weren't happy together. He didn't even love her.

Then Lydia testified and he heard the most unbelievable thing.

"I shot Antonio…"

Had Lydia confessed to the murder? His heart started pounding in his chest when the two women were found not guilty. The courtroom erupted in noise; people expressing their disbelief. He sprang from his seat and ran blindly into the hallway. Two of his men were there waiting to hear the verdict. Their plan, already set into motion.

"Victor, what happened? We heard the courtroom erupt with noise," one of the men spoke. "We tried to get into the courtroom, but the room was full, and they wouldn't allow us to pass through."

"Were they found guilty as you said?" the other man questioned.

Victor hung his head and shook it. "No, they have been released. Lydia, Isabella's friend, has confessed to the murder. She has already been taken into custody."

"Does the hit order still stand? Do we take out the sisters before they can leave this courthouse?"

"NO! Not here, not now. We will deal with Sarah Lawson later. Lydia, on the other hand, is guilty. Tell the others that she has been arrested for Antonio's murder. She is the one who must pay the price."

The two men nodded their understanding. One of the men immediately pulled his phone from his pocket and dialed Jorge.

"The two sisters are innocent. The hit is now on Lydia Palmer, the friend of Isabella. She has confessed. Victor wants her eliminated!"

With that, Victor left the courthouse and instructed his driver to take him to the plane. He then called the private airstrip and asked that his plane be brought to the runway for his departure. He made one final call to his cousin, Louis, who had connections to the prison in Gatesville.

He drove in silence and in shock at the fact that Lydia had been the one to kill Antonio. Had she planned this all along? It didn't matter how it happened; she would be eliminated soon. He arrived at the airport where Antonio's plane was waiting. Just as he was about to board, two FBI agents stepped from the hanger.

"Victor Sanchez?" one of them called out.

As he turned to face them, one of the Agents flashed his badge and began speaking as the other agent placed him in handcuffs. "You are under arrest for money laundering and for the murder of John and Mindy Bercher. You have the right to remain silent. If you give up that right, anything you say can and will be used against you in a court of law.

As Victor looked closely at the second agent, he realized it was Dom Chavez. Shock spread across his face and his body felt weak. He had been tricked.

"Hello Victor Sanchez. I'm Special Agent Miguel Chavez. We've had our eyes on you and your organization for quite some time. With the death of Antonio Alvarez, that puts you in command of his operation. We have been working very diligently for the past several months knowing you would all be in Texas for the wedding of Sofia Alvarez. We had planned to arrest you and Antonio for money laundering. But before leaving the courthouse yesterday, Sarah Lawson made a positive ID on Antonio Alvarez and also on you for the murder of John and Mindy Bercher, owners of the Luxe Loom Designers Jewelry store chain.

"I cannot believe this!" yelled Victor. "What about Isabella? She was involved! What about Enrique? Where's Luna?" He kept firing questions in his disbelief.

"Enrique has been working with us to infiltrate your operation. He had hoped to convince Isabella to join him, but she still feels as though she can manage Botella de Agua legally with the help of her son."

As the second agent led Victor away to a waiting vehicle, he said, "Luna was persuaded by the feds and realized the error of her ways. She is working with the prosecution against you. She had much to say about you."

Victor was placed in the back of an unmarked vehicle and was soon on his way to the Bexar County Correction Facility. As the two detectives walked towards their own car, shots rang out as a semi-automatic weapon began firing. The vehicle swerved and rolled onto its side. The lone shooter ran from a side building and headed towards an SUV as Agent Chavez reached the overturned vehicle. A lone bullet had pierced the head of Victor Sanchez, ending his life. Something else was at play here. The detectives rushed to their vehicle and radioed headquarters as they sped after the shooter.

"It appears that we have had a cartel hit on Victor Sanchez. The vehicle carrying him to the correctional facility was just hit! We are now in pursuit of the shooter. All available officers needed in the vicinity of the airport, pursuing a black Cadillac Escalade license plate PG9S97. Send an ambulance and back up to the airport. It would be advisable to contact the Linda Woodman State Jail where Lydia Palmer is being transported. Her life may also be in danger."

Enrique Martinez sat next to Isabella in the empty courtroom in complete shock. The jury box was empty, and the gallery cleared. The bailiff had turned the lights off not realizing they were seated in the back. This was not how they thought things would go today. Though Enrique was thankful that the innocent women were allowed to go free, he was worried for his sister. The Los Zeta cartel was not forgiving of mistakes. She might be held responsible in some way. The entire situation was surreal.

"Were you aware of Lydia's part in all of this? Did you ask her to do this for you?" Enrique asked his sister.

"I can assure you; I am as shocked as you. I was so afraid they would pin this on me because I wore that wig to his room, but I had no idea she went to his room after I left her alone. My heart is broken." Isabella quietly began to cry. She cried for the loss of her husband, and she cried for the future of her dear friend.

As they made their way out of the empty courtroom, two FBI agents approached them and immediately escorted them both into a secure room.

"I am Detective Johnson, and this is my partner, Detective Carson. If you would both have a seat, please."

Inside the conference room Detective Carson spoke up. "We were just informed that Victor Sanchez was shot and killed after being apprehended moments ago. We have the suspect in custody at this time. He is a known member of the Guadalajara cartel. His name is Jorge Lopez."

"My God! I thought they had all returned to Mexico!" Isabella exclaimed. "Jorge killed Victor? It is evident where his loyalties lie," she said as she glanced towards Enrique.

"The flight log at the private airstrip listed all the names of Antonio's men already departing the country except for four. Victor Sanchez, Jorge Lopez and two others. We are looking for the other two now. They were all scheduled to leave today with Victor," Detective Johnson informed him.

"If anyone else is in danger, at this point it would be you and your sister. We are placing you both in protective custody until the trial of Jorge Lopez is over. We have heard from our intel that you are the final hit ordered."

"But Jorge is loyal to me. He would not carry out an order for such a hit. I can assure you of that," Isabella said, her head held high.

"Ma'am, nothing is of any certainty when dealing with the cartel," Detective Johnson retorted.

"Where are you taking us that we can be safe?"

"Mr. Martinez, we're placing you into protective custody. As for you, Ms. Alvarez, you will have to face the courts for your involvement in the murder of John and Mindy Bercher of Austin. You and Lydia Palmer provided sworn affidavits as to the whereabouts of Antonio Alvarez and Victor Lopez the night of the crime. That's perjury under the law. You might be able to secure immunity in exchange for your testimony to help wrap up the case, but you will need to consult your attorney. We will make sure Antonio's men can't get to you," Johnson said. He held the door open to a waiting U.S. Deputy Marshal. "Sir, this way please." Enrique was led from the room and headed to an unknown location. Isabella was headed to the detention center until her pre-trial motion could be made.

Rick drove the sisters to the law offices of Sisco, his vehicle trailing close behind with his investigator in tow. Their excitement was palpable as they approached the stately brick building, its polished glass doors reflecting the afternoon sun. Just as the sisters stepped toward the entrance, the screech of tires shattered the quiet. Two black SUVs careened into the driveway, gravel spraying as they skidded to an abrupt stop. Sarah screamed recalling the screech of tires moments before the murder of the Berchers. Four FBI agents emerged in a flurry of movement, their expressions tense and purposeful. Without hesitation, they surrounded the group, ushering them swiftly into the building. The heavy doors slammed shut behind them, and the agents secured the entrance with a precision that left no doubt about the gravity of the situation. What was going on?

With the building and its occupants secure, an agent informed them of the entire situation. There had been a cartel hit, and Victor Sanchez taken out. "We are keeping you here and secure until we have word that the situation is under control."

"Do you think they will come after us? What about the inmate at the prison who stabbed me? Was that also Sanchez and his men?" Emily questioned. Would this nightmare ever end?

"We have witnesses that say Victor Sanchez entered the prison and delivered the message himself. That is under police investigation at this time."

The group sat huddled together, each deep into their own thoughts. After a couple of tense hours, it was clear that the threats against them were over. They were given the go-ahead that they were free to leave and head home. The agents left as quickly as they had arrived.

Chapter 52

The sun was shining, not a cloud in the sky. With a blend of ideal weather and the lake offering a sense of tranquility, it was, by all accounts, a perfect day. There was a gentle breeze blowing as Michael and his kids hiked down the trail to the lake, with Morrow following a safe distance behind.

Tall pine trees lined the trail casting shadows across the path and creating a warm glow on the trail ahead. Sounds of birds could be heard overhead as well as the sounds of squirrels scampering through the woods in search of food.

The air was filled with the invigorating scent of pine. As they hiked, they could catch glimpses of the lake ahead. It was indeed a perfect day in every way. A perfect day, except for the fact that Sarah was on trial for murder, and the Lawson family might be torn apart soon.

Michael was fully aware that the defense would be presenting their case that day. That was the reason for the hike. Sitting in the cabin, alone in his thoughts and imagination of how the trial was going, would be more than he could stand. The kids were getting antsy and needed a distraction as well.

At the suggestion of Deputy Pierce, they packed a wonderful picnic lunch complete with sandwiches, fruit and energy-boosting snacks. They spread a blanket in the sun and settled down to enjoy a leisurely meal with a soothing soundtrack performed by nature around them. They could hear the birds overhead, the sound of the lake lapping the shore, and the rustle of leaves.

"I wish mom was here," Jordan said. "This is a nice distraction, but I am still thinking about her and wishing we were home. How much longer do we have to stay hidden away?" she asked as she fingered her mother's necklace.

"Isn't the defense presenting their case today?" questioned Zach.

Michael sighed. "Yes, today is the day. Rick and Sisco are calling their last witnesses. I'm not sure how it will go. Sisco thinks it could go either way, but Rick said he had a plan."

"How long before we know something?" Zach asked.

Michael shrugged. "It could be as soon as today, but it might go until tomorrow, or even into next week. It will all depend on how the prosecution follows up with questioning, and how late the judge will let each day run. And of course, how the jury decides to rule in the matter. Rick thinks the judge is in a hurry for this to end."

"Dad, aren't we all in a hurry for it to end soon?" Jordan commented.

Michael nodded agreeing with Jordan.

They sat in silence for several minutes. Zach had brought his ball and glove along and enticed Deputy Morrow to join him for a game of catch. He was itching to get back to the team and show them his heat.

Jordan stretched out on the blanket to soak in the sun and daydream about boys as she played with Nova, her new kitten. Michael was left alone in his thoughts about the trial.

The sound of the ball hitting the glove blended in with the sound of the water hitting the shore. "Good one Zach, now throw me a curve. Excellent."

Moments later, Deputy Morrow's phone rang. "Hang on Zach, I need to take this call." He was all businesslike and professional on the phone. "This is Deputy Morrow. Yes. Yes Sir, I understand. OK sir, put him through. MICHAEL! MICHAEL!" Morrow yelled. "MICHAEL, I have a call coming through for you!"

Deputy Morrow ran down the trail towards Michael, phone in hand, with a look of determination on his face. "It's Rick on the phone. You're going to want to take this call." He shoved the phone at Michael.

This was it. The verdict must be in already. Michael lifted the phone to his ear, both children standing next to him. Jordan reached for his hand as he answered.

"Hello?" he answered hesitantly.

"Hey, buddy. Rick here!"

"Hey, Rick. What is happening? Why are you calling me so soon? Did something happen in court today?" Michael fired the questions at Rick.

"Slow down there, Michael. I have Sarah here with me and she wants to speak to you. Hold on, here she is."

Sarah took the phone in her shaky hands. "Michael?"

"Sarah, oh my God, what happened? Tell me now, before I lose my mind," Michael said.

"Could you put this call on speaker, I think you and the kids should hear it from me at the same time. I don't think I can say it twice," Sarah requested.

"Hold on." Michael put the phone against his leg so Sarah couldn't hear what he said. He looked into the eyes of his children. "Mom wants me to put the phone on speaker so she can deliver the news to all of us together. Please be strong for her. This may be difficult news."

Jordan shoved the kitten into Deputy Morrow's arms as Michael held the phone in the middle of the circle they formed around each other. Jordan put her arms around her dad and little brother, Zach did the same. "Go ahead, Sarah. Tell us."

"You are not going to believe it. I am on my way home! We have been released. The wife's best friend committed the crime. Rick somehow got her to confess!" Sarah shouted. "Did you hear me? I'm coming home!"

Michael slowly slumped and dropped to his knees as his body began to release all his pent-up stress and worry. Huge tears began to fall as he cried. "Sarah, my sweet Sarah..."

Jordan and Zach were screaming and jumping in the air. Then they flooded Sarah with a multitude of questions. "What happened? How did Rick get you off? Is Emily innocent, too? When are you coming home? When can we go home?"

Sarah chuckled. "Slow down guys. I just found out myself and I'm still a bit overwhelmed. I can tell you all more about it when we're home. Michael, could you take the phone off speaker for a moment."

Deputy Morrow, with kitten in hand, called to Jordan and Zach and asked them to follow him back to the cabin to share the news with Pierce. Though Pierce probably already knew, he needed to give Michael some time alone to speak with his wife.

When the three of them headed up the path, Michael spoke to his wife. "Sarah, I thought I was going to lose you."

"You can't get rid of me that easily. We're in this together ..."

"Together forever," Michael finished. "But I just have to know, how in the world did the crime scene have YOUR hair?"

"Crazy as it sounds, when we donated our hair to Strands of Hope, the person who received the wig with our hair just happened to be staying at the same hotel at the same time. That girl's mother put the wig on and committed the crime. It's all just so surreal!" Sarah gave Michael a few more details of what happened in court that day. It was quite a story to tell, and one they'd not soon forget.

She also told him about the murder by the cartel. It was horrifying to think it could have ended that quickly for her and Emily.

"Are you safe? I need to know that we are all safe to return home. I couldn't bear it if something happened to you or the kids after all of this."

Sarah reassured him. "I have spoken with the FBI and the detectives on the case. They are certain that it was a hit on the people who worked for Antonio Alvarez. They have assured me that we will all be safe. And Michael, my memory of that horrible night in college came back to me. Crazy as it sounds, Antonio Alvarez and his assistant, Victor Sanchez, were the ones who committed the murder of John and Mindy Burcher. That part of my life is over, too. I've already given my sworn statement."

"Are you saying the guy that was murdered at the hotel was the same guy that murdered the Berchers? Seriously?"

"That's what I'm saying. It was all a tangle of unforeseen coincidences. One thing led to another and another and so on. The whole thing is crazy!"

"Do you think Libby Burcher will be able to leave the witness protection program? Would she want to after 20 years living as someone else? Michael wondered.

"I don't really know. I just know you get to go home and so do I! That's all that matters to me right now."

"What are Emily's plans? Is she considering a return to New York?"

Sarah smiled to herself. "At this point, no. It seems that Stephen swiped her job at The Mezcal Room, something he's wanted to do for quite some time. There's another story in the works for Emily, but for now, just know she plans to move home closer to family."

When Michael made it back to the cabin, he had a new spring in his step. He couldn't stop smiling. The day turned out even better than it started. The cabin was buzzing with excitement as the kids were packing and telling jokes, laughing with Deputy Pierce and Deputy Morrow. The mood of the cabin was certainly different than the first time he had set foot inside.

Michael found a moment to speak privately with Deputy Pierce. He wanted to know what had happened on the interstate the day they arrived at the cabin. Pierce had already explained to him that an unmarked van had crashed and burned.

"Was it supposed to be us in that van? I have to know for my own peace of mind," Michael asked.

"This I can tell you; it was not a hit directed at you or your family. The cartel was involved, but it was a rival drug hit. All of our sources indicate that you and your family are safe and free to go home. If there was any doubt, you would not be leaving today."

Two hours later, the Lawsons were heading down the pig trail towards interstate 40. Their destination, the Little Rock Airport. The van was full of conversation and laughter, much different from the trip there.

Michael thanked the two Deputy Marshals for all they had done for him and his family, even if they were just doing their job.

"Can I have my phone back? Please!" Jordan asked. She was behind on the gossip and had quite a bit of her own to add. "If I'm lucky, I might be able to get a date for the Valentine dance if it's still a thing."

Zach rolled his eyes. "Dance? *I'm* not going to a Valentine dance. I'm ready to go to the 'Big Dance'.

Deputy Morrow laughed. "You still have a lot to learn, Zach. The Big Dance is for the basketball playoffs. You're a baseball player. You look forward to the playoffs and, if you're lucky, the World Series."

Everyone laughed, including Zach. It felt good to have things getting back to normal.

As Lydia reached the Linda Woodman State Jail in Gatesville, she was put through all the humiliation that Sarah and Emily had gone through. Her life, as she knew it, was over.

After all the processing was complete, she was escorted to her cell. Her cellmate was there waiting when she entered.

"Hi, I'm Marysol. I've been waiting for you." She smiled a half smile that sent chills down Lydia's spine.

She extended one hand forward for a handshake, the other hand palming a blade.

Emily and Sarah stepped off the plane and into the bustling terminal of the airport, flanked closely by their lawyer, Rick, who carried a quiet air of reassurance. The two sisters exchanged a glance, a mix of exhaustion and relief washed over them as they scanned the crowd.

Moments later, a joyous cry broke through the noise. Sarah's husband, Michael, stood with their two children, Jordan and Zach, rushing toward them. Zach, with his lopsided grin, threw his arms around his mother, while Jordan began to cry, hugging her Aunt Emily first and saving the best hug for her mother. Michael's embrace was firm, his relief palpable as he held Sarah close, his voice thick with emotion. Emily smiled warmly, stepping back to give the family their moment, tears glistening in her eyes as she watched the reunion.

For a moment, the chaos of the world melted away, leaving only the warmth of love and the comfort of being home. The kids hugged both of their parents together making a human sandwich. The reception at the airport was overwhelming. It felt so good to be in a familiar setting with the people you loved.

Rick stood next to Emily; a huge smile spread across his face. "I showed you my skills in the courtroom and I'm anxious for you to show me your skills in the kitchen. Let's get these folks home and make an amazing meal together for them."

Emily turned and smiled, looking up at Rick. "What are your thoughts on Barcelona? There is a beautiful, secluded castle there called Castell de Tamarit. Have you ever been?" She took him by the hand and led him towards the waiting car.

Epilogue

Two months later...

The baseball diamond was set in a green field that had been mowed in swaths like a vacuumed rug. The red clay on the baselines had been newly raked and striped with white lime and the cinder-blocked dugouts freshly painted red and white. Multicolored plastic banners advertising local sponsors were tied to the chain-link fence and lightly flapped in the breeze.

Zach walked to the pitcher's mound with the swagger of a seasoned pitcher. He threw a few warmup pitches before the umpire called, "Batter up!" This was his moment to shine, to show that his two-month stent away from the team, time spent with only four other people, was beneficial and advantageous.

Zach stood for a moment, facing the batter with his pivot foot touching the pitching rubber. He brought the ball to the set position, both hands in front of his chest, concentration visible on his face. For just a brief moment he closed his eyes and heard Morrow's voice in his head. "It's just you and your catcher having a catch. Just throw the ball to him with all you've got."

Zach looked at his catcher waiting to take a sign. The catcher signaled a fast ball. No problem. Zach sent the ball sailing over the plate right into the catcher's mitt. "Strike one!" the umpire called.

In a matter of minutes, it was three up, three down. Zach strode off the field, holding back a grin. He wanted to look unphased by what was happening out on the field.

Coach Bennett grabbed hold of him as he was walking into the dugout. "Boy! Let me see the magic in your glove." He took Zach's glove and let out a low whistle! "This is an official Cardinal's glove autographed by Jim Morrow! Are you kidding me?"

Zach just shrugged. Things were back to normal. No, things were better than normal. His family was home, Jordan was in the stands with his mom, texting on her phone no less, his favorite aunt was sitting behind them with 'Uncle' Rick, and his dad was at the fence yelling "atta boy" after every pitch. It couldn't get any better than this. Could it?

Just beyond the center field, in a deserted parking lot, sat a black SUV. Two men were looking towards the field through binoculars, but they weren't watching the game.

Acknowledgements

I would like to express my gratitude to everyone who supported me throughout the process of writing and publishing this book.

First and foremost, I extend my heartfelt thanks to my husband, Rick, whose relentless encouragement pushed me to finish, believing in my ability. As my first critic, you were a sounding board, listening to all my ideas, and providing invaluable suggestions and a great book title. Thank you for your patience, understanding, and love.

Special thanks to my daughter, Kaley, for her encouragement in finding a starting point by challenging me to participate in NaNoWriMo. You read my first draft, told me all my flaws, and motivated me to try again. Also, for promising a book cover design when I finished. Your book cover is perfect.

I would also like to acknowledge the exceptional help I received from Janie and Laurie, my beta readers. Janie, your keen insights and attention to detail greatly enhanced the quality of this work. As a professor and lover of books, you saw things in my story that needed attention. Laurie, you encouraged me not to throw the project in the garbage, but cheered me on, knowing I could do it!

To my former students, I have to say, I finally did it. After donating my hair to a company that makes wigs for children with alopecia, I posed the question to each of you. What would happen if someone wearing MY hair committed a crime? You all encouraged me to write a book telling what I imagined.

I would be remiss if I didn't offer thanks to my 92-year-old father who read the entire book in just a few days and told me I did a great job. That means a lot. Thanks, Dad.

Made in the USA
Coppell, TX
18 June 2025